THE
REBEL
TRAP

LANCE ERLICK

Finlee Augare Books (Chicago)

This is a work of fiction. All of the characters, organizations, and events portrayed herein are either products of the author's imagination or are used fictitiously, and any similarities to actual persons, organizations, or events is entirely coincidental. Also, though locations used in this work exist, for dramatic effect details have been altered. Accordingly, they should be considered fictitious.

Edited by Arlene Robinson

Finlee Augare Books, Chicago, IL
ISBN: 978-0-9914643-0-2 (print)
ISBN: 978-0-9914643-1-9 (e-book)
Library of Congress Control Number: 2014904761

Printed in the United States of America

To Sue for putting up with my crazy ideas.

To Dave and Jason: Discover your dreams and follow them.

ONE

I won. I lost. I'm out. I'm in. I cannot tell a soul. It was enough to spin my head, to make me wish I was back in that zoo of a high school I just left.

My thoughts darkened with the implications of what I'd done and the commitment I'd just made. I hurried out of Commander Hernandez's sparse office; even the khaki-colored corridors looked darker than I remembered only an hour before. The drab lobby of the Tenn-tucky Mechanized Warrior compound brimmed with sister warriors, a gauntlet I had to squeeze through on my way out. Yet, I could no longer call them "sister" anything.

"Loser!" someone yelled. It sounded like one of Dara's girls. Defeating the amazon bully in the mech tournament final hadn't silenced her, or her posse.

"Hey, Annabelle," Dara yelled, "how's it feel to wash out?" She stood a head taller than the other girls like some ruling monarch.

Joke's on you. I took deep, steady breaths while I marched toward the exit. *Don't get into a fight,* I reminded myself. That was what she wanted, bringing up how after the tournament I'd refused to kill my male opponent in the separate arena final.

Hot, locker-room bodies surrounded me, sweat-soaked from their own arena fights to the death against boys pumped up with steroids and chemical enhancers to make the challenge even tougher. Some two dozen male corpses lay in the arena morgue, testament to the training and bravery of these recruits. Unlike them, I couldn't bring myself to kill Morgan for sport, even when I

1

had him pinned in a chokehold. For that failure, they took my title and kicked me out of the Mech Corps. *Well, to hell with them.*

Things weren't that simple, though. They never were for me.

"You don't have what it takes," Dara shouted. The amazon's large face tightened like a monstrous fist. She growled, "Weakness finally caught up with you."

"They'll strip away your title," scrawny Margarite said from behind Dara.

I inched forward through the crowd, my eyes fixed on the tinted, bulletproof door that promised freedom. *Don't fight. Only a few more feet.*

Dara stepped in front of me to block my exit. "You know what that means? I'll have the title that's rightfully mine. All that work for nothing. Sucks, doesn't it?"

Not like getting a title you didn't earn.

Brandy, my closest mech friend, cowered in the corner, face hidden beneath auburn curls. She brushed the hair aside and glanced up, eyes pleading. I hated letting her down. During training, she'd latched onto me as her lifeline. I sensed she wanted to talk, to get answers, but I was a pariah. I embarrassed the entire program by winning the tournament and the arena contests, yet disqualifying myself on a technicality.

I wanted to reassure Brandy, and thank her for being a good friend, but that would make her life hell with her sister recruits. I couldn't do that to her. I looked for a path around Dara, one I could take without stirring a fight with one who needed no provoking.

"What ya do, fall in love with that redhead?" Rox yelled. The dark-complexioned loner must have decided to align herself with Dara now that I was out.

The jibe bit hard. *Yeah, I'd like to get to know Red—Morgan. Even if I didn't, I won't kill for sport.* Maybe if I hadn't saved him several times before the arena match, I might have acted differently, but that wasn't it.

For the past six weeks as a mech trainee, I'd counted these girls as friends, with the exception of Dara. Now, their scornful looks reminded me of high school. Escaping at 16 had been a gift. Now I longed to return to a cage I understood.

I held my head high, squeezed between Dara and Margarite, and pushed the weaker girl out of the way. I ached to yell out the truth, but Commander Hernandez had been clear and insistent: "Tell no one you're still in the program."

Instead, I kept moving and endured jabs to my arms, already inflamed from my fight. Morgan had been a tougher competitor than Dara, and almost killed me twice. Yet, I couldn't hurt him. *Stay calm.*

Dara grabbed my arm and pulled me back. "I'm not finished with you."

"Yes, you are." I yanked free and pushed through the glass door into sticky heat. Haze drifted in from Knoxville. I was tempted to take my mech-cycle and race to the Outland border to make sure Morgan crossed safely. Then the mechs would follow me and catch him for sure. *Patience, Annabelle.* Besides, the commander took my electric cycle when she officially kicked me out of the program.

The forest-camouflage guardhouse across the concrete clearing seemed miles away. My adoptive mom and her electric sedan weren't waiting for me outside the gate, where the commander had arranged for her to pick me up. Nor was Mom's car among the line of other cars and buses leaving the arena parking lot. Sweat soaked my neck and beaded up on my forehead.

On unsteady legs, I moved toward the gate. It felt like nightmares where I reach for my birth mother while mech-warriors tear me from her arms and send her to prison for trying to help my dad escape. That happened when I was three. Yet the horrid ache returned to me nightly as a fresh wound. To spare me from an institution Mom adopted me and raised me as her own.

I picked up my pace to get away from the taunts that echoed from Dara and her crew on the steps behind me. I had to get outside the compound, which reminded me of a prison with its high concrete walls, concertina wire, and hidden cams.

Still shaken by the mess I'd gotten myself into, I also reeled over having just witnessed someone try to assassinate Tenn-tucky State Senator Cora Scott, my adoptive mom, in the middle of my life-and-death struggle with Morgan. What a cluster. I prayed no one would connect his escape to Mom or me.

She still wasn't outside the gate.

While getting out of here sounded great, I couldn't face Mom's disappointment at my failure or relief that I was out of the mech program. I wasn't out. Yet. But I couldn't tell her. I didn't need Janine's probing questions either, or her attempts to comfort me as if I were the younger sister. At least with me officially out of the program, she wouldn't feel the need to join the mechs to follow me.

Where are you, Mom?

I reached the guardhouse. Still no car.

The stocky guard with coal-black hair stepped out of the shadows and blocked my exit. Though shorter, she had the commander's solid build and looked ready to take my head off—me, the true winner of the Spring Mech Tournament. She probably could. Even though I'd gone through grueling mech qualifications, I hadn't completed my training yet.

I hung my head. "Sorry, Sandy."

She grabbed my arm and spun me around to face the building. "You will be. Commander wants you back in her office." She pushed me toward the mech building and that gauntlet of angry recruits.

"What's going on?" I looked behind and still couldn't see Mom's car.

"Don't cause me any grief," Sandy said. Her thick fingers dug into my forearm, making me gasp.

She pushed me back to the building. "Whatever it is, I suggest you humble yourself. The commander has never recalled a washed-out recruit before."

"Come on, Sandy, give me something."

Dara, Rox, and Margarite glowered at me from the top step. They blocked the door.

"I don't know, but good luck," Sandy said. "For the record, I had my money on you."

She pushed me up the steps. "Everyone out of the way."

Dara looked like a giant next to Sandy, but the great amazon stepped aside. Sandy dragged me along the khaki-colored corridor back toward the commander's office. My eyes watered. It was like getting a pardon from prison, only to have the judge reverse her decision.

"Haven't you had enough?" Dara yelled after me. "Had to come back for more?"

I dropped my gaze to the concrete floor. Moving toward freedom had given me courage. Now, as my nerve bled away, I could only imagine what had gone wrong.

<Don't be alarmed,> a muted bass voice said directly into my skull.

You know how when someone says think fast, you can't? My brain scrambled to make sense of this male voice deep inside my head, given that I'd never heard a masculine tone until six weeks ago.

Sandy tugged me forward. "Don't keep the commander waiting."

I pulled back. *Morgan, what are you doing in my head?* It felt like the mech com-link that allowed you to hear another's projected thoughts. I couldn't imagine how to turn the blasted thing off, or how to talk to him without Sandy overhearing. I couldn't let her or the commander think I was crazy on top of everything else. I considered that possibility.

<I haven't much time,> Morgan said. <My brother hacked your com-link's auditory implant. Your escape plan failed. Mechs are rounding up the other boys. Your mom's in danger.>

I froze. I wanted to see Morgan's face. Yet I didn't trust all this craziness inside me, as if I wanted more than just to see him. His tone did sound comforting, though, the only really friendly voice since I ran the gauntlet.

Sandy yanked me forward.

<Sorry for being such a bother. I need your help,> Morgan said somewhere inside my skull.

I followed Sandy, shook my head, and mouthed, "No." As if somehow, he could see that. I'd done my bit. I'd tried to help him escape.

The gravity of my situation sank in. Had Commander Hernandez caught the nurse helping the boys, or connected the escape to Mom? The entire idea had been stupid, a rushed effort because I really liked Morgan, despite having to fight him. I should have had a better plan, but I was not a planner.

TWO

Numbed by the day's string of events, Senator Cora Scott severed the com-link with Commander Hernandez and steadied herself against the trunk of her blue government-issue sedan.

Janine grabbed her arm. "Mom, what's the matter?"

Cora straightened up. She forced a smile and smoothed the lines on her face, a practiced move from a long political career, in the unpopular opposition. "Commander Hernandez needs more time with your sister. She'll find Belle a way home. Don't worry."

"Can I drive?" Janine asked.

Cora released herself from her daughter and moved to the driver's side. "That won't be necessary." She couldn't decide what shocked her most: the attempt on her life, how sweet little Janine stopped the cop-intern in time, that Belle got herself kicked out of the mech program, or that Belle had talked her into helping those boys escape.

The senator slid into the driver's seat and disabled the autopilot. She pulled the sedan out of her parking spot and glanced across the half-empty lot at the grotesque Roman-style arena, where Annabelle had fought that redheaded boy just a short time ago. She prayed that Nurse Wells had been able to move the boys out of the arena dungeon, beyond the mech compound, and safely to the Outland border.

Cora shivered at the thought that an assassin almost took her from her daughters during Annabelle's fight. She shook that off. She needed to be strong for her girls.

It seemed as if all of the approximately 300 personal vehicles from Knoxville had been at the arena. Thousands of spectators waited by the exits for buses to take them down the hill to public transport: the train and bus connections into town. She had mixed feelings about Belle's situation. She was proud of her adopted daughter for doing the right thing against all odds. Yet, she had to wonder at how Belle always took the tough roads in life. The senator had worked so hard to make up for what had happened to Belle as a child, but she had other daughters to consider.

Janine had that frightened look again, which she did whenever Belle got into trouble.

"Everything will be fine, Janine. You'll see."

Cora drove toward the gated exit and checked vehicle stats on the dashboard. A flashing red light caught her eye. Next to the light, a faint message flickered. She strained to read, "Don't be alarmed. I'm in trunk. Morgan."

She took a deep breath and cursed to herself as a driverless limo cut her off. Morgan's message might explain the commander's call and Belle's delay. The senator wiped sweat from her brow and froze a smile on her face. Instinct urged her to rush into the mech-base to demand Belle's release, but that would cause her daughter more grief.

"Why kick Belle out of the program?" Janine asked. Her face twisted into a studious pout. "It makes no sense. She did everything better, even better than that bully Dara. I'd think—"

"I didn't like you girls fighting. Maybe this is for the best." She glanced at her daughter with mixed feelings. At 15, Janine was still a child. Yet she had confronted their attacker while Annabelle's drama unfolded, and saved both of their lives.

"I need help," Morgan wrote on the dash. "Drop off J."

Cora gripped the wheel and tried to keep a sickly taste in her throat from distorting her public face. While she prayed being a Tenn-tucky state senator might exempt her from a vehicle search, the attempt on her life had shaken her confidence. Threats were some of the risks of being in the opposition. Other attackers might be roaming the parking lot or on the roads. She looked around, and tried not to act paranoid. She had to get Janine safely home.

"I mean, after we've rounded up all the boys and they're gone," Janine said, "there won't be any left to fight in the arena. When they don't expect her to kill, they'll see how good Belle really is."

Cora sighed, let another limo cut in front of her, and inched toward the exit. Her political efforts to oppose treating males as outcasts had been futile, something she couldn't discuss with Janine. Like other leaders, she had supported entrepreneur Adrianne Picard's EggFusion Fertilization program for its ability to solve infertility problems. After the Second American Civil War, EFF made an all-female society a possibility. Choice was one thing; the round up, expulsion, and abuse of males was another. Sure, you didn't get far in life without getting hurt by someone, but this vendetta by the political elite had gone on too long.

"Drop me off by the gate," Janine said. "I'll wait for Belle. She shouldn't have to go through this alone."

The senator shook off her melancholy. "I'm sure the commander doesn't want you hanging around." She reached the gate, rolled down her window, and waited for the brunette guard in her pressed green-camouflage outfit.

<∞>

The gray steel door with the nameplate "Commander Samantha Hernandez" opened. The guard pushed me inside the sparsely decorated grayish-beige room I'd left only a short time ago. The door slammed behind me. The commander looked as if a thunderstorm had blown through. The ruby-red scar down her right cheek blazed.

I sucked air into my lungs; my chest tightened. My heart thumped harder. I held my face as still as stone, the product of keeping too many secrets in a communal family.

She paced across a worn spot on the tile floor. "Sit!"

I dropped into a wooden seat that made me feel as if I were back in high school, forced to sit in the corner of the Harmony Director's office for skipping class.

"Forty-five boys escaped. Forty-five!" Commander Hernandez poked at her virtual screen. "In my 20 years running this facility, we've only had a few breakouts. Hell, we haven't had half that number in the entire 20 years."

My breath came in shallow bursts, then a deep sigh. Except for Morgan's voice in my head, I could have enjoyed a moment of pride. My hasty escape plan had been the biggest in Mech Corps history, payback for what they did to my family. Except, it failed.

The commander clenched her fists. Blood rushed to her face.

She looked as if her head would erupt like a volcano and spew blood all over her gray-beige office. *Well, the room does need some color.* My attempt at humor didn't ease my jitters.

When she turned away, I wiped sweat from my forehead. I needed details of what had gone wrong. *Yet, nothing eludes the commander's attention.* Those words stuck in my throat, choking off my questions.

"I hold myself responsible for their escape," she said. "I focused so much on orchestrating your transition from official recruit to covert operative I took my eyes off security." She slumped into her seat, eyes staring at the ceiling.

Then she lowered her head and studied me with such intensity I felt her reading my rebellious thoughts. After all, she ran the Mech Corps back when they took my birth parents. I didn't hate the commander, but I did hate what the corps did to my family and still did to boys like Morgan.

"We've caught all but three of the boys," she said with a sigh. "That's not good enough. We've never failed to catch every last one."

I took a deep breath and stared at a pink spot on her long, narrow scar that had faded to dull gray. "Do you need me to help search, Commander?" I needed information on Morgan, but asking would signal my interest. *Too many secrets.*

I should have realized she'd have mech-warriors between the compound and the border. My role had been to provide a diversion. All I did was distract the commander until the boys got out of the building. It wasn't long enough.

With a jolt, she seemed to wake up. Her face took on its usual composure. She jumped to her feet. "No. I want you to review cam footage with me."

<∞>

Cora Scott gripped the steering wheel.

The guard looked at the long line of cars still waiting to leave the arena parking lot. She shrugged and approached the senator's sedan. She looked in the backseat and paused over the trunk.

Cora bit her tongue and stared straight ahead. There was nowhere to run. The heat of Janine's attention bore into her. Thankfully, her daughter said nothing.

The guard returned to the side of the car. She hesitated, stared at her wrist-com, and then triggered the gate to open. Cora drove through, and eased past the front gate of the mech compound, where Commander Hernandez had originally said to pick up Belle. *Slow and easy. Don't draw unwanted attention.*

"Let me out," Janine said. "I'll call if—"

Cora grabbed Janine's wrist and sped down the mech road toward Knoxville.

"Belle shouldn't be alone," Janine said.

"That's enough."

Janine settled into her seat with her characteristic pout. "Do you think Belle should've killed that boy in the arena? She's much too sweet to do that."

"I didn't raise killers." Cora glanced at the dashboard, engaged the autopilot, and prayed for no more messages that Janine might glimpse.

On the way home, Janine peppered her with questions. "What will happen to Belle?" "Will they send her away now that she's out of the mechs?" "Why can't we go back and wait for her? She needs us."

Cora expected nothing less from her straight-A student. Right now, her concern was for her daughters' safety. The boy in the trunk threatened them all.

When she reached Pleasant Acres, the mile-square gated community that held her duplex, she stopped outside the iron gate. Concrete walls surrounded their cluster of homes. She didn't want to test the community sensors that might pick up the cargo in her trunk. Assuming he wasn't dead from the sweltering heat. She shuddered at that thought.

"I need to stop by my office," she said.

"We could've done that on the way home."

"It should be safe for you to walk home from here."

Janine's stubbornness settled into her intense eyes, her father's eyes, a father who had to leave before she was old enough to remember how much he wanted to be a part of her life. The attempt to help Morgan and the other boys had brought back all that history. The senator tried to concentrate on the road. When she couldn't, she was thankful for the autopilot.

"Why can't you tell me what's wrong?" Janine asked. "I've never seen you so worried. I know you're not telling me everything about Belle."

"There's nothing to worry about, dear. She'll be fine. You won't be, unless you go straight home and report in with Mama Grace."

"Stop treating me like a child. I'm 15." Janine climbed out of the car.

Cora waited until Janine entered the gate to their community before she drove off. Her daughter might fight, but she was still obedient. Most of the time.

THREE

I watched Commander Hernandez push a button on the wall behind her desk. A gray panel slid away. She motioned for me to follow her into a dark opening I hadn't seen before. Inside was a much smaller version of the main command center, where her team oversaw missions and mech activities on dozens of vid-screens that lined the walls. Hernandez tracked the movement of all warriors by means of their implants, and all males by means of collars: blue for day laborers, green for students, and maroon for criminals: namely the rest.

With barely enough space for the two of us, the room hugged me like a wool blanket on a warm day. Wall-screens displayed views of the mech compound, with timestamps that indicated this was all in the past.

I froze.

Under the blazing sun, images of the back of the mech facility were clearer than any I saw earlier from the main command center. These even covered blind spots I'd believed were there. Nine groups of five boys ran out the back of the compound, along with one woman, Nurse Wells. "I can't believe this," I muttered, realizing my mistake.

Hernandez changed the images to follow the boys. "I've had suspicions about Wells. Stockholm syndrome. She spent too much time with the boys. What do you see?"

"She led them out of the compound and guided them toward the Outland border," I said, stating the obvious. I needed to leave before I saw something I'd regret.

"What else do you see? Count bodies." She pointed to a frozen image of the back of the compound.

My mind fogged. "Some 50 boys plus the nurse."

"Forty-five." She motioned to a different scene unfolding under a shaded canopy of green. "How many do you see in the woods?"

I slowed my breathing and counted the boys, scattered in groups of four or five. "Forty-two boys and a woman."

"That's not Nurse Wells."

I looked closer at the shadows and prayed it wasn't Mom. I should never have talked her into helping. The image was fuzzy. I couldn't be sure. Despite air-conditioning, sweat dripped into my eyes and stung. At least the vulture commander had allowed me to change out of my sweat-soaked haptic fight outfit and into my civilian skorts and blouse before she sent me through the gauntlet. It wouldn't do for a civilian to have mech high-tech haptic gear.

"Do you recognize her?" Hernandez asked.

"Does Nurse Wells have an assistant?" I tried to focus and not focus at the same time. "Someone mech recruits don't see?" I stared at the image. Nurse Wells could finger Mom.

What have I done?

Hernandez frowned. "Only one woman came out of the compound." She sped the images forward in time.

"Wells must have had an accomplice on the outside." I forced myself to watch as mechs surrounded the boys. Most fell to their knees, hands over their heads. Two boys broke into a run. Mechs sliced them in half with machine-pellets. I recoiled at the viciousness and braced myself not to reveal too much. The rest of the boys dropped to the ground. The woman with them wavered, and fell onto her face.

"She's dead," the commander said. "Poison, no doubt. Autopsy will tell."

"Who was she?" I held my breath.

"We've identified her as part of the Underground Railroad. I doubt her body or her home will provide much more. They've been very careful."

"What about Nurse Wells?"

Hernandez pointed to another wooded scene. The GPS tracking showed a woman running north, through thick brush. Given the shaky image, the vids must have come from an airborne cam-swarm. Those could follow you anywhere unless the wind picked up. I felt chilled.

The middle-aged nurse tumbled down a ravine, out of sight. When the aerial swarm picked her up again, she was facedown on the ground, a gun in her right hand. Her head looked like road-kill. I bit back tears.

At the sight of Nurse Wells, my stomach churned. I liked her. She cared. I could tell from my many visits to the nurse's station. Now she was gone, because of me. Aware of the commander studying me, I steadied my breathing and held my practiced calm exterior.

"She should have known better," I said, not liking how shaky my voice sounded. *What about Mom?*

I looked at another screen, this one with no time delay. Two boys ran hard up a wooded hill in the heat. This image was so clear I saw sweat trickle down the backs of their necks. I recognized them from earlier arena matches. The boys urged each other forward at a sprint. The scene erupted into a splatter of red as their bodies disintegrated under the withering fire of mech machine-pellets.

I willed myself not to lose it. Seeing those boys die was more graphic than anything I had seen in training. I blamed myself for giving them hope. With cams everywhere, it was crazy to have thought I could help them escape. *I'm sorry.*

"The only one who eludes me is Morgan." Commander Hernandez studied me with the same intensity she did during training. "He's the boy you refused to kill."

I stood up straight and thrust out my chin. "I told you I couldn't kill for sport."

"You really like that boy, don't you?"

"Why would that matter? I'll never see him again. Fighting to the death in the arena isn't the best relationship builder."

"You think this is funny?"

"He's a human being, Commander. Fighting him to prove I'm worthy is one thing. Killing is another." I scanned the other screens for signs of Morgan or Mom.

"If you get caught on a mission in the Outland, it'll be a fight to the death. I have to know you're ready."

I returned my attention to her. "You doubt me?"

She grinned. "Guts you've got, but you can't play nice in real combat."

"You'll have to trust me to know the difference between the arena and being captured in the Outland."

She studied me like some lab animal. "Now that you've seen the escape, what's your assessment?"

I had to give her something. "Whoever helped them had to be into electronics. A geek maybe."

"What makes you say that?"

"They had to be, to bypass our security and escape as far as they did."

"You said 'they.' Who else do you think is involved?" Her eyes narrowed.

"I don't know if the geek is male or female." I returned my attention to the screens, praying I didn't see Morgan or Mom.

The commander's eyes burned into the back of my head.

"According to these timestamps, I was in the arena during the escape," I blurted out.

"You're acting guilty. I wasn't accusing you, but do you have something to confess?"

Not yet. I couldn't be sure what she knew or guessed. "I don't like how you're interrogating me like a suspect, Commander. Particularly after that cop-intern attacked my mom."

"Ah." She circled around to face me. "You don't have to call me 'Commander' when we're alone."

"Sir ... ma'am ... Sam."

"Sam will do. Get used to tough questioning. You'll get far worse at the hands of Captain Voss and her sidekick when you return to work. I daresay daily interrogations will be their delight."

I wanted to say I could handle Voss the Boss, but my legs felt rubbery, my stomach in knots. I wanted no part of Sam's special secret mission.

I'm in over my head. There, I admit it. Can we move on?

I needed to escape her command center before I broke down and quit. Then for sure, she would suspect my involvement in the escape. I couldn't do that to Mom or Morgan. I couldn't leave poor Janine to fend for herself, even though she had stunned me by how she handled the attacker.

"I called you back," Sam said, "because this escape could have something to do with your mission. As you suspected, Captain Voss washed out of the Mech Corps."

"I knew it."

"She'll lord it over you that you failed. She'd like nothing better than to discredit the Mech Corps, and me. She's recently made spectacular captures of escaped boys, and is using that as leverage."

"You think she could have been involved in this escape?" *Yeah! Let's shift attention from me to Voss.*

"I can't say. If I'm right, your mission is more critical and dangerous than I anticipated."

"And you don't think I can handle it."

"I have no doubt you can," Sam said, "only whether you'll buckle down and focus. Secrecy is paramount. You can't tell anyone I've kept you in the program: not your mom, and certainly not your sister. You'd best put on a convincing performance for them and everyone else."

I nodded at her third warning, while staring at the scar below her right eye. She could have had the scar removed—softened and faded actually. Yet she chose to wear it as a badge of her bravery during the Second Civil War, when the Federal Union swept the entire nation except for the Outlands. The war had started over economic and social conflicts, but when men flocked to help the rebels, the Federal Union, under the banner of New Harmony, looked at all males with suspicion. Peace didn't ease the tensions.

The hard part for me was Janine. We told each other everything. Well, most things. I never had the heart to tell her that Mom adopted me. Besides, Mom swore me to secrecy on that and a dozen other topics.

"We need to catch this Underground Railroad," Sam said, "to stem the tide of escaped boys before they grow up and take arms against us. If Voss does, she'll rise in favor with the governor. That'll put her in position to close down or absorb our Mech Corps into the police force."

This was growing into Sam's personal vendetta against Captain Voss. I didn't want any part of this. I certainly didn't want to have to choose sides, but I was already stuck in the middle.

FOUR

"You want to tell me why you're in my trunk?" Cora Scott asked as she drove toward the river. She had to make this look to those who tracked her vehicle as if she was taking a drive to clear her head. After what had happened, they might give her some latitude.

Morgan's muffled voice came from the trunk. "Mechs were on our trail. I tried to create a diversion. I was too late."

The senator steadied her nerves as she drove along empty secondary roads she had used before. She strained to hear him through the padded backseats. "What do you mean, too late?"

"Mechs were waiting for us. Someone tipped them off."

"What about the women who helped you?" She clutched the controls to keep from shaking and drove east along the river, wondering who would be monitoring the many cams and tracking devices along the way. The cams were too small to see these days.

"Both killed themselves." His voice sounded shaky. "I'm sorry. I couldn't help—"

"Why my car?"

"Only way past the mech compound."

"You put my family in danger after my daughter saved your life." She glanced in the rearview mirror, saw no one following, and turned. "What about all the parking lot cams?"

Morgan coughed and cleared his throat. "I had them blinded. It would take too long to explain." He coughed again. "Sorry for all the trouble. I'm grateful to you and Annabelle. I didn't know where else to turn."

She eased her way along the river road. "I'll get you close to the border. You'll have to find your own way across."

"I'm not crossing," Morgan said. "Not until I get my brother out of the Oak Ridge Institute."

"What? That place is more heavily guarded than the mech compound."

"I know."

She turned away from the river and drove toward an older part of town, where there would be fewer cams, she hoped, and vacant buildings. It was on the way to her office, a reasonable excuse for coming this way. "How will you do it?"

"Best you don't know." Morgan sounded in pain, probably boiling in the stuffy trunk. "Can you find me a safe house for the night? Then I'll be out of your hair."

She pulled behind an abandoned store, one of many along what used to be a high-traffic corridor before the city banned most cars. "This place will do for a night, no longer. Good luck with your brother." She released the trunk latch and stared through the mirror.

Morgan climbed out and stretched. With a shock of red hair, he was big, too muscular from the steroids Commander Hernandez had pumped into him before his fight with Annabelle. He had strikingly masculine facial features like her husband, Bret, who had crossed into the Outland 13 years ago. She sighed.

"I can't thank you enough," Morgan said. "I'm sorry for your friends."

"Please don't put my family at risk again."

Morgan smiled and hurried toward a side door. "I'll be in touch."

<∞>

Sam glanced at her wrist-com and motioned for me to join her back in her office. "I hope you see the importance of returning to work for Captain Voss. Find out what she's doing with the money she's skimming. Money will lead you to what she's really up to."

"How?" I asked. "I don't have access to her data files."

"I wish I had more time to give you details. I have a boy to capture, and—" Sam led me to her gray steel office door. "Janine's heading back, no doubt looking for you. You can't let her know any of this. You should leave before she gets here."

"Does that mean I can keep my cycle?"

Sam shook her head and pushed me out into the dim corridor. She led me in the opposite direction from the front door. "You're officially out of the mech program. No mech-cycle."

"Then how do I get home?"

"You'll have to cab it." She handed me a cab-chip. "Until I can work something else out, I have an older cycle for you. It's at that U-Store facility across from your home. Here's the key-chip. Hide your face around the facility so cams can't ID you. Don't speed, or give your cop friends any reason to stop you."

"Won't they be able to track me?"

"I've given you special transit authority around the metro area. I'll also remove you from all databases except mine. Your wrist-com tracking device will mysteriously begin to malfunction." She handed me a thumbnail-sized cube. "This will allow you to check your cycle for tracking devices the cops might apply. Press the button and scan it over the entire cycle like a Geiger counter."

"Is it radioactive?"

She laughed. "It uses electromagnetic waves. Just don't abuse your cycle privileges. And don't let anyone at home, in the mechs, or on the police force know, particularly that inquisitive sister of yours."

"I have to tell her something," I said. "She's persistent."

Sam's eyes narrowed. "Don't make me regret my decision to keep you. I was sure you could handle the secrets required of this mission. If not, then I can't use you. If you tell Janine, you're out."

I nodded. "What about the rest of my mech training?"

She handed me a tiny plastic case. "Com-link contacts. They'll allow me to communicate with you. Wear them at all times." She motioned for me to put them in.

I opened the case and struggled with the left contact. She kept talking. "We'll have to improvise on the rest of your training. Until your mission is over, you can train on weekends and evenings. You'll get the full treatment later. It'll take longer, but in the end, you'll have experience the other recruits won't have. Now go."

As soon as I had both contacts in, Sam pushed me out the mech compound's side door into steamy daylight and a waiting green cab. I hated having to sneak around, as if I were doing something illegal instead of beginning an official mission for the elite Mech Corps I distrusted.

<∞>

Lieutenant Brita Scarlatti savored intense relief as Captain Voss pulled her electric police sedan out of the mech-arena parking lot. The place gave Scarlatti the creeps. It had ever since she lost her arena fight to a man who delivered a paralyzing blow to her right shoulder before she could rip his head off. She'd moved an instant too slow. Each time she saw this place, Scarlatti had to relive the assault that motivated her to try out for the Mech Corps in the first place. A double humiliation.

Scarlatti couldn't imagine why her chubby-faced captain insisted on attending this year's spring mech contests, given that she also had washed out of the mechs. Yet, watching Annabelle get kicked out was worth it. Scarlatti enjoyed the rising body count, each dead boy a stand-in for the bastards who not only attacked her, but also escaped to the Outland, where they could gloat.

"Wish I'd put more money on Annabelle washing out," Scarlatti said when they reached the main road. Along the roadside, arena spectators impatient for buses walked the half mile down to public transport.

Voss pulled onto the road and headed toward Knoxville. "We did well enough. While you're celebrating, consider your other good-news-good-news bit."

"What?"

"Good news: we've found you a partner."

"Annabelle?" Scarlatti said.

"Since she's out of the mech program with a high-profile finish, we get to take her back."

"She has the worst attitude of any intern. She's a waste of uniform and space."

"Now for the really good news," Voss said in her high-pitched whine. "You get to destroy the little maggot. She has nowhere else to turn."

"Can't we put her with Brooks?" Scarlatti studied the lineup for the train into Knoxville. "The girl is worse than no backup at all."

"I'm giving you the assignment of watching her and her family. While you're at it, dig into the connection between her mother and Commander Hernandez. See if you can trick them into giving us something juicy."

"How did we get stuck with both Annabelle and her sister?" Scarlatti asked, sulking that this fell on her.

"It helps to pull strings."

"You wanted them?"

"I have an idea how to deal with all our ghosts at once." Captain Voss' jowls pulsed in a joyful laugh. "In the meantime, we need to pay a visit to Governor Battani. You impressed her last night by taking down those Oak Ridge boys."

Scarlatti grinned over the prior night's operation at the Oak Ridge Institute. It had been like netting fish at the country club. *It pays to have inside information.*

FIVE

Janine waited until Mom turned the corner. Then she headed away from the community gate and home.

She was tired of all the family secrets, and Mom not sharing, as if Janine was too young to understand. Annabelle was in trouble. Janine felt it almost as she had during mech training when they shared the mech com-link. The device allowed warriors to share thoughts faster than talking, which Commander Hernandez said helped in battle. While using it, she couldn't read Belle's mind, but she could hear projected thoughts and sense her sister's emotions, something that frightened her at first and then felt like a warm sauna on a cool winter night.

Without the mech com-link, Janine had to get face-to-face to confront her older sister before things spun out of control. Annabelle had become a puzzle, a conundrum, and Janine liked nothing better than solving brainteasers, especially the human kind.

Janine entered the U-Store facility. *Guess what? I have my own secrets.*

She covered her face, unlocked her narrow storage unit, and removed the black, old-style electric cycle. After she put on her helmet, she eased out of the facility.

Having a sister who was a year older allowed Janine to experience more than other girls her age. *Time to put that to good use.*

She turned onto Kingston Pike and spotted a cop's front bumper beside a boarded-up store. She slowed to the limit.

Commander Hernandez had been explicit: "Don't call attention to yourself, and don't let the cops know you have this cycle." People treated Janine like wallpaper, which everyone sees yet few really notice, like the bland, government-approved pastel wallpaper in her home. The trick was never to stand out in dress or actions. Always be plain.

She followed the roads Belle usually took, yet didn't spot her on any of a dozen cycles, or in any of the half-dozen cabs or private cars along the way. In case Commander Hernandez had reduced Belle to taking the bus, Janine checked bus transfer centers, with no luck.

When she reached the mech compound, buses were gone and the drive empty. No guard stood near the camouflage-colored guardhouse. She scooted past the main gate, along the high concrete wall topped with wire and cams, toward the side entrance.

Commander Hernandez told her to avoid the other mech recruits. They weren't to know she was training on the side. A svelte black guard waved and smiled as Janine passed.

In her dress blues, Hernandez greeted Janine by the steel doorway to the building complex. "I'm glad you're back."

By monitoring tracking implants, she always knew when Janine was on the way and usually greeted her, like Mama Grace welcoming Janine home. She almost gave Hernandez a hug, but decided that wasn't appropriate. Besides, the commander was already heading down the hallway.

Hernandez led Janine into her small office and closed the door. A simple Marine Corps plaque looked lonely on bare, beige-gray walls. The office was modest for a hero of the Second Civil War and Commander of the Mech Corps.

Janine pressed herself against the wall and steadied her breathing. "Now that the tournament and arena contests are over—"

"I want to talk to you about that." Hernandez offered Janine a stiff wooden seat that faced the clean metal desk. "With Annabelle returning to the police force, you need to decide if you'll join the Mech Corps. Think carefully before you decide. Many lives depend on your decision."

Janine shifted in her seat, her eyes fixed on her commander, and on the scar Hernandez could have had medically removed yet chose not to. "I … I only signed onto mechs because of Annabelle. I don't feel right continuing without her. It would be a slap to her face."

Sam's smile softened the scar on her cheek. "I realize at 15 you're our youngest-ever recruit, but you learn quickly. You've excelled in every aspect of training so far … in an accelerated program, I might add. You handled yourself very well this afternoon with that assassin."

Janine's cheeks burned at the memory. "I had to protect Mom."

"I want to continue your training, in secret."

All Janine wanted was to come clean with Belle so she could push her sister to do the same. "Can I at least tell Annabelle? We share everything." *At least we used to.*

"If you do, you're out of the program. Our code requires mechs not to share corps activities with outsiders."

Another reason not to stay. "I—"

"I'd rather you didn't make a hasty decision," Hernandez said. "Becoming a mech will serve your family, Annabelle, and you. Don't blow this opportunity."

"But, Commander—"

"You can call me Sam behind closed doors. Don't waste your life. Give this some thought. Open your mind to the possibilities. Now that you've completed your orientation and initial training, you're far ahead of where the fall recruits will be. You'll be a shoo-in to win the tournament and become a mech leader."

"Why are you doing this?"

"Because, my dear, sweet Janine, you're not the innocent, helpless girl Annabelle takes you for."

Janine smiled. *You have no idea.*

"You do want to help your sister, don't you?"

Janine nodded.

"You want to be like her."

"Yes, but—"

Sam leaned forward. "Then we'll continue your crash training with Renee. If we have time, I'll put you through intensive training before the tournament and arena. That should give you an edge."

Janine squirmed in her seat. "Is that legal?"

"Unusual, but I believe you're ready. You'll still have to compete in the tournament and do the arena tests in order to become a mech-warrior. Your confidentiality agreement remains the same. You can't tell your mom, Annabelle, the police you work with, or anyone else. Consider this an honor. I assure you, Annabelle will be so proud of you. Can you do this for her?"

Janine stood erect. "I stand ready to deliver." *And to find out what's really going on.*

"Excellent. Keep using the cycle in secret. Don't let anyone see your face while you have it until I can arrange official transportation. I want you to use these." She handed Janine a contact lens case. "They will allow me to communicate visually with you. Go ahead and put them in."

Janine examined the contacts and wondered how much deeper she was getting in. "Is Annabelle here?" she asked, remembering the reason she came.

"She left," Sam said. "Are you sure you can keep this a secret?"

No, but as plain wallpaper, it pays to be agreeable. Janine nodded and smiled.

<∞>

I slipped lower in my seat in the back of the cab. After my humiliation, I didn't want anyone to see me.

I tucked the key-chip into an inside pocket of my skorts. I longed to check out the cycle Sam left me at the U-Store and go as far from Knoxville as I could. What if I zoned out and cops picked me up speeding or in one of the forbidden zones? I didn't need the additional humiliation of the shortest mech mission ever.

On my wrist-com, I scanned newsfeeds for anything about the escape. "Keep your doors locked," one report said. "Keep your eyes open for suspicious activities," another repeated. *Rat out your neighbors,* I said to myself. The news spin was that the Underground Railroad had struck again. For 20 years, the Federal Union had kept the peace by segregating males. Now we needed to beef up our police to stop this new threat.

So, facts were scant about the escape. What newsfeeds had ample supply of was my spectacular humiliation in the final arena contest. I clicked off the news feature and deleted dozens of messages from ill-wishers who felt entitled to comment on my new celebrity status. I wondered if Sam had leaked the story.

I couldn't face going home and having to spar with Janine trying to pry secrets from me. I needed to talk to Mom. She had to be hurting after the attack on her life, and worried about me. Yet, I was too wired to have that talk. I didn't need Mama Helen and

Mama Grace, my two other moms, hovering over me, or any of my other seven sisters looking down at me as yet another disappointment, a black stain on the family. I recognized this for what it was, the hell promised for all I'd done wrong so far.

After I got the cabby's attention away from her dash display of the daily news, I directed her to let me off at my cop station. It was time to reacquaint myself with my new-old surroundings. The cabby frowned when I held out Sam's cab-chip. She probably hadn't seen one before. I smiled and tucked the chip into my pocket. The cab sped away.

I dragged my bruised and reluctant bones up the steps and through the concrete archway into my cop station: Captain Voss' actually. The rows of metal desks looked unchanged from my last visit. I shrugged. I hadn't been gone that long. What did I expect?

Saturday afternoon, the station was empty except for Lieutenant Becky Brooks, hunched over her desk. Before she could spot me, I slid along the outer wall of desks to the cafeteria, and behind it, the small station gym and lockers. I was surprised to see my name still on my cabinet.

I checked for a clean cop-intern uniform, navy skorts and beige blouse, before I stripped out of my street clothes. In a nearby mirror, my blonde hair looked like the fur-ball my cat coughed up. I took a warm shower I hoped would wash away the day's events. It couldn't erase the fight, the escape, that cop-intern who attacked Mom, Sam kicking me out of the mechs, or this super-secret assignment Sam pinned on me. At least I was clean.

My fresh outfit made me look pudgy despite all my fight training. My hair fell to my shoulders: beyond regulation. I tied it up. I didn't need demerits on my first day back.

When I reached the great hall, Brooks sat slumped over her metal desk. She looked up, smiled, and waved for me to join her. I glanced at Lieutenant Scarlatti's office. Door closed, blinds open. At least she wasn't there.

"I hope you didn't lose too much betting on me," I said as I approached my former partner and mentor. Brooks was alone at the station because she drew the short straw, and Janine, her new partner, had gone to the arena finals to watch me.

When Brooks smiled, her coarse face softened. She looked much older than her 40 years—a tough life, I gathered, that put my issues into perspective. Yet she never lectured me. I liked Brooks. I gave her up so Janine could have the best partner in the station.

Brooks pushed e-files aside and faced me. "I lost enough," she said with a sigh. "Don't worry. I didn't gamble all of my earlier winnings. I'd never bet against you."

"Thanks. I don't want to talk about it." I eyed the seat next to her, but wasn't up to sitting.

"It's Saturday," she said. "You don't have to be here until Monday."

"Becky, please."

She lifted herself out of her seat, stiffer than usual. Too much sitting, she would say. "Let's take a ride."

Glad to be out of the station, I crammed myself into the passenger seat of her two-seat electric squad car, her punishment for being out of favor with Captain Voss. The rest of her punishment was getting me as a partner when I started. Janine was a much better student. She rarely caused anyone trouble.

"Is your mom okay?" Brooks asked, looking concerned. "It's been all over the newsfeeds. I can't believe a cop-intern would attack her."

"Thankfully, she wasn't injured," I said.

"I'd imagine she was quite shaken. I hope it won't slow her down."

I closed my eyes. "I haven't spoken to her since—"

"Belle, you should go home."

I forced a smile. "I'm not ready to face everyone." I clenched my hands in my lap. "I pray betting on me and having me as a partner hasn't made your life too much of a hell."

Brooks laughed. "I'd take you as a partner any day. It sounds as if the mech experience humbled you."

I nodded. "It was my safety net. I blew it." I ached to tell Brooks that wasn't so, but something told me Sam would find out. She always did. I took a deep breath. This was harder than I imagined.

Brooks pulled out onto the empty boulevard, heading west. "I'm glad you stopped by. It gives us a chance to catch up. There've been a few changes."

"Captain Voss retired?"

"No such luck." Brooks eased past a packed bus. Bicycles

scattered as the bus lurched forward.

"Lieutenant Scarlatti was reassigned to another station," I said, hopeful.

"Voss has adopted a military mentality, as if in watching you, she remembered trying out for the mechs."

I shrugged. "You want me to behave."

"Try harder not to irritate Voss and Scarlatti. They're on some mission. Last night we caught more escaped boys. Scarlatti got inside info. Now Voss has the governor's ear."

"Didn't the governor put Voss in this job?"

Brooks stopped and turned to me. "That was years ago. Now Voss is making moves to advance the governor's interests. She's bucking for promotion."

"That sounds great. I mean, if she gets reassigned elsewhere."

"Ah, my young protégé. You have much to learn about politics. If Voss moves up, she'll promote Scarlatti to captain. That'll give them both more power."

"I don't get it," I said. "Voss doesn't strike me as sharp enough to pull off these captures, even with inside information."

Brooks pulled out behind a bus. "I thought you should know about their new attitude before you encounter our dynamic duo."

"I miss having you as a partner, but I couldn't do that to Janine."

"She's doing well," Brooks said, "but she's been distracted lately."

"I'm sure she's only worried about me and the mech tests," I said, to deflect any problems from Janine. "What can you tell me about the raids?"

Brooks headed up a tree-covered hill. "The Belleville Prison was last week. Six boys bypassed their new security system. We caught all six within two hours. Yesterday was the Oak Ridge Institute. Three managed to activate the fire alarms and escape during the drill. With the help of insider information, we caught all of them in less than two hours."

"Voss and Scarlatti did this?"

"It's hard to argue with facts," Brooks said. "In any case, Voss will receive some award from the governor, and probably more latitude in how she operates."

"Meaning she'll make our lives more miserable." Was Voss' success what worried Sam?

Brooks received a call. When she disconnected, she turned to me. "Our benevolent dictator wishes to grant her humble subjects an audience."

SIX

After Voss and Scarlatti spoke with Brooks, it was my turn. Climbing the narrow steps toward Captain Voss' office was like rising up out of the dungeon to face the firing squad. I should know. I'd had that pleasure once, without the actual firing squad. I would prefer the single bullet to the back of the head over machine-pellets to the gut, which left you in misery until you bled out or the toxins took you. A miserable way to go, and no open casket. That sent shivers up my spine.

I took a deep breath, reminded myself of Sam's mission, and entered the office. It was larger and better decorated than Sam's office, if you didn't count the mini-command center behind it. Captain Barbara Voss, the round-faced cow, stood behind her heavy mahogany desk. Off to my right, Lieutenant Brita Scarlatti's lean, no-nonsense figure stood by a polished round conference table. I could still flee down the stairs. *Then what?*

I forced a smile. "I'm ready to devote myself to serving this station and the citizens of our community."

Voss scowled and brushed back her shoulder-length brown hair, obviously dyed and longer than regulation. "Cut the bull. You aren't happy to be here and we aren't pleased to have you." Her voice was much higher pitched than her large frame would indicate. I stifled a laugh.

"My experience has prepared me to be a better police officer." I tightened my fists inside my pockets and held my face as placid as I could.

Captain Voss kept the desk between us. "The 'experience' humiliated you and left you nowhere else to go. So let's not play games."

Oh, let's. I grinned. "A little humility could be a good thing." *For you*, I wanted to add. I pushed that snide remark aside. "We've all gotten Sam's boot." I looked down, yet kept them both in my peripheral view.

Scarlatti looked away.

Voss grimaced and gripped the edge of her desk. "You're nothing like us, so don't go there." She grunted and cleared her throat. She sounded ready to launch into another monologue, so I braced myself.

"While you're on the force, might as well put you to good use," she said. "I'm assigning you to Lieutenant Scarlatti. She'll be your mentor and guide. Do whatever she asks, whenever she asks. You're to make yourself available to her 24 hours a day, seven days a week."

Blah, blah, blah.

"Can I have a cycle so I can respond quickly?" I asked when she took a breath. While I dreaded being under Scarlatti's thumb, I wondered how to use this partnership to complete Sam's assignment as quickly as possible. My mind went blank.

"She can pick you up whenever you're needed." Voss returned to her seat, but didn't sit down. "You don't qualify for a vehicle at this time."

Or ever, I imagined. "So I'm a full-time police officer?"

"Yes, yes." Voss waved her hand. "You're not returning to high school. If you want your GED, you'll have to get that on your own time." She nodded to Scarlatti.

The lieutenant strode up to me and held out her hand. "Welcome onboard. I trust Brooks has taught you enough so I won't have to start from scratch."

I shook her hand, a firm grip. "I'll do my best. I aim to serve."

Voss shook my hand, more like a cold fish. "I might be hard on you, but I have many lives to consider. Don't give me your guff and we'll get along fine."

"Thanks for giving me a second chance, Captain. I'll do my best to honor my service." *Not you.*

<∞>

Morgan McDermott sat on the dusty concrete basement floor

of the abandoned hardware store where Senator Scott had dropped him off. He mopped the sweat streaming down his cheeks and adjusted his e-contacts, the ones he almost lost during his fight with Annabelle.

As much as he could complain about his day, he wouldn't trade for hers. Through the hack into her contacts, he studied her conflict with her police captain with interest and decided not to bother her. He needed her help. That would take more finesse than when he broke out of his prison six weeks ago, the first time he met her. As a cop-intern, she hadn't turned him in. In fact, that was when she had helped him escape the first time.

His e-buds clicked. A familiar voice resonated in his ears. "Get me out of here." Seth's voice sounded thin and mechanical, its usual cadence.

"I hear you, bro. By the way, thanks for setting up these com devices. You saved my life today."

"Your fight was cooler than vid-monkeys," Seth said in a monotone. "She is pretty."

"Not your type, bro." Morgan smiled. He had to be patient with Seth, who rarely showed anything resembling an opinion, let alone emotions. It probably kept the younger boy alive, while locked away in that geek institute where they picked his brain.

"They will kill me," Seth said, as if stating a mathematical fact.

"Be patient. It'll take time to figure something—"

"I cannot stay."

"I know," Morgan said.

"They're going to move me."

"Where? When?"

"Tomorrow, they move two boys. Then it is my turn. I want to go home."

That was the most emotion Morgan had heard from his brother, even after they lost their parents. He got the message. Seth was scared. Morgan wanted a home, too, but they had no home, at least no place where they could return. Their mom had disappeared in the middle of the night. Neighbors said she worked with the Underground Railroad, which was a convenient excuse to eliminate those who disagreed with relocation policies. Their dad took them into hiding, and then vanished one night.

"I'll do what I can," Morgan said. "Can you guide me to our safe house?"

"Too far. Too many cams."

And women, Morgan reminded himself. A tall male would stand out. He needed to wait until dark.

<∞>

It was time to go home to face my family, and the shame I brought them by getting kicked out of the Mech Corps. Lieutenant Brooks dropped me off at the gate to Pleasant Acres. The sprawling mile-square community contained hundreds of four-bedroom duplex townhomes for community families like ours. Most housed three moms and up to six kids; my family had nine girls. The eldest three, like me, were adopted around the same time.

After Brooks drove away, I was tempted to cross the street and check out the cycle Sam had left me in the U-Store facility. I could use it to find a quiet place to think down by the river. The evening was warm and clear. Twilight drifted in, my time of day. I could walk to the river, but the cycle called to me.

I also missed the solitude of the tiny suite off the mech-gym I used during training while other recruits went off partying. Sam no longer wanted me hanging around the base, where my presence might raise uncomfortable questions among the other recruits.

Janine stood by the gate. She saw me and froze, not the reaction I needed after the day from hell. I expected disapproving looks from Therese, one of our older adopted sisters who acted as if she had a future except for the shame I hung over the family. My heart ached to tell Janine I was still in the mechs. That I hadn't failed her.

She smiled, came over, and hugged with none of the usual joy. I gazed into her sweet, intelligent eyes and couldn't bear the distress I saw.

"I'm so sorry I disappointed you," I said.

<Be careful what you say,> Morgan's bass voice thundered in my head, an alien resonance that bypassed my eardrum. <Your commander probably told you the contacts allow her to communicate with you. They also let her see and hear everything you do.>

"What?" I clenched my fists, willing the voice to go away.

"Belle? I'm not disappointed in you," Janine said.

<Don't say anything,> Morgan said. <The cams in the contacts and listening devices connect with your auditory implant.>

I let that sink in. "I did what I had to." I wondered whom I wanted to convince.

While gazing into my eyes, Janine took my right fist, unclenched the fingers, and traced a figure 8 on my palm. That was our signal at home that there were prying ears, lots of them. She flicked her hair and tilted her eyes toward the cams by the gate. "I wanted to find you," she said. "Mom said to stay in, but I figured you'd be hurting."

"So you snuck out." I was still trying to figure out the implications of Sam watching me.

Janine shrugged and smiled up at me.

It tore my heart to keep secrets from her. I steeled my resolve. "How's everyone taking this at home?"

"Mom's surprisingly calm."

I sighed. "She puts on a brave face for us. What about …?"

"Therese? Oh, she tried to whip everyone into a frenzy. Our lives are over because you got kicked out of the mechs. Everyone else is too shocked over Mom to blame you."

"They're all proud of you."

"You would've done the same," Janine said. "Let's go home. It's a good night to be surrounded by family."

"I want to talk, but I need time alone. Go home. I'll see you in an hour or so."

Without putting up her usual fuss, Janine walked toward the gate. She looked different. I couldn't help wondering if standing up to the assassin had changed her. I felt chilled, as if, despite the figure 8, things weren't okay between us. I'd been the strong one Janine looked up to. Now who did she have?

<∞>

Janine moved past the gate and slid behind a stone pillar. With the sun setting, shadows hid her civilian blue blouse and skorts. Even her tanned legs blended into shadows, just like pastel wallpaper.

She wanted to go home before Mom got upset, before her two other mothers worried about her being out late by herself, but she couldn't leave her sister. Belle was hurting, worse than Janine had seen in a long time, yet she wouldn't share. Janine replayed Sam's words, "Tell no one," and cursed this veil of secrecy Sam had thrust over her.

Well, Belle wasn't a "no one." She was the closest connection Janine had, a bond stronger than with Mom. Belle had always been there when Janine needed her, while Mom was off doing political

34

things. Her two other moms worried, but they had their own daughters.

Janine didn't know how to deal with Sam kicking Belle out of the Mech Corps while the commander wanted Janine in. Maybe the sisters could find other activities to share now that they were off their high-school basketball team.

Instead of following Janine home, Belle crossed the street. Janine stepped out from behind the pillar and stared. Her sister covered her face from the ever-present cams and entered the U-Store facility. Belle turned the corner, out of sight.

Stunned, Janine waited a moment, then dodged a bicyclist and ran across the street. Covering her face, she entered the U-Store. She sprinted to the far end of the first drive and around to the next. She froze. Belle stood before one of the narrow storage units. With a hand over her face, she looked both ways before unlocking the unit. A moment later, she emerged on a cycle, an old-style electric like Janine's.

What's going on?

While Belle rode toward the exit, Janine sprinted to her unit. She unlocked and removed the cycle Sam had given her. Then she rode out after her sister. At the exit, she caught a glimpse of movement to her right. Belle. She raced after her.

"Don't speed and don't follow too close," Sam said as if hovering inside Janine's ear.

Janine looked up, but of course, Sam wasn't there. She was speaking into Janine's audio implant.

"I'm sorry, Commander."

"Watch the road."

"Sorry, Commander."

"Just focus!"

Janine slowed and followed her sister's cycle at a distance. They drove past the cop station, then up a tree-covered hill beneath solar-powered streetlamps. There were no other cars on the road and few cycles. Belle stopped before a brownstone Janine recognized as belonging to Captain Voss. It looked big enough to swallow both sides of the duplex Janine called home, and Voss only had one wife and three kids.

"What's your sister up to?" Sam asked.

"I don't know, Commander. I swear." Janine pulled her cycle behind bushes and studied Belle, a block away. *You're not planning something, are you?*

A large round head appeared in an upstairs window. Captain Voss. Janine didn't like the big woman, just as she didn't like that bully, Dara, but she sensed much more anger coming from her sister. Belle moved onto the property, looked up at the window and then hopped onto her cycle.

Janine was relieved as she followed Belle away from the captain's home. *You don't need more trouble, Belle. Come home and talk to me.*

She hated letting Sam see what Belle was up to, in case it involved breaking more rules, but since Belle was out of the mechs, maybe that no longer mattered. Janine kept a wary eye on shadows all around her. She hated the night, and took comfort that Sam was listening in if she called out.

After riding up and down an endless stream of tree-lined, hilly roads, Annabelle stopped at Scarlatti's high-rise condo in Farragut with a fancier stucco exterior than the homes in Pleasant Acres. Scarlatti had been married to a younger woman. Now, she lived alone, no kids, in a very nice home for a lieutenant.

Belle climbed off her cycle and walked to the side of the building.

"Follow her," Sam said into Janine's head. "Stay close, but not too close."

"Yes, Commander."

"You don't need to respond. I don't want her to hear your voice."

Janine caught herself before she said anything more and parked her cycle around the corner. She followed Belle, and looked up to see if she could spot Scarlatti's windows. When she returned her attention to the side of the building, Belle was gone.

"Check her cycle," Sam said. "Don't let her leave without you."

Janine hurried back to the street just as Annabelle rode off in the direction of home. Janine panicked. If Belle got home first, she would know Janine was up to something. Janine took shortcuts and pushed the speed limit. She got her cycle put away just as Belle rode in. She ran home with more questions than before, and disturbed by Sam's voice in her head interrupting her own thoughts.

<∞>

After I returned my cycle to the U-Store facility, I crossed the street in the dark. The gate at Pleasant Acres accepted my biocode and let me enter. It disturbed me that I even considered the alternative: that it wouldn't. I was in over my head, yet I couldn't back out. If I lost Sam's lifeline, I had no future.

I didn't know what I hoped to accomplish by riding out to Voss and Scarlatti's places. I was tempted to break in, find whatever I could for Sam to end this mission, but I didn't know how to break in and I didn't know what I was looking for. I felt like the blind leading the deaf, all coming together in the partitions of my own brain.

Working for Captain Voss before mech training had been like rebelling against school rules. Working for Sam called upon everything I'd learned in mech training, and more. There were things Sam wasn't telling me, like how she saw what I saw and heard what I heard. If I had no privacy before, now I didn't even have my mind to myself. I wished Morgan would say something to shake this despair. I imagined his face: bristled whiskers over chiseled chin and cheeks, soft green eyes, the reddest hair, and freckles. Janine had freckles, but Morgan had a forest of them, though only visible up close.

The image faded. Rows of identical duplex townhomes drifted by, lit by LED porch lights powered by our community windmills and rooftop solar cells. Solar-powered streetlamps played out long shadows. As I kept walking, the light from the next lamp dissolved my shadow from the light behind me to nothing. That was one way to hide in plain sight. Not even our community-assigned maintenance crews were out this late.

I waited until my younger sisters were in bed before I entered our duplex. Janine greeted me at the door with a big hug. "I'm not disappointed in you," she whispered into my ear. "I swear." She looked worried. I had taken much longer than an hour.

Mom's light showed under her office door. She would be preparing for next week's legislative session. Mama Helen put down her e-pad, likely some medical report, and stood up. Mama Grace placed her knitting on the table and got to her feet. The rest of the room was empty; my seven other sisters were upstairs.

Janine's face was flushed and moist, though she didn't look as if she'd been crying. I mouthed, "What's up?"

Mama Grace reached me next and hugged me as if she hadn't seen me in months. She was the heart of the family, the glue that held us all together. "I'm so glad you're out of that terrible fighting. It breaks my heart to see girls brawl like little boys."

"I'm okay, Mama Grace. No permanent scars." Unless you counted the ones inside.

Mama Helen studied me, giving me her medical once-over. Then she hugged me. "Do you need medical attention?"

I shook my head, let go, and squeezed her hand. Then I entered Mom's office and shut the door.

She was staring at a large picture of Niagara Falls hanging on the wall behind her desk. Bret had proposed to her behind those falls. Mom took me once, before the Federal Union restricted travel. I'd never met Bret, Janine's dad. Mom hadn't seen him since she adopted me right after mech-warriors tore me from my birth mother's arms. That night, I traded places with Mom's only son, George, when his father took him to the Outland. I lost my dad that night as well, and had nowhere else to go except a state home. I suspect Mom took me in to fill some of that hole left by George. She talked to me about him almost every night.

"You okay, Mom?" I didn't see any bruises or cuts.

She hugged me, and clung as Janine used to at night. "It's hard to know who to trust these days." She pulled away. "I'm sorry mechs didn't work out. Maybe it's for the best. Not that being a cop isn't dangerous. I dread you getting stuck in the Outland."

"I'm fine, Mom." I closed my eyes and took a deep breath before I said too much. "Any idea who wanted to hurt you?"

She returned to her desk and let her face take on its stoic look. "Any good democracy is based on healthy argument over how people want to be governed. Some people can't stand dissent."

"I know the theory, Mom. As a cop, I'm asking if you have any idea who pushed that intern into attacking you."

She laughed, half sobbed, and caught her breath. "You're only 16, Belle, ready to take on the world. Leave this for the mechs and more experienced officers. You're too close to the incident to go digging. I'd hate for those involved to hurt you."

"Mom! Do you have any leads?"

"No, my dear. I don't." She leaned heavily against her desk. "I'm begging you to drop this. Just do your job for Captain Voss."

"Because one more cluster, and I'm off to exile." I sighed.

Having two bosses made that twice as likely. Or was this one of Janine's exponential functions where it got four times worse?

"Get some sleep," Mom said. "It's late. I have more work to do."

"No bedtime stories?" I asked, referring to her nightly reminiscence of Bret and George and the Outland.

"Not tonight, Belle."

Mom's refusal saved me, saved both of us. Realizing what I'd almost done, I closed my eyes and reminded myself that Sam could hear and see whatever I did.

SEVEN

I left Mom's office, feeling guilty. I couldn't help thinking she wanted to talk. Something troubled her, and it seemed to be more than the attempt on her life. Whatever it was, I didn't want to share with Sam. I kissed Mama Grace and Mama Helen goodnight, then went upstairs.

Sporting a cheeky grin, Therese stood in the pastel-wallpapered hallway, between two of the bedrooms. Her muddy brown hair looked slept in. Her blue eyes were bloodshot. The grimace on her face wore thin and began to fade. It added nothing attractive to her otherwise plain countenance. She carried that annoyed look that accused me of being the cause of all her problems in life.

Want to trade?

She blocked the end of the hallway and the bedroom I shared with Janine and our youngest sister, Sarah.

"As if this family didn't have enough problems," she said.

"So why make more?" I pushed past her, my body prepared for any of a dozen mech moves to land her on her rump in the corner. I forced a smile.

"You've made the entire family the laughingstock of Knoxville."

"Then move to where people don't care about petty things."

"It's not petty. You've ruined our chances of finding good jobs, good partners, and good homes."

You wouldn't be so high and mighty if your adoptive mom wasn't a doctor. I kept that to myself. If Mom hadn't been in the opposition in the

40

Tenn-tucky senate, my prospects might have been better. I didn't blame her.

I entered my bedroom with lights out. Sarah snored like a chainsaw. Somehow, I'd not only gotten used to her rhythm, but silence disturbed me when I'd stayed on the mech-base. By the hall light, I counted two lumps on the three beds pushed together along one wall. Janine and Sarah. *Good.*

Our calico cat entangled herself in my feet to welcome me home. I picked her up and we nuzzled noses. The family believed I named Dot for the black spot above her eyes, but Dot was short for Dorothy Montgomery, my birth mother, wherever she was. I placed Dot on the bed and went into the suite's bathroom, leaving the lights out.

After I finished in the bathroom, I located my bed by the closet and slipped under the thin sheet. Within moments, the furnace was at my back. Janine. "Where did you go?" she asked.

"Down by the river to clear my head." The lie came too easily, one of many I'd have to get used to telling in order to keep the secrets Sam demanded of me.

"You want to talk about it?"

I did, to the point a pain stabbed behind my left eye, reminding me I was still wearing my contacts. "I'm exhausted. Maybe we can talk in the morning."

Janine turned away. I tried to sleep, but I had too much adrenaline racing through me.

<Thanks for helping.>

I started to say, "You're welcome," then realized the voice was deep and male. *Morgan!*

<I'm sorry you lost your mech-warrior opportunity because of me,> he said into my audio implant.

I stiffened.

"You okay?" Janine asked.

I broke out in song. "If I had a hammer—"

<Don't say another word.> To stress his point, I got it as text visual in my right contact, with my eyes closed.

Though he couldn't see me in the dark, I mouthed, "Leave me alone."

<I need your help to rescue my brother from the Oak Ridge Geek Institute.>

<∞>

41

Sunday morning, Janine pestered me the moment we got up. "How do you feel?"

I shrugged. *Wonderful, for a girl with a guy's voice stuck in her head.*

"Will you talk to me about yesterday?"

Love to. Then I'll be in bigger trouble. "Later."

"You want to go down to the river?"

I smiled. *Great. Then you'll have more time to pester me with questions I can't answer.*

"Or we could go downtown," she said.

The guilt mounted. I needed to talk and she wanted to listen.

I volunteered us for church, the Universal American Church of Christ branch at the corner of our Pleasant Acres community. It was our Federal Union's very own church, a unification of all other faiths into one that would support the Federal Union. Despite being in the opposition, Mom said it was good to put in an appearance now and then. Church would silence Janine and the mounting questions that floated behind her eyes.

With my small backpack as a pillow, I dozed through the service. After church, I looked for Janine, and couldn't find her. She must have already left for home, so I popped my backpack over my shoulder, ran after her, and caught up about halfway home. "You want to grab lunch?"

"I've waited since yesterday afternoon for you to make time for me. I've made other plans." She walked faster.

"You want me to come with you?"

She hurried on. "I'm late."

"You shouldn't travel alone," I said. "There've been too many escapes and kidnappings."

"Stop mothering me. Maybe you'll be in a mood to talk tonight."

She broke into a run. Her words stung. I wanted to tell her everything. Maybe with the day to think, I could figure out how to handle this.

<Good morning, sunshine.> The cheerful male voice reverberated in my head.

"Don't—"

<Careful what you say. You can't be too sure who's listening. Nice church service, by the way, though you nodded off.>

Blood rushed to my face. Sweat trickled down my neck. I

wanted to reach into my skull and gouge out whatever implant carried his voice.

<Keep walking and listen,> Morgan said. <Our hack into your auditory implant and contact lenses allows me to hear and see what you do, just as Sam can.>

I walked fast to stay ahead of the rest of the family, the gaggle of sisters gathered around Mama Grace and Mama Helen. I didn't need a public scene. When Morgan's bass voice continued, I sang, "Got to get you out of my head. Da da da da da dum."

<Stop that or Sam will figure this out.>

"Sounds good to me."

<Don't say another word.>

"Sam, I'm in over my head."

<If you tell Sam, she'll know that you helped me.>

"Soldier, focus on your task, not your doubts," Sam said into my auditory implant.

That answered the question of whether she paid attention or was recording me for later. I wanted to scream. Instead, I took a deep breath and struggled to recall everything I'd said since I left Sam's office. "I stand ready to deliver." I passed our townhouse.

<I take it you didn't believe me that Sam had you bugged.>

I pursed my lips. I couldn't think of anything I'd said today that would compromise things. I couldn't be sure about yesterday and before that. How long had Sam been listening? Had she overheard Mom and me talk about the Outland, about Bret and George? Had Sam seen me hunt for my birth mother? Maybe this explained how Sam seemed to know my thoughts. I was a guinea pig in some horrid experiment.

I wanted to yell at Morgan without Sam hearing.

<I need your help,> Morgan said. <You're the only one who can, but you have to be careful.>

As if I needed more trouble. "How can I do what I have to do?" That sounded plain enough.

<Ah, how can you talk to me?> Morgan said. <Or rather, give me a piece of your mind. I'll get to that. Keep walking.>

"Soldier," Sam said into my head, "you need to take a moment and think this through. This is no time to act flustered."

<Your commander set up your auditory implants so she could talk to you and hear everything you hear. We can't bypass her

hearing you. She set up the contacts so she could see what you see, and send messages in both contacts. My brother modified the links so I can hear and see everything your commander can, including what she says. Sending to you is trickier. To avoid Sam catching on, I have to flip a switch to talk or send images, and only to your right side. I can't do that often, or for long, or she'll grow suspicious and change the contacts and implants to fix the problem.

<When I have the switch on, the only way you can communicate with me is visually. You'll know because I'll be talking to you. Make sure you're in a stationary place, so your commander won't suspect you're hiding something. Then close your left eye and write. I'll be able to see, and she won't. You'll know when I respond. If you understand, nod.>

I passed through our community gate, nodded slightly, and crossed the street.

<I'll take that to be a yes. Maybe a demonstration would help. Find a place where you can remain still.>

With my face covered, I entered the U-Store facility and got my cycle. I rode down toward the river, parked, and stared at the gentle flow of waters that originated up in the forbidden Outland.

<Are you ready?> Morgan asked.

Ready? I was beyond confused, between my implants, contacts, and the wrist-com the police department had provided me. But I refused to admit this. I closed my left eye and waited for Sam or Morgan to say something. Neither did. I pointed to my wrist-com.

<Okay, but make sure you delete and don't send. I don't think they can trace that.>

I typed into my wrist-com: "I hate you. Get out of my head."

<Not until you agree to help me free my brother,> Morgan said into my right ear. <Before they kill him.>

My wrist-com vibrated. I remembered in time, and carefully cleared my message to Morgan before I checked the incoming message. It was Scarlatti: "Get your butt out to your gate. You're wanted at the station. I'll pick you up."

When I reached the U-Store facility, Scarlatti's squad car sat across the street at the rest stop, next to a silver city bus. I wondered if Janine was on the bus, if she was safe. I didn't like her being on her own, a concern Mom should have had, except she was often busy or distracted.

I wanted to change out of my church pantsuit, but didn't see how to sneak past Scarlatti. I returned my cycle to its locker and ran to the facility entrance. Scarlatti looked around, and then stared at the community gate. When a bus obscured her view, I ran across the street and pretended to be returning from the woods. Sam didn't want my cop associates to know about the cycle.

Scarlatti rolled down the passenger window. "Hurry it up."

When I climbed in, the seat was hot from the sun. I checked the time. "Less than five minutes. That's not bad."

Not answering, she spun out onto the street between two groups of bicyclists and swerved to miss a bus.

"What's our first assignment together?" I tried to act cheerful.

"The captain called everyone in. You'll find out when they do."

I love being in the dark like fungus. Well, surprise, ground fungus might be the smartest life form on the planet. It terraforms its environment and spreads like a brain's neural network. It's quite resourceful for a low-life. That gave me something to aspire to.

When we reached the station, Scarlatti parked out front and tossed me the key-chip. "Move the boxes from the trunk and wash the car. I want it to shine before we head out."

Yippee, my first assignment. I looked at the mud-caked wheel wells and rear bumper. "It's illegal to wash cars on the street."

"Captain Voss said to do as you're told. Wash the car, after you bring the boxes to my office." Scarlatti hurried up the front steps and disappeared inside the maw of the station.

Make nice, I told myself. I'm more of an outside girl anyhow.

Then again, I couldn't look into what was happening inside our station while stuck outside. I glanced up and down the street—no cops ready to arrest me for washing Scarlatti's car. Yet, this was a cop station. Yeah, Scarlatti would delight in my arrest on my first day on the job. *I'm not a dumb blonde.* That sounded like what a dumb blonde would say. *Just do the work.*

I moved the car to the alley behind the station. Less chance to get caught. Then I recalled that Scarlatti wanted the boxes moved first. I opened the trunk and stared at the frayed cardboard of two old-style file boxes. The government had banned paper over ten years ago. Everything was digital so they could monitor everyone.

A single strip of tape sealed each box. I was tempted to open them, but I wasn't sure how Sam would react, and Scarlatti would know, since cams faced both ways up and down the alley. Besides, there wasn't any tape in the trunk to reseal the boxes, and Scarlatti might intercept me before I could hunt some down.

I adjusted my backpack over both shoulders and lifted the first box. It was heavy; contents inside shifted. I wanted a peek.

When I reached the bullpen, the rows of metal desks were vacant. Everyone gathered by the screens at one end of the great hall, surrounding Captain Voss and Scarlatti. Janine stood by Brooks. She glanced my way and smiled. I let out a long, deep sigh. She was okay.

"The governor wants an end to Outlanders crossing the border and stirring up trouble," the rotund captain said in her high-pitched voice. "We have some good intel that could lead to the capture of the Underground Railroad and end all these border crossings."

Scarlatti noticed me, pointed my way, and flicked her fingers to tell me to keep moving.

Her door was closed, but unlocked. I entered the dark office and dropped the box onto her cluttered desk. I pushed aside her e-pad, thin purse, and knickknack souvenirs she'd collected on various raids, including a couple of carefully hand-carved bird sculptures. The rest looked like tacky, cheap ornaments, yet might have had sentimental value to the lieutenant, reminders of successful stakeouts.

I looked through the open blinds. There wasn't a soul outside Scarlatti's office, and I was pretty certain there were no cams inside. From the shadows, Voss sounded like a squeaking mouse. My mind played tricks like that, which got worse after Morgan took up residence in my head. Thankfully, he'd been silent since Scarlatti called me.

I considered eavesdropping on Voss for some hint of what was going on, but I'd find out soon enough. The boxes called to me.

Never the cautious type, I peeled back the tape and was surprised it didn't rip the cardboard as it pulled free. I glanced inside. By the light from the bullpen, it looked like another collection from a raid: banned paper books and a ledger. Boys rarely kept anything electronic we could trace. I frowned, and wondered who had owned these.

I opened the ledger and flipped through the pages. Echoes of the pages appeared in my left contact. The scribbling made no sense, a jumble of letters and numbers. I pushed paper and books into the box and rummaged through Scarlatti's file drawer for tape.

The first drawer contained a half-eaten sandwich with enough odors to send me to the door, gasping for air. I shut that drawer and opened the next. It contained collections of key-chips and cards. I couldn't decide if these went to something important, or were themselves raid trophies.

"Get that box sealed and move to the next," Sam said, directly into my brain.

I jumped, as if caught napping in church, or worse, in one of Sam's training sessions. I found tape in the bottom drawer, gobs of it. I re-taped the box and slipped the tape into my backpack.

When I passed to return to the car, Voss still ranted about the Outland. She loved to hear herself talk and could keep her captive audience entertained for hours. I carried the second box to Scarlatti's office and eased back the tape, which tore some of the cardboard. The box was so battered, I doubted Scarlatti would notice. Inside were file folders: more banned paper the government couldn't access electronically.

I flipped through the files, page by page. Janine's puzzle-solving skills would have helped for what looked like codes, locations, or something. With how easily I scanned all of this, it interested me that Scarlatti hadn't done so, and destroyed the paper. I couldn't tell if I was looking at a list of boys and locations, or a clever mnemonic for recalling someone's grocery list.

By the time I resealed the second box and headed outside to clean the car, Voss was winding down; she had to pause to catch her breath after every few words. I hurried outside with a bucket of carwash liquid and scrubbed at the mud. It had a clay-like consistency that reminded me of the lands east of the mech-base: no-man's-land. We had robots for things like car cleaning, but Scarlatti was teaching me my place in the pecking order.

"Scarlatti," I whispered for Sam's benefit. "What are you doing in no-man's-land?"

"Finish your work and get inside," Sam said.

"Aye, aye," I said.

I scraped off most of the mud and cursed that I'd ruined my Sunday pantsuit. I should have changed into my cop outfit.

After I hosed down the car, I returned it to the front of the station. Aside from messing up my clothes, which Mama Grace would give me hell over, I didn't mind the work. Physical labor was like training. It allowed me to work off some of my muscle tightness after Saturday's fight.

Inside the station, the bullpen was full of officers and detectives. Janine sat with Brooks. Scarlatti called me into her office. The boxes were stacked in the corner, with knickknacks neatly rearranged on her desk. "You're on stakeout with me tonight."

"What are we looking for?" I asked.

"Another escape."

I didn't want to capture boys, not like this. I forced a smile. "Where?"

"You'll do exactly as you're told. Is that clear?"

I nodded. "What can you tell me so I can prepare? The captain must have talked for an hour."

Scarlatti laughed. "Short version: we got another tip. Boys crossed from the Outland, possibly a kidnapping raid. We don't know how many. You'll act as backup."

"Look, Lieutenant. I know I got off to a terrible start. I really want to do well this time. The more you tell me, the better job I can do for you."

She studied me and sighed. Before she could say anything, Voss knocked at the door. "Tonight you're there to learn, nothing more. Lieutenant, I need a word."

Scarlatti pushed me out of her office and locked the door. "We leave at eight. Until then, clean the cafeteria and the common areas." She followed Voss upstairs.

EIGHT

Nothing was messier than a cop cafeteria after Voss called everyone for a meeting. I guess my school cafeteria could be worse though. I'd cleaned that often enough. I wanted to bar the door when officers and detectives strolled in, grabbed decaf, bagels, and such, and left their mess for me to clean up. *A fun Sunday afternoon.* At least Brooks picked up her trash before she left.

While I swept bagel crumbs and mopped up decaf spills, I pondered the connection between Scarlatti's boxes and insider information for tonight. I wanted to review the files and try to make sense of them. As if by magic, they popped up before my right eye as a display. While I stared out the window at the alley and a concrete wall on the other side, documents floated before me, projected on the glass. Eye movement allowed me to sort through the documents I'd seen in the boxes.

A jumble of letters and numbers popped up, nothing to indicate times or places or what this meant. Janine's puzzle-solving skills would help, but I couldn't involve her when Sam explicitly said no. Besides, I had no way to share this information with Janine without implicating Morgan. She wouldn't approve.

Janine stopped in, saw me, and hurried out. This rift reminded me what a good team we usually made. In basketball, I'd been the point guard and she the shooting guard, a deadly combination against every team until we ran into Dara the Terror, the amazon who'd dogged me throughout mech training.

"Keep your chin up," Brooks said the next time she dropped in.

I wanted the day to end and yet, I imagined the same for tomorrow, and the next day, for the rest of my life. I wasn't cut out to be a cop or security, yet the state gave me no choice.

Sam clearing her throat pierced my thoughts. I scrambled to answer my wrist-com. When that showed no messages, I realized the voice was in my head, left side. I hurried into the restroom and checked the stalls. Empty.

"Yes," I said.

"Hope I didn't startle you," Sam said.

You know you did. "No, Sa—" I stopped and added, "Commander."

"We have a situation: a distress call. I want you to respond. Be careful and discreet. You can't reference this call." Sam gave me the address. I froze. It was Governor Battani's residence.

"Adrianne Picard is there, as part of the governor's fundraiser," Sam added.

I knew from discussions with Mom that Picard's inventions made an all-female society possible. The wealthy entrepreneur had also been instrumental in the Federal Union winning the war. She had supplied thousands of mech outfits and performance enhancement drugs that allowed Union armies to sweep the nation. What prevented a complete victory had been opposition leaders like Mom and Dorothy Montgomery, who pushed for a ceasefire and shaky peace. Battani and others never forgave Mom.

"Return to the cafeteria," Sam said. "When the phone rings, pick it up and reply in the affirmative. You'll reference that call if anyone asks."

"How do I get there?" I asked. "I don't have a vehicle at the station."

"You're wasting time. Show me how resourceful you can be. Remember, what's called for is discretion, not arrests."

"Understood."

I bolted out of the restroom. My mind swirled with questions, such as where to find transport. When I reached the cafeteria, the phone rang. I didn't recognize the woman on the line explaining their emergency. I nodded. "Uh-huh. Yes."

She hung up. I was stunned, as astounded as I was during the tournament when I almost embarrassed myself in a quick loss I turned into a victory. Then I remembered: *Sam's watching.*

I changed into my cop skorts and blouse, and hurried out into the bullpen trying to think, or not to. I'd get to meet Picard. A legend. The one who enabled our world without men by promoting EggFusion Fertilization, a laboratory process whereby two women could have a child without the need for a man.

It would take several buses and transfers to get home to my cycle. What would I say to Picard? Taking buses to Governor Battani's would take as long, and I didn't know the schedules. I checked my wrist-com for any news items. There was nothing about the governor.

Janine sat next to Brooks, listening, asking questions, and trying to soak up everything she could from her mentor and partner. I approached.

"I need to borrow your car," I whispered.

Brooks shook her head. "What's this about?"

"Trust me. I don't have time."

I glanced at Scarlatti's office. She hadn't noticed me yet. When she did, she'd have more busywork for me. I took Brooks by the arm and pulled her up and toward the station lobby. She moved stiffly.

Janine followed. Her intelligent eyes barely masked wheels turning inside. *Not tonight. Please.*

"We have an all-hands stakeout tonight," Brooks said as I pulled her down the front steps.

"Please, Becky. I need you to trust me."

"Last time you borrowed my car, you got yourself arrested," she reminded me. "I can drop you off. That's the best I can do. I need the car."

"I'm coming with you," Janine said, with her dig-in-her-heels persistence.

I stared at Brooks' boxy two-seat squad car next to Scarlatti's now-clean sedan. "We won't all fit."

"Then tell me what you're up to," Janine said, pouting.

"I don't have time for this," I said.

Brooks shook her head, muttered something, and unlocked the car. She scooted the passenger seat back as far as it would go, almost into the little trunk. I stuffed my five-eight frame in. Only slightly shorter, Janine pushed my backpack aside and climbed onto my lap. I fastened the seatbelt around both of us as Brooks climbed into the driver's seat.

Without giving the address, I directed Brooks street by street toward Battani Estates, the elite gated community where many city and state officials lived. They excluded opposition members like Mom, though I don't think she wanted to be that close to the governor.

"What's this all about?" Brooks asked along the way.

"While I cleaned the common room, I received an emergency call."

"And you decided not to run it through dispatch."

"We're on a real assignment?" Janine asked. I didn't have to see her face to feel her excitement.

"Yes," I said. "I didn't want Voss or Scarlatti deciding I wasn't ready."

Brooks sighed and shook her head. "Where exactly are we going?"

I waited until we were close and pointed to the entrance to Battani Estates. "In there."

"You're kidding," Brooks said.

"Are we going to meet the governor?" Janine asked.

Her enthusiasm for the official who hated Mom sent chills up my spine. I dreaded this, and was glad I'd brought Brooks.

"Spill, Belle. Give me all the details." Janine squirmed in my lap, trying to look into my face. The movement pinched the nerve in my right leg.

At least she couldn't give me her inquisition eye. I stared at the back of her silky brown hair, and wished she would give me a break while I figured how to handle this.

"Yes, little one, it's the governor's address. That's all I know."

"Don't call me little."

Brooks stopped at the gate. "Why not let Voss send someone? You'll get us all kicked off the force."

"Tell them we're responding to an emergency at the governor's mansion," I said.

Janine poked me in the ribs. "No more secrets."

I'm with you. I took her hand and drew a figure 8.

Brooks spoke into the gate security system. Doors opened. From the street, all that was visible was the ten-foot, steel-reinforced concrete wall topped with concertina wire and covered in ivy. Trees didn't overhang the wall, to prevent outsiders from climbing over. Inside the community, huge, two-story stone buildings lined a wide boulevard. This was where our leaders lived. Well, most of them.

Tall trees gave shade as well as privacy from satellite cams. There was an otherworldly aspect, a scene both out of the past and from the future. Old-style structures featured the latest in solar, wind, and advanced technologies only special people could acquire, including personal quad-copters for some of the residents.

I expected dozens of cops at Battani's residence. I found a single sleek black quad-copter and a collection of special-design new and vintage cars, some that never saw the streets of Knoxville. The mansion took at least twice the land area of nearby homes.

Brooks parked on the street. "You sure you want to do this?"

"I have to," I said.

Janine crawled out of the passenger seat. I took a moment's deep breath and poured myself onto the pavement before standing up, stiff, my right leg half-asleep.

Good thing Sam didn't want me to arrest anyone. There was no more room in Brooks' car, except for the trunk. That brought memories of stuffing Morgan in there the first time I helped him escape, six weeks ago.

"What do you know?" Brooks asked.

"Only that there was a disturbance." And the last person Governor Battani wanted at her front door was me. I hadn't thought this through. *No plan.*

I knocked at the door. A mid-twenties brunette in a slim black suit greeted us. I realized only Brooks wore a cop uniform. Janine and I still had our intern clothes, since Scarlatti hadn't issued me a new outfit.

"Knoxville police," I said. "We were told of a disturbance."

The brunette nodded and led us into a royal foyer with a stately chandelier dangling ten feet above my head. She left and hustled into a wide hall where dozens of well-dressed women smoked (illegal), drank (illegal), and watched entertainment that wasn't so well dressed: a man with no shirt. I stared with thoughts of Morgan. The first time I saw him up close, six weeks ago, he was soaking wet, the first boy I'd ever seen without handcuffs.

<Stop staring,> Morgan said.

I looked away, disturbed that he was watching this. "Now what?" I mumbled under my breath.

"Patience," Sam said. "I know you can't talk, so don't. I'd rather you had gone alone, but I applaud your resourcefulness. Remember to exercise discretion."

<I've been that boy,> Morgan said.

"I'm sorry," I said.

"No need to apologize," Sam said. "Focus on getting in and out without a fuss."

Ahgh. Leave me alone!

I forced a smile when the brunette in black reappeared with a tall, big-boned woman in an elegant evening dress. Governor Battani.

She scowled and said in a husky voice, "You! Of all the—"

A slender blonde with dark eyebrows stepped in front of Battani. Adrianne Picard looked more stunning in person than in the photos of the hero of the Second Civil War. Despite being over seventy, she looked twenty, her complexion the product of the biomed empire she built and controlled.

"I trust we can expect the utmost discretion from Knoxville's finest," Picard said, while she shook Brooks' hand.

"Absolutely," Brooks said. "Can you tell us the nature of the emergency?"

"Best we show you," Picard said.

She cast a puzzled glance at me and led the way through an ornate archway into a long, high-ceiling hall with rooms on either side. In one room, I recognized state congresswomen, senators, city officials, and others, like Picard, who supported Governor Battani. A dark-haired woman with an olive complexion stood out, stiff postured, dressed more in a gray uniform than formal attire.

"Antonia Rossi," Sam said into my head, anticipating my question. "Haven't seen her in ages. I'm surprised she'd lower herself to attend one of these fundraisers."

In the corner sat Emily Battani, the governor's daughter and a former classmate of mine. She looked miserable, an only child in a world of community families like mine. She headed toward me. A black-uniformed woman stopped her.

The hallway reeked of banned tobacco and other aromas that could get a girl like me years in prison. Governor Battani took Brooks aside.

Janine followed close beside me. "How did you—"

I cast her a sideways glance to back off. She looked annoyed, but dropped it.

I made sure to look at each of the oil paintings on the walls, at every table along the way covered with half-empty glasses, smokes, and ritzy knickknacks, and into every room that we passed. I had no idea what to look for. The replay feature of my contacts would come in handy later, to help me figure out not only who was here, but who, besides Mom, wasn't invited.

A tray on one of the hall tables caught my attention. It held a tiny needle from an injector gun. I stared at it and hoped my gaze would bring Sam's comments. It didn't.

Picard took my arm and pulled me along. "We must deal with this quickly."

I studied her youthful features. "It's amazing to meet you." She could have passed for a high-school student, with no wrinkles around her eyes, mouth, or neck. Yet, her eyes had the aura of a much older woman, at odds with the rest of her appearance. "I've read all about your work before the war and—"

"This isn't a social visit," Sam said. "Act professional. Keep looking around."

"I hope whoever disrupted your party didn't cause too much trouble," I said when we stopped before a closed door.

"What?" Picard said. "No, indeed." She unlocked and opened the door to a darkened room. She entered and waited for Brooks, Janine, and Governor Battani to join us before she closed the door and turned on overhead lights.

"I daresay he frightened some of the women," Picard said.

A dark-haired boy, Morgan's age and size, lay on the hardwood floor, wearing boxer shorts and his maroon collar. His neck looked charred from the activated collar. They must have left the electric shock on full until he was well past dead. I hadn't seen charred flesh like this. The smell filled my sinuses, a distinctive sour odor that had me gagging.

I couldn't breathe. All I could think of was Morgan, and how Sam had wanted me to kill him in the arena. Janine stood over the boy and studied him like one of her biology projects. I wanted to close my eyes to keep this from Morgan. Instead, I took it all in, scanning the nearby carpet, a sofa pushed out of the way, and empty bookshelves along the wall. Empty, except for a tray of needles: drugs, meds, something to enhance performance or dull senses.

<Will you help me before this happens to my brother?> Morgan asked.

"Discretion," Sam said.

Brooks knelt over the boy's neck. "This looks like excessive force. He could have been useful in the arena. How did this happen?"

I stepped between Brooks and Picard. "I suppose you need us to dispose of the body."

Picard nodded. "Unfortunate accident. People got carried away."

Not like he will be. "We only have a two-seater," I said, "which was a tight fit for the three of us."

Picard's face lit up. "Ah, being new to the force, you don't have your own transport."

The governor pushed between Picard and me. "Annabelle, this is *not* the time."

"That's all right," Picard said. "This is a practical problem with a practical solution. I believe I can help." She turned to me. "For your discretion in these matters." She handed a key-chip to Brooks. "Leave your two-seater, and consider this a gift from a grateful citizen. It'll allow you to transport and dispose of the body." Picard turned to me. "As for you two, how would you like shiny new electric cycles?"

<They're buying you off,> Morgan said.

My stomach cramped as if Picard had punched me. "I don't think—"

"Take the gift," Sam said.

"I don't know what to say," I said. "Thanks for your generosity."

Janine gave me a funny look but didn't say anything. I felt all twisted inside with all these voices in my head. I expected God to chime in at any moment with my next punishment, though I'd also expected Her to weigh in on my birth mother for some time.

Silence.

Brooks looked at me and then at Picard. "We'll remove the body for you. Do you have a way out that avoids the crowd?"

<You're going through with this?> Morgan asked.

"There's a side exit that leads to the car," Battani said.

"Adrianne knows the way. I'll make sure you're not disturbed." Battani left in a huff.

I expected Janine to object. Instead, she knelt over the boy's head and covered him with a blanket from the nearby sofa so we could no longer see his face. Brooks eyed me, and with good reason. I was wallowing in sin.

"Let's do this." I grabbed the boy's feet. He was heavier than I imagined, perhaps my burden of treating him as less than human. I needed to get out of Battani's home, out of Battani Estates.

Picard held the door while Brooks and Janine helped me carry the boy out of the room, across to a small kitchen and out a side door. The four-door car parked nearby was new, sleek, and much more spacious than Scarlatti's four-passenger sedan. It had no police markings, but we could easily add those. No markings would be a bonus in disposing of the body. The thought covered me in filth. I had just done a favor for whom? The governor, and the saint of the Civil War.

Discretion.

NINE

Under the cover of a large oak, we dropped the boy's body, wrapped in the blanket, into the trunk of Brooks' new car, and collected her things from the two-seater. Janine climbed into the back while I stretched my legs in the passenger seat next to Brooks. When she pulled out of the drive and down the street, I took one last look at Picard's sleek quad-copter. I wondered how many of the governor's neighbors were at the party, participating in whatever we were cleaning up.

"Care to explain what happened in there?" Brooks asked as we approached the community gates.

Not really. I braced for another lecture. "The call said there was an emergency, a disturbance at Battani Estates. That's all I knew before we got here."

"Where did the call come from?"

"Keep that to yourself," Sam said. "I have another task for you. Outside the gate, a van will meet you. Deliver the boy to Dara and Margarite."

"Are you ignoring me?" Brooks asked.

<You know what they'll do,> Morgan said.

"We should bury the boy," I said. "Give him that, at least."

"Turn him over to Dara," Sam said. "That's an order."

"Earth to Annabelle," Brooks said. "You didn't answer the question."

"Which question?" I asked.

"This is so unlike you," Brooks said. "I'd have expected you to

58

delight in investigating this."

"To what purpose?" I asked. "Picard was there along with … everyone. I don't want the shortest cop career on record."

"That was good," Sam said.

"Mech training *has* changed you," Brooks said. She pulled out past the gate and turned. A black van cut us off. Brooks careened up onto the curb and into a row of forsythia. Before I could say or do anything, Dara's big face loomed over the windshield like a Halloween mask. She stood outside Brooks' door, banging on the window with her gun.

Brooks glared at me. "Did you know about this?"

"I swear I didn't." *Until a moment ago.*

"Open the trunk," Dara said. "We'll take it from here. And keep your mouths shut."

I climbed out and went to the trunk with Dara. The lid popped open.

"Hey, loser. How does it feel to be a lowly cop?" Dara rubbed it in.

"This is a police matter," I said.

"The boy was meant for the arena. He slipped police custody and ended up here. So, excuse me if I don't trust cops. We're taking him back." Dara glared at me. "You haven't become a boy-lover, have you?" She stroked my cheek.

I pushed her hand away. "Regardless of what you think of him, he's a human being. He deserves a proper burial," I said, not only because I believed it. I hoped it would silence Morgan for now.

"I think you have." Dara lifted the boy's head. "No wonder you lost."

I helped Margarite with the feet, as we carried the boy into the van. She closed the back of the van, and with quick movements that never seemed to match her frail appearance, she climbed into the driver's seat.

Dara grabbed my arm. "Thanks for the assist. Just don't forget your place in the pecking order. You can thank Sam for ordering me to cooperate with the cops." She shoved me toward the car and swaggered off. I looked over to see Janine behind the car. She held her stun gun in one hand and a pistol in the other, a pistol interns weren't allowed to carry. I nodded for her to get in the car. I'd have to talk to her later about the gun, or not, with Sam watching.

It was hard not to hate Dara. Now, I had to deal with Brooks and Janine. I waited behind the car as the van drove off, trying to think of something clever to say to get them to stop asking questions, while not getting Sam upset or having Morgan interfere.

I sank my hands deep into the pockets of my skorts. My fingers curled around the contacts case. *Of course.*

I made sure Janine was in the backseat before I pulled out the case and removed my left contact. Before I could place it in the case, Sam's voice blared into my left auditory implant. "Put the contact in or return to base this instant."

"Is this going according to plan?" I asked. I squirted a dab of eye drops onto the lens and eased it onto my eye.

"You can thank me later for the cycle," Sam said.

"You knew?"

"Picard knows how to repay favors," she said. "Unfortunately, you've become a liability to the governor."

"Thanks. I need more enemies. So you *can* see what I see." I could imagine the smile on Sam's face stretching her scar.

<You're playing a dangerous game,> Morgan said.

"Did you see what you were looking for?" I asked.

Brooks rolled down her window. "We're late."

"Thanks for getting me inside the party," Sam said in my ear. "It helped. Now extricate yourself from your companions."

<∞>

With the sun setting, Janine and I had to push Brooks' new car out of the bushes and over the curb onto the street. Janine eyed me while we moved the car. It was much heavier than the two-seater. When she climbed into the backseat, Janine looked poised to ask me something. I closed my eyes and climbed into the front.

"Who alerted the mechs?" Brooks asked as she drove toward the station.

"Don't look at me," I said, pretending to nap.

"Open your eyes," Sam said into my implant. "Don't you dare remove your contacts."

"Then how did they know … and what the hell happened back there?" Brooks asked.

I obliged Sam by opening my eyes, and staring out the side window. Janine kicked my seat to let me know she was upset. Brooks hammered me with questions I couldn't answer. I waited for Morgan to weigh in. I hadn't ever felt so muzzled, and I was used to holding secrets. I hadn't signed on to being watched twenty-four-seven, but the alternative was exile.

The only break from questioning came when Brooks took a call from Captain Voss and looked shaken. She stopped the car and turned to me. "You've done it this time. And you won't even give me the satisfaction of answers. I'm disappointed, Annabelle. I expected better."

"I'm sorry, Lieutenant. That's all I know." Thankfully, I didn't have to look at Janine.

Instead of driving to the station, Brooks turned around and headed to Bakerton, a planned community on the east end of town. The plan had been to create a mini-downtown next to a bus transfer interchange, with all the government-approved stores clustered together to create a community. Sadly, it was too close to the border. Few women agreed to move this far east, so it remained a bus interchange, with one active restaurant for commuters. Most of the stores were vacant. *That's what happens when people don't follow the government plan.*

Brooks parked next to Scarlatti, who scowled; she no longer had the best car on the force.

Captain Voss ambled over and collared Brooks as she got out of her car. "Don't think this buys you anything. The governor said something about returning a favor. That doesn't excuse you being late."

Scarlatti grabbed me and pulled me away before I could come to Brooks' defense, which would only have dug a bigger hole for both of us. I wanted to ask why this was our problem instead of the East Knoxville station's.

"You know how to piss people off," Scarlatti said.

She led me to the side of a complex of stores, most boarded up with no signs. Despite being new, the Union Burgers & Subs looked in need of repairs, with a cracked window and debris outside.

"We're behind schedule," Scarlatti said. "Our source reported several Outland boys in the area, no doubt working for one of their cartels on another kidnapping raid. These empty stores are a magnet for such trash. They can't hide for long."

A fresh scowl on her face, Scarlatti took me across the narrow lot from Union Drugs and parked me beside an unlit lamppost. "Stay here and wait for further instructions."

With the sun having set, the sky darkened more than I was used to. The eastern fringe of town had few working streetlights and the stores were shuttered. I wasn't afraid of the dark, but I wanted to keep an eye on Janine. "Can I help with the raid?"

She shook her head. "Stay here."

I studied the well-lit drugstore, and saw no one inside. "The boys could be here for the meds."

"I *said*, stay where you're at and report anything unusual."

"Do I get a firearm?"

"You aren't trained," she said.

"Actually, I am."

She handed me a single-shot stun gun. "Make do with this, and don't move from this spot."

She headed around the back of the building, leaving me on my own. That would make it hard to get close enough to Voss or Scarlatti to get the answers Sam wanted.

<I need your help, Annabelle,> Morgan said into my right ear. <Seth. You didn't ask, but that's his name. He's 14, scared, alone, isolated. They pick his brain until he wants to kill himself. He knows if he dies, others will do the work. Help Seth, please.>

I closed my right eye and stuck a wad of tissue into my right ear.

<Closing your eye won't send me away. I know you want to help. You're a good person, the best I've met.>

I opened my eye and removed the tissue. There had to be a way to get him to leave me alone. I had enough trouble.

He was right about my wanting to help. Then what? Did he care that I could lose my second family? Of course he didn't. No one but Mom knew about my birth parents.

From beneath the darkened streetlight, I scanned the boarded-up stores to my left, the empty parking lot except for four cop cars, and the woods to my right. Using my wrist-com infrared, I looked for the boys, and other cops. Most of the cops were still out front. I looked behind me, in case boys tried to grab me.

It had been a long evening and I needed the bathroom. I spotted one inside the pharmacy. I didn't see Voss, Scarlatti, or anyone else. It was like my teachers sending me to my high school's Harmony Director's office when I violated some school rule, so I could get a lecture while I stared out the window at Morgan's school-prison, as it turned out.

The pharmacy looked deserted. I found the door unlocked. I headed inside and checked all the aisles with half-empty shelves of personal care needs before making my way to the restroom in the back. I felt self-conscious, all eyes watching me. "I deserve some privacy," I whispered as I entered the restroom. I removed my contacts and put them into their case. This time Sam and Morgan didn't protest. They could still hear.

The stalls looked recently cleaned and stocked with sanitary cleanser and Insta-flush. Nonetheless, when I finished, I washed my hands and stared in the mirror, a moment of privacy. I looked up above the door; probably nano-cams made sure no one lurked in the restroom.

I tied my hair up to keep it regulation, off my shoulders, and headed out of the restroom. I had to get back before Scarlatti caught me away from my post. I came face-to-face with two ragged boys with bushy, unkempt hair and beards, both bigger than me. They froze. I froze, and then reached for my stun gun. I pointed it at one and then the other boy. I only had one shot. The other boy might try to overpower me. They looked to be brothers, twins. But I hadn't seen many boys. Maybe it was their scruffy beards and rags.

They each carried backpacks. As I'd thought, they were after meds they couldn't find in the Outland. Our benevolent Union wouldn't trade Picard's wonder drugs with them. One boy looked ready to run. The other assumed a fighter's pose.

<What are you up to?> Morgan asked. <I told you closing your eye wouldn't send me away. Neither will removing the contact. It'll only alert your boss.>

Thinking of these boys as Morgan and his brother, I put my finger to my lips and motioned them toward the back door. One dropped his meds on the nano-tiled floor. The other stuffed his handful into his backpack. I motioned with my hands for them to hurry.

"Get your contacts on, soldier," Sam said.

I scanned outside the pharmacy, and didn't see any cops. I motioned for the boys to go out the back, and moved to a dusty window display out front. Shadows shimmered outside, beneath dark parking lot lights with no infrared images in view. I eased down onto the tile floor and put on my contacts.

"What happened?" Sam yelled into my left implant.

"I heard a noise. Someone hit me from behind. When I came to, I didn't see anyone."

"Why don't you have a partner?" Sam asked. "Don't answer that. And don't remove your contacts again. I could've sent help."

Thanks, Sam, but I'm not sure which side you're on. I nodded. Then it hit me. "Does that mean you have warriors in the area?"

I heard movement in the back of the pharmacy and crouched down. I should have called this in to Scarlatti, but I felt sorry for those boys.

I held out my stun gun and inched forward. Crutches on a display caught my eye: an additional weapon, in case. I hesitated. Earlier, when I bumped into those boys, my contacts were out. That was stupid, yet Sam hadn't said anything. I couldn't remove the contacts again.

A clean-shaven boy with tussled brown hair knelt down and picked up the meds the other boys had dropped. I scanned the rest of the pharmacy to make sure he was alone. I didn't see anyone else in direct light or infrared.

"Did you get lost?" I asked. *Careful,* I told myself, mindful of the contacts.

The boy looked tall and muscular. Yet, he cowered and raised his hands over his head. "Don't shoot. Don't turn me in. Pa's ill. We can't get meds. If I don't help, he'll die."

Eyes bore down on me: Sam, Morgan, probably Voss and Scarlatti. I knew what I would do for family. And I'd already let two boys go.

I waved my stun gun toward the door. "Outside." I puzzled over how to let him go without getting caught. "Where are you from?"

"The Outland."

I raised the crutch and nudged him toward the front door. "Where, exactly?"

"Biltmoor."

"Where in Biltmoor?"

"My pa works in a warehouse. We live near it."

"How did you get this far? Did you have help?"

"I've done this lots of times," the boy said. He looked ready to cry.

I marched him outside, toward my post. There was a clump of trees beyond the lamppost, where the two boys might have gone. I could give this one a chance to knock me out, though I didn't fancy that, and Sam already suspected me over Morgan's escape.

"You got a name?"

"Hank."

"Have you been caught before?"

The boy shrugged and dropped his shoulders.

"Are you working with others?"

"You ask a lot of questions for a cop," the boy said.

"What other cops do you know?"

"Please don't turn me in. I did prison the last time."

"Who else is with you?"

"I'm alone," Hank said. "Look away and I'll disappear. You'll never see me again."

<It's a trap,> Morgan said. <The boy's lying. Look to your right, by the power transmission shed.>

I did, and spotted the glint of metal: a rifle with a scope.

<Something's not right. Don't let him go. You know I wouldn't lie about this.>

I spun the boy around and cuffed him. Then I pushed him to the ground.

"Please," the boy said. "My pa—"

Several cops rushed out from behind the transmission shed. Brooks and Janine came from the front of the building.

Scarlatti appeared over my shoulder. "I told you to stay put. If you can't do as you're told, you're no use to me."

"I caught him."

"We have reason to believe there were two other boys. Did you see them?"

Beneath the heat of various flashlights, I stared at the boy on the ground. "Were there others?"

The boy seemed to withdraw. Tears filled his eyes. *Damn. I should have helped him.*

"I smell a rat," Sam said.

The image of that rifle and scope burned into my mind, or was it a replay in my right contact?

Captain Voss stood over me. "Get him out of here. Place is empty. If there was anyone else, they're gone."

Scarlatti hauled the boy away. She didn't offer to give her partner, me, a ride back to the station. I couldn't loosen the tightness in my heart that I'd had the chance to help Hank, and hadn't. He'd only wanted meds for his pa.

TEN

Instead of giving me a hug or seeing if I was okay, Janine headed out front with Scarlatti and Voss. I tried to shrug it off.

"You did well," Brooks said. "Come on, I'll give you a lift. We might as well make use of my new luxury car."

We both laughed, which lightened my mood. I followed her toward the car.

<Admit it,> Morgan said. <I saved you from a terrible mistake.>

I wasn't ready to admit that. I just wanted to shut him off, but that would take surgery. I closed my right eye.

<I don't blame you for not trusting me,> Morgan said. <I need your help. Nod your head once if you agree to hear me out.>

The mech com-link connection, which was like telepathy, gave me comfort. I could turn that off. These incessant others in my head were infuriating.

"A ride would be great, Becky," I said to Brooks. "Home sounds good."

"After I file my report on your little sideshow."

<Agree to listen, and I'll leave you alone the rest of the night,> Morgan said.

I gave a slight nod while I got into the passenger seat. Janine climbed in the back without saying a word. I longed for a mirror so I could gauge her expression. She was pulling away, as if her standing up to Mom's assassin meant she no longer needed me.

"You two have had a busy couple of days," Brooks said. "You deserve a break."

"I'm fine," Janine said, though her voice told me otherwise.

My right contact pulled up what at first looked like a swarm-cam view of the boy's capture, though it was too steady for a swarm. I hadn't seen any reporters. Then I noticed all the views came from the buildings: security cams. My wrist-com newsfeeds showed the same views, in too much clarity for regular security cams, as if ... as if Voss had staged the capture for publicity.

The contact viewer showed me escorting Hank from the pharmacy to the light post, and then cuffing him. The newsfeed on my wrist-com showed Scarlatti escorting the boy out front and stuffing him into the back of her squad car. There was no view of Hank's face, and no indication anyone else was involved except Scarlatti.

"This is bull," I said. "I captured the boy and Scarlatti gets the credit."

"At least you survived your first mission," Brooks said.

Yeah. And if I had let Hank go, Voss would have had enough evidence to send me to prison. *Thanks, Morgan.*

Brooks left me in silence the rest of the way to the station. My head told me Morgan had saved my butt; my heart wasn't convinced.

"You two can wait in the car," Brooks said when we reached the station.

I wanted to take Janine home, which involved three buses with two transfers. Even if I couldn't share with her, I could keep her safe.

When I held the car door for her, she climbed out and ran inside the station.

"You two okay?" Brooks asked.

"She's still trying to make sense of what's happened," I said, and hoped that was all.

"If you want to talk, I'll make time."

I shook my head and followed Brooks up the steps. I considered checking Voss' inter-mesh access, but the last time I did, to hunt for my birth mother, Voss caught me and almost sent me off to resocialization. This time I would look for Sam's mission, but I needed to be sure Voss and Scarlatti were out of the station, and that they didn't have cams or spies checking up on me.

Brooks stopped me inside the station. "I know that look, Annabelle. You don't have to go through this on your own. You did fine at the pharmacy. Your instincts are good, better than some experienced cops. Don't beat yourself up over what Scarlatti said."

"I want to learn the ropes and do my job well." I gave her the vanilla version, while I eyed the stairs to Voss' office. The captain and Scarlatti whispered across the large station hall. *Too risky to go prowling.* "How do I handle Scarlatti, when she hates my guts?"

"You can be a good cop or a dutiful cop," Brooks said. "Tonight you tried to be a good cop."

"You think I should have waited outside while the boy grabbed meds and made a run for it."

"If you want to get along with Scarlatti, you need to listen to her. You weren't the only cop out there. You could have called for help."

"So you don't think I 'did fine' at the pharmacy."

"Don't twist my words. You asked for my advice. Give a little in your dealings with Scarlatti. Don't keep stomping on her toes. After all, today was your first day with her and you disobeyed her express orders."

Because Scarlatti was wrong! "I had to use the bathroom."

"You don't have to sell me," Brooks said.

I expected Scarlatti or Voss to jump in and continue belittling me. Instead, they headed for the elevator to the basement. I'd only been down there once, to tour the jail cells I almost occupied six weeks ago. That was when Sam gave me the alternative of trying out for the mechs. *Some choice.*

At the other end of the basement, Voss kept the mech-cop outfits she would never let me use. Cops trained there, a mild version of what I went through for Sam.

"Is there another mission tonight?" I asked Brooks.

"Nothing to concern yourself with." She headed toward her desk in the middle of the great hall.

I hurried to the elevators as the doors opened. Voss stepped inside. I caught my breath. "Captain, I'm sorry I broke protocol this evening. I had to use the restroom. Then I saw that boy. I didn't want him to get away. I'm still learning."

Voss nodded toward Scarlatti. "You should make amends with your partner."

Scarlatti scowled. "We'll talk in the morning, now run along." She flicked her hand my way.

Follow orders or seize opportunity. I'm not one to sit on my hands. "Beg your forgiveness, Lieutenant, but if you have a mission using mech-gear, I'm trained."

"How did that work out?"

"I promise to follow the letter of your commands, Lieutenant. I could be a valuable asset." *And figure out what you're up to.*

"We have all the units briefed and ready to go," Voss said. "I'm afraid you'd slow us down."

"I'm a fast learner. Is this another escape attempt?"

Voss nodded involuntarily. "You'll have to wait your turn. You've had enough excitement for your first day."

"I'm the lieutenant's partner," I said. "Shouldn't she have backup tonight?"

"Go," Voss said. "Don't make us late."

The elevator doors closed. Something told me to follow Voss and Scarlatti, that doing so would bring me closer to what Sam wanted than hunting through Voss' net access. Besides, too many cops lingered around the station. The sooner I got this mission over, the sooner I could get my life back and reach out to Janine

Across the bullpen by the entrance, she stood talking to a woman in a black and white penguin outfit: formal wear. I recognized the brunette from Battani's party.

I joined them. "What's going on?"

Janine grinned and handed me a chip. "This nice lady is delivering our new cycles."

That was quick. I studied the thumb-sized electronic key. Despite wanting a cycle I could use anywhere, this was dirty money, a bribe. I held out my hand to refuse it.

"Take the cycle," Sam said.

I nodded, took a deep breath, and thanked the woman.

"Meet you at home," Janine said. She ran out of the station and down the steps.

"Do I owe you anything?" I asked the woman in black.

"I was only told to deliver them to you and your sister. They're charged and ready to go."

The woman shook my hand in a firm grip and left. I wanted to wash off whatever taint came with the cycles. A better idea came to me.

I headed outside, into the night. My shiny new black cycle stood alone under a streetlamp next to Brooks' new car. Janine was gone.

"Remember what I showed you," Sam said. "Do an electronic sweep of the cycle."

When I did, I discovered a tiny tracking chip below the seat. I removed it, and attached the rice-grain-sized chip to Scarlatti's car. Then I pulled out onto the street, dodged a city bus, and headed around the building.

The streets were quiet. Only the occasional bus and a few civilians hurrying to the nearest bus stop. Brooks left, along with a few other cops who weren't on this mech-cop mission. I did a count and roster check. In total, six cops were unaccounted for, all Voss insiders, including the veteran lieutenant, Terry Scandia, and a fresh sergeant, Dot Montrose. When they weren't doing undercover work, those two kept to themselves, or hung around Scarlatti. Both had trained with mech-cop gear.

Two armored vehicles pulled out of the alley and headed east. Between East Knoxville and the border, escape action would be hottest. Yet that was Mech Corps territory, Sam's responsibility. Voss *was* stepping on toes. The vendetta went both ways.

Beneath the halo of city lights bouncing off the partly cloudy sky, I kept my distance. It wasn't hard to follow the armored vehicles, given their grumbling motors. They weren't quiet or stealthy like Sam's mech models. Still, it was too dark to see the puffy clouds of smoke, mostly water vapor, except when they came near streetlamps.

Morgan weighed in. <You shouldn't go east on your own. It's too dangerous.>

His concern was touching. To stop him from crowding the rest of my thoughts, I turned on the cycle's radio and ran through the familiar music stations. The tunes were too bland for me. They threatened to put me to sleep while I rode.

One of the talky stations blared another ad for Adrianne Picard's EggFusion Fertilization. It was late night, after all, when young minds were supposed to be in bed.

"With EFF," the announcer proclaimed, "you can have a daughter with your partner whenever you're ready."

I wasn't, and I didn't have a partner.

It was half-past ten. I flipped to another talky, another commercial. "Thanks to new medical advances, Picard Enterprises offers new, noninvasive cures for brain cancer."

Every month or so, Picard's company announced a new cure. The last one had been for breast cancer. Women flocked to clinics for the preventative treatments. No more surgery, no more chemo.

The ad ended and the talk show came on, threatening to put me to sleep with lectures on the seven steps to promoting the New Harmony. I turned it off.

East of town, artificial lights dimmed. The stars that poked out between clouds looked brighter, closer. The armored vehicles passed through a guard post on the main road leading to no-man's-land. I hesitated, waiting for Sam's warning. When I didn't hear from her, I figured it was okay, or she'd dozed off. She did sleep, didn't she?

I walked my cycle along the concertina wire-topped chain-link fence until I found a break, a spot where rains had washed a gully beneath the fence. Thankful it was dry, I crawled through and pulled the cycle after me. Mama Grace was getting used to getting stains out of my clothes.

From there, I crept past the checkpoint guards before resuming my ride. When the roar of the armored vehicles loomed up ahead, I stopped and pulled off the road.

I'd never been this close to the border before, and wished I could see more than moonlit shadows. My skin crawled with the thought that someone could drag me over the border to an uncertain future. Yet, part of me hungered to find George, Mom's son, the only boy I really knew, though we'd never met.

Clouds faded away, leaving a sky full of stars and a half moon. Not far away, I watched mech-cops in dull black-shielded gear in the armored vehicles' headlights. Special coating on the shields made them almost impossible to see in the moonlight when they stepped away from the vehicles. At first two mech-cops appeared and then four, not mech-warriors, who operated in threes.

After they lined up, the four mechs sprinted toward the border. I imagined myself in one of the black exoskeletons, making my way into the Outland and freedom. Except freedom didn't sound so great when you didn't have meds, a tyrant ran the place, and women were treated as slaves. Despite all the warnings, I found the last part hard to believe, just more propaganda.

Hidden by bushes, I waited. Could these boys be so stupid as to cross the border when we had mech-warriors and mech-cops waiting to intercept them? Those two boys I let go had been quite brave. Using my wrist-com infrared, I watched the characteristic mech-suit exhaust move toward the border and fade away.

Voss and Scarlatti sat in one of the armored vehicles while two cops sat atop the vehicles with what looked like small cannons. I wished Morgan would talk to keep me company. I hadn't gotten the chance to get to know him in our brief encounters. He had my attention in ways that felt comforting, and confusing.

The first time we met, six weeks ago, I acted petrified, like a cornered mouse. I still couldn't believe he fit into the trunk of Brooks' two-seater, or that I'd been foolish enough to help him escape. The second time hadn't been much better. I was on a stakeout to capture boys squatting in an abandoned college dorm. When he jumped out of nowhere, I couldn't use my stun gun. If I hadn't been so petrified, I might have followed him then. When we fought in the arena, he had me. Then I had him, yet I couldn't kill him. It was my idea to help him escape the arena, and I failed. Sam caught all of them, except for Morgan.

The two cops atop the vehicles scanned the surrounding area. I curled up into a ball so I wouldn't give off a recognizable infrared signature.

Cat's-eyes wandered nearby. A spooky set of eyes I took to be a raccoon's moved in the distance, too far away to see well. An owl hooted from behind the vehicles. A flutter of animals scurried for cover. The stomping of mech-suits squashed the remaining silence, as unmistakable as the bass of male voices. I looked toward the vehicles to see the first of the mech-cops return carrying two figures.

"You godless Feds got no right crossing the border," a male voice said.

"Take us home," another said.

That got my attention. "Voss is crossing the border to capture boys," I whispered.

"I see," Sam said. The immediacy of her response unnerved me. She'd been with me all night.

"What in the world for?"

"Why do you think?"

"Scarlatti said she expected two more boys," I said, scooting around to get a better view.

"Now they have them."

Like the governor on newsfeeds, Scarlatti and Voss complained about Outland raids into our lands, but never these. No wonder the Outlanders kept fighting.

"Stay low and small," Sam said. "I don't fancy blowing your cover tonight. I can't rescue you out there."

I curled up and gazed from behind some rocks at the floodlit scene below. Three other black-shielded mech-cops returned. They stuffed six males into the back of one of the armored vehicles. Two mech-cops climbed in after them. I stayed low as the vehicles pulled out and sped down the road toward Knoxville. I wanted to follow, but with their infrared checking for pursuers, they would spot me.

Not wanting to see the Outland reaction to a raid, I ran to my cycle. With lights off, I headed west along the dusty road, stopping now and then when moonlight didn't show enough of the road. I had to sidetrack near the roadblock, and cross beneath the chain-link fence.

By this point, I was beyond exhausted, burning my last reserves of energy, and amazed Sam had been so quiet. I considered stopping at the base, but not at the risk of getting shot or facing too many questions. When I reached within sight of the first active residential development beyond the base, I stopped to relieve myself.

Hearing turmoil behind the community walls, I covered my face with a scarf, scant protection from our ever-present cams. I grabbed some broken branches and bush trimmings, and climbed the wall. I placed branches over the concertina wire and placed bush trimmings over that. Then I froze.

Two armored vehicles parked inside the entrance to the community. Mech-cops stood nearby. I used my wrist-com night-vision to get a better look. I recognized the two cops on top of the vehicles as Scarlatti's friends. I heard male voices between the vehicles and me.

"This way." "It's a trap." "Let's stick together." "We'll do better if we split up."

Switching to infrared, I spotted one of them, running between duplex townhomes not unlike my home. Three others followed.

High-pitched gunfire shattered the night air. One of the infrared figures fell onto his side. His signature split in two—mech machine-pellets. The other figures dove into bushes. One doubled over. Lights came on all around the development from homes and security posts. Mech-cops, with "SWAT" emblazoned on their dull-black titanium shields, rounded up the remaining boys.

"Are you seeing this, Sam? What is this, a war game to train Voss' mech-cops?"

Sam's voice rattled around in my head, causing me to jump. "Voss is getting bolder. I don't know what she's up to."

"Other than impressing the governor."

"Dig deeper."

Three boys surrendered. Another ran for the wall to my right. A mech-cop fired into the boy, sending him sprawling onto the grass. He twitched and lay still.

My stomach knotted up. My throat closed.

<That's what your glorious Union does at night,> Morgan said. <Sorry to interrupt your pleasant thoughts, but that awaits Seth when they're done with him.>

I nodded. *I'll help.*

For an instant, I imagined helping the three boys who had surrendered. They knelt with hands over their heads. Two female figures in the shadows made their way toward them. Could they be Underground Railroad? I looked away before Sam saw, in case Mom was one of them. Hope evaporated when three mech-cops surrounded the last boy and carried him to the armored vehicles.

<Be careful,> Morgan said. <They'll kill you for watching.>

That explained why Voss didn't want me here.

"Get your butt out of there. Now!" Sam said. "Head east to the base. I can't protect you out there."

ELEVEN

You don't have to tell me twice. I dropped from the wall and spotted two cops heading my way on foot. I ran along the wall, behind bushes and trees, and reached my cycle. Keeping lights out, I sped away from the development down a dirt path heading east, beneath a wooded canopy that blotted out the stars and the moon.

At least I hoped it was a path. Unable to see much, I was too busy avoiding rocks and branches to use my wrist-com night-vision. *This is nuts.* I should have hidden and taken my chances, but with their infrared, they would have caught me.

I kept my head low, dipping below the top of the visor when branches whacked the cycle. At least they couldn't get their armored vehicles down this path. On the other hand, they could send the mech-cops after me. Mechs could run at 30 miles an hour, and with experience up to 40. In the dark, I couldn't afford to ride faster.

Engines roared behind me. Floodlights sent long shadows, illuminating the path on either side. I prayed they didn't have cycles. In their places, I would have.

"Your path will dead-end into a steep ravine," Sam said. "Turn 60 degrees left."

For once, I wasn't annoyed that she could see and hear me. I ran through a gap between bushes and veered left. My bones rattled over rough, rocky terrain. The path was too narrow. I wouldn't put it past Voss to call in choppers, unless our captain didn't want that much visibility.

"Where are they, Sam?"

"Two mechs took off along your path. Their infrared picked you up. The other two are in armored vehicles that split up. They're taking wider paths to your left and right. There's a dirt road ahead of you. They'll use it to close off your escape."

At least if Mom or her friends were there, I'd provided them a distraction and time to escape.

"Focus!" Sam said. "In a moment, turn right 60 degrees and head straight east."

Bushes tore at my bare knees and elbows. Swatches of my ragged blouse and skorts flapped in the wind. A branch bypassed my visor and smacked my helmet. I didn't slow down, didn't dare to. Mech-cops thrashed behind me. In the distance, the roar of diesel-powered vehicles rumbled over the quiet purr of my electric motor. I couldn't outrun them.

"I'm sorry, Sam. I got careless—"

"Shut up and focus," Sam said. "This is just like your training. When I give the signal, ditch the cycle and run due north, to the left."

Trees to my left and right took on the appearance of mechs, surrounding me. Moonlit shadows loomed all around. Now and then, the mech-cop beams cut through the darkness, lighting up nearby trees for what they were. Then all fell dark until my eyes adjusted to moonlight. I avoided hitting a tree, found the path, and picked up speed.

"Now!" Sam said.

I skidded the cycle into a ditch I hadn't seen. My bare left leg scraped against leaves, dirt, and rock. Pain jabbed like nails. I scrambled out from under the cycle and sprinted just as Sam taught us during training: as if my life depended on it.

"Turn slightly left," Sam said.

I crashed into tree branches. All around, flashes blazed like fireworks, though without noise, like a light show. The flashes continued as I made my way to the south wall of the mech compound. I expected an open door, or at least a "Welcome, you're approaching the finish line." My wrist-com night-vision showed only the stark concrete wall and a closed steel door.

Lights flashed behind me, illuminating my path. There were no lights along this side of the complex itself. Sam would use infrared, microwave, and a dozen other silent trackers. How had I been so naive to imagine I could help boys escape from the mech compound? Yet Morgan had gotten away. That was something.

When I reached the steel door, I saw a mech in the shadows and froze.

"Get your sorry ass inside. That's an order, soldier."

The door swung open. I broke into a sprint. Flash-decoys scattered behind me. The mech closed the door and removed her helmet.

"I won't ream you for brazen behavior," Sam said while she led me down a narrow khaki-colored passage. "I trust you'll do enough of that to yourself. I'm glad you made it in one piece."

"You were expecting this?" I asked, bending over to catch my breath. Shreds from my blouse hung at my sides.

"I wasn't sure what Voss was up to. This doesn't surprise me, though. She's been trying to undermine the Mech Corps ever since she washed out."

I took a deep breath. "Why couldn't you warn me?"

"Come on. While you're here, might as well get some training in."

I was too exhausted for that, but Sam delighted in pushing me harder when I was down.

She led me down corridors toward the mech-gym where I'd trained for six weeks.

"I wasn't sure how you'd use what limited information I could give you," Sam said. "And if I was wrong? I know how you feel about Voss and Scarlatti, but one slipup, and your knowledge could doom you and the mission. It's best you work this out on your own."

"Best for whom?"

Sam stopped and opened a door I hadn't seen before. Inside was a smaller version of the mech training gym.

"You let me fall into a trap without warning me," I said. "How does that make any sense?"

A matted ring sat in the middle of the small room, with a handful of lockers along one wall. She removed her mech-glove and opened one. "Sit," Sam said.

I dropped onto a padded seat, and studied my muddy skorts and scraped leg. She lifted my leg and cleaned the wound. Then she applied ointment and wrapped it.

"What aren't you telling me about this mission?" I asked.

Sam put the ointment into her locker and pulled out an injector.
I cringed. "What are you giving me this time?"

"Something to speed your recovery." She parted the tatters of my sleeve and jabbed the injector before I could protest. "You need to be on top of your game."

"I don't like being a guinea pig."

"It's nothing I haven't used myself. Get changed." She opened another locker, handed me a haptic fight outfit and grabbed another. Later, Sam would expect me to revisit this training exercise and relive the fight in the VR chamber, thanks to downloaded input from my haptic suit sensors. *Oh, joy.*

I looked away so Morgan couldn't see Sam undress, and wondered why I hadn't heard from him since I fled Scarlatti's phony arrests.

Beside me, Sam used the mech-gear's quick-release system to drop her mech-suit onto the floor by her locker. She moved in front of me, still wearing her dress blues. "You have much to learn, Annabelle. You tend to learn best by doing. Therefore, it'll be by doing that you'll learn. Now suit up."

"Another riddle?" I pulled off my torn blouse.

"If I gave you all the answers, you'd absorb none of it." Sam changed into her haptic uniform.

For the first time, I saw Sam in something other than her dress blues. Without her uniform, she was both stocky and lean. Her muscles weren't bulky like the boys in the arena, but measured, tight, and well toned.

I stared at my bandaged leg. "I'm too exhausted for training, Commander. I—"

"That's when your enemies will take advantage of you, now suit up."

I changed into the haptic suit. I should have gone home with Janine. Instead, I was stuck with Sam, who never let up.

"Tell me what you learned out there tonight," Sam said.

"Captain Voss shouldn't be anywhere near the border, yet she used her mech-cops to jump the border and kidnap boys." I adjusted the haptic head-shield and stood up.

Sam attacked. She dropped me onto the padded floor and pinned me. I struggled for breath. All I could do was kick and grunt.

"What was that for?" I asked when she got up. "You wanted a report. We weren't even on the mats yet."

"Do you imagine your enemies will play fair? Don't. Never let your guard down. That could cost you your life."

I got to my feet, stepped back, and assumed a fighting pose. I had no delusions of defeating Sam.

"Continue with your report," she said.

"Report or fight?"

"Both." She faked a blow.

I flinched. She advanced, caught me off guard. I twisted away at the last moment, blocked three blows, and fell back. "Voss must have allies in the border patrol, or they'd report her to you."

"Exactly." Sam attacked with a kick-punch-spin-kick that sent me sprawling across the mat.

I tumbled, rolled to my feet, and faced her. "She must have allies in the East Knoxville station, since she operated in their district."

"And?" Sam moved in.

"It's a political move to get you removed as commander."

"Maybe I should retire. I've run this command for over 20 years. Retirement might suit me."

"You don't look old enough to retire," I said.

"Thanks, but despite appearances, I'm almost 50, which in military terms is getting old." She poised to attack.

I faked an attack and pulled back at the last moment. She countered with what would have slammed me onto the mat. "I don't think that's your plan, Commander. You don't like where this is heading."

Sam grinned, stretching the scar on her cheek. "Good observation."

"Then why send me after a money trail?"

"What can you tell me about how Voss uses police department funds?" Sam grabbed my shoulders and twisted to get behind me.

I dropped to the mat, kicked her feet from under her, and scrambled away. "She might be bribing border guards. I don't think she bribed the East Knoxville captain. Could Captain Chou be in cahoots with Voss?"

"What makes you say that?"

"Something Dara once said. Besides, it would be easier to bribe a guard to look the other way. It would be much tougher to pull off a raid in another captain's district."

"Very good." Sam attacked, kicked.

I grabbed her foot, twisted and threw her to the mat. She pulled me with her and grabbed me from behind. She had me in a chokehold before I landed on top of her. I struggled to remove her grip on my neck. Her hold was like steel, as Morgan's had been during my arena final.

Morgan. Where was he? I'd expected him to pipe in with an idea. Maybe the base shielded the signal, or he was afraid base sensors would pick up his transmission.

Sam let go and moved away. "You need to watch that terminal chokehold."

"I keep forgetting. There are no moves you haven't seen in combat." I got to my feet and rubbed my neck. I could have used Janine's soothing ointments, though I couldn't let her know why I needed them.

I resumed a fighter's pose. "So you arranged for Picard to get me a cycle."

"Not exactly."

"Sam? You sent me to Battani's, and now I have a cycle."

"A fortuitous turn of events, I'd say. Very well, I was monitoring communications in and out of the Battani residence, on account of the players at that party. I had no way to get inside."

"You tried to get invited?"

"Mine is a political position," Sam said. "It pays to kiss the babies now and then, and to bow to the wishes of powerful people who would rather I wasn't there. I intercepted the distress call, saw it as an opportunity to look inside, and got you involved."

"You used me, in other words."

Sam stood up straight and brushed off her haptic suit, as if announcing the fight was over. "Of course I used you. You're my agent. Tonight you were my eyes and ears."

"You could have warned me."

"You need to be more flexible. You did well with limited information, better than if you let yourself get distracted with too much."

"I could get into deep trouble with Voss and Battani over this," I said. "Neither would have allowed me to be there." The fatigue of today, plus yesterday's fight and disappointments weighed heavily. Yet some engine inside pushed me along.

"Very possible. Remember, without my lifeline, you were heading into exile."

"Thanks for reminding me. What did you inject me with?"

Sam gave the briefest of smiles before her face hardened. "The meds I gave you will heal your leg and your bruises, so you won't have to make excuses to that sister of yours. Now concentrate on your mission."

"What does Captain Voss hope to gain by this kidnapping and raid?" I asked.

Sam advanced, looking more determined than before. "Aside from discrediting me, you mean. Why do you think?"

I backed away, considered Sam's words, and prepared to avoid another spill to the mat. "More recognition from the governor. More money."

Sam kicked, spun, and kicked again, following with a series of punches. "I'm sure Voss wants to advance her political career. More ribbons won't satisfy her. I suspect she found some additional sources of money for her little adventures. That's what I want you to investigate."

I blocked, retreated, and blocked again. "Do you think her raids might have something to do with recent protests over the treatment of boys?"

Sam faked a blow and stopped. "I don't like coincidences."

"The escapes raise fear among the people, so they'll support the governor in the upcoming election."

"Something stinks. Something premeditated." Sam swept my legs from under me and sent me sprawling onto the mat.

I recovered and got to my feet. I should have been flat on my back, but my adrenaline levels kept spiking. Sam's meds? "Who's pulling the strings?"

Sam sucked in a deep breath. "That's the most important question."

"And?" I braced for her to attack.

"Come on, I'll bet you could use some real coffee. And something for your blood sugar. You look shaky."

I changed into my dusty, tattered cop uniform.

Sam shook her head. "We can't let you leave looking like that.

Too many questions." She headed out of the gym. "Let me see what I have in your size."

"What about my brand-new cycle?"

I followed Sam to her office, where she poured me a cup of coffee from an urn behind her desk. The aroma was rich and mouthwatering. "Sit," she said. "I'll have your cycle returned to you after it's cleaned."

I took a sip and savored what I missed when away from the mech-base: real, caffeinated coffee. "What about Voss and—"

"She knows better than to tread on my lands. By 'clean,' I mean remove the tracking devices someone saw fit to attach."

"You mean ... Voss knew I was out here?"

"Someone did," Sam said, "which is why you can never let your guard down."

"I checked the cycle before I left the station."

"Always check it again for backup tracking devices. Now drink up. I need you alert."

The coffee tasted rich, much better than that watered-down, decaffeinated slop at the cop station. "Did you capture all the boys who escaped the arena?"

Her dark eyes bored into me. "All except the one you took a liking to."

"I won't kill for sport."

Sam laughed. "You'll have to learn to obey orders in combat, or you'll lose your team and your life."

I looked down at her battered metal desk. "Yes, Commander."

"You want to know what I learned by interrogating the other boys." She took a sip of coffee and studied me. "They all confirmed that your redhead broke away to create a diversion. They misjudged how many mechs we had in the field. I don't know how that boy got away, but I'll find him."

<Get her to drop this.>

Morgan's voice surprised me. "What about the cop-intern who attacked Mom?" I asked.

"What about her?"

"Who did she work with?"

"She was an intern for the East Knoxville station," Sam said, "a loner with no family, no close friends."

A fanatic, Mom would say.

"Interns aren't allowed to have guns," I said. "She knew where

Mom would be, and attacked when I was in the arena. That took planning, coordinating, and help."

Sam straightened up. "Let me pursue the assassination attempt. You concentrate on Captain Voss and the money trail."

I took another sip of the coffee, which had already perked me up enough to worry how I could sleep later. "How do I research the money when I don't have access to the captain's records?" I stared at the worn tile floor. "When I pried into her net access before, you know what happened."

"Look at me."

I looked up. Sam's eyes intimidated, as if they contained lie detectors. Probably did.

"You're not to touch Voss' or Scarlatti's network access. In fact, you're not to use the inter-mesh for anything related to your assignment. Doing so will leave a trail for others to follow and trace your work to me. Is that clear?"

"Yes, Commander, but without access—"

"I know how hard this assignment is. That's why I put you on it."

My chest swelled until I realized she was manipulating me. I deflated. "How do I find out anything, then?"

"Whatever money Voss is using has been removed from the electronic ledgers."

"Meaning we can't trace it," I said. "How does she convert from ledger to off-ledger?"

"Good question. You don't have much time. Voss will act soon. Besides, the sooner you complete your assignment, the sooner you can move forward in the mechs, and the sooner you can get your life back. I need you on this full-time."

"That's hard when Scarlatti has me cleaning her car and the cafeteria."

Sam laughed. "What did you find?"

"Books and ledgers from capturing boys."

"What was in the ledgers?"

I shrugged. "A jumble of numbers and letters."

"I see you need more training." Sam projected ledger images on her blank wall. "We haven't deciphered these yet, but I can tell you we're dealing with millions of credits diverted outside our electronic system."

My eyes popped. "Where does it all come from?"

Sam's next projection showed numbers in columns. "Good question. Now get me some answers."

"If I had access to bank files and—"

"I can't let you do that. Electronic prying is too easy to trace."

"Should I interview officers from the East Knoxville station?"

"No." Sam turned the wall images off.

"Then how do I get information? Who can I talk to? What records can I look at?" All this reminded me of my high-school history classes, where teachers expected me to memorize answers and not dig too deep. I finished my coffee, letting the last drop linger on my tongue.

"Get some rest. I'll put you up for the night. Your cycle and a change of clothes will be ready at five so you can return to your station. Call your family and give them a good reason for not coming home tonight."

"Like what?" I asked. "You don't want—"

"Soldier, in combat you can't take this defeatist attitude. Show me what you're made of."

I straightened up and swallowed hard before I spoke. "Fine. I got stuck on the other end of town. I'm staying with a friend rather than ride home so late."

"Better."

"Why can't you give me more to work with so I can do my job?"

"Learn to be flexible," Sam said. "When you're on a mech assignment, you won't have the specificity you think you need."

"Sam, I can't do this without access to records or people."

"Can't, or won't?" I didn't think it possible, but her gaze on me hardened even more.

"I don't know how to figure this out on my own. This is nothing like mech training."

"It's exactly like mech training. You didn't think you could do that, either."

"That was all about physical stamina."

"Was it?" Sam checked her wrist-com and a private screen on her desk. "Wasn't it also about mental toughness? Isn't that how you defeated Dara and the redhead? You're the perfect person to pull this off, because no one believes you can."

"Including you?"

She laughed. "It's up to you. No one will expect this of you.

Voss and Scarlatti don't think much of you."

I shifted in the wooden seat, surprised my leg offered no pain. "Neither do you, or you wouldn't have humiliated me and kicked me out of the Mech Corps."

"On the contrary, I've given you the credibility to succeed in this assignment."

"Then give me a more specific assignment. Tell me what I can look at."

"Learn to trust your instincts … and those who can help you."

"You've told me there *is* no one I can share this with. And I certainly can't trust Voss or Scarlatti."

Sam chuckled, stood up, and paced. "Let's call it limited trust, then. Part of your success will depend on learning to trust others to behave in certain ways. That requires you to make an effort to open yourself up, so you can learn what makes them tick."

"Their habits?"

"It's more than that. You have to dig deep, very deep. Find out what motivates people. Not the easy stuff, but deeper down."

"How do I do that without interviewing people?"

She kept pacing, keeping her gaze on me. "People don't like being interrogated. For now, I need you to show me what Voss is up to. Get me eyes inside, so I can assess the threat and deal with it. If what she's up to is a ploy to get me to retire, so be it. If it's more than that, then you have a real opportunity to serve your country by exposing her."

I should have felt more than faint twinges of pride for this honor. Yet it could get me killed, or worse: hurt the only family I knew.

TWELVE

None of my questions had answers, it seemed. Sam checked her wrist-com again, excused herself, and entered the mini-command center behind her desk. She didn't invite me, and closed the door before I could ask. I took a deep breath and tried to clear my head. The fog of weariness spread over the jumble of everything that had happened, plus Sam's meds, whatever she'd given me, and still not knowing what she expected from me.

A worm of a thought wiggled its way through my mind, stimulating sensory regions I didn't want disturbed. Something tore at my gut, ripping the heart out of my three-year-old chest—a child too young to understand, except that the elite Mech Corps I now belonged to was bashing my world apart. My heart raced. *Mommy, where are you?* I hated the mechs. I wanted the entire corps destroyed for killing my dad and putting my birth mother in prison.

The worm didn't stop there. It moved to my visual cortex, and headed to Sam's data access only feet away. I was in the most secure facility in the state, one of the most secure in the entire country. If anyone had access to where the state held my birth mother, Sam would.

I sat behind her desk and began to search. Her system didn't ask for a password. But why would it? Sam was the only one with access to this room, and had been here moments before.

I pulled up files on prison records and looked for out-of-state facilities. Something else caught my eye, a file labeled "Voss." I opened it and scanned the contents. Page after page showed my captain's life, down to her brief journey through mech training. She had been a bright star with potential, had won her early tournament and arena fights. She had the skills and drive Sam wanted.

Voss broke the rules with other recruits by crossing the border on a dare. In the arena, she made a single, fatal mistake. Judges had to jolt her male opponent to stop him from killing her. That disqualified her in the final round.

The story didn't end there. Sam recruited her to continue in the mech program on a secret mission. Like me, Sam gave her a second chance. On special assignment, Voss was to cross the border and capture three escapees from a local boys' prison. Voss did, then massacred the boys rather than bring them to the arena. Furious, Sam kicked Voss out for good. That was why Voss hated Sam. No wonder Sam suspected Voss of undermining her command.

"I could have you court-martialed for less," Sam said from behind me.

I scooted back from the desk, but not in time; she grabbed me in a chokehold. "Never turn your back on a potential opponent."

Unable to breathe, I patted her arm and pointed to my throat.

She dragged me out of her seat and let go. "You don't need me as an enemy."

I fell to the tile floor and scrambled away before she grabbed me again. "I'm sorry, Commander. I wanted to see what you weren't telling me about my captain." I was glad I hadn't begun the search for my birth mother.

"Did you find anything worth getting caught?"

"No, Commander." I sat up. "Except you recruited Voss for a secret mission, and she failed you."

"She didn't fail me. She deliberately disobeyed orders." Sam's pupils narrowed, boring into me. "Learn to pick your fights."

I stood uneasily and leaned against my chair. "This was a test, wasn't it?"

"You know where the suite is. I suggest you sleep. I'll be at your door at five." She pushed me out of her office and closed the door.

I was no closer to finding my birth mother. I needed this assignment to end, but I'd have to go through hell beforehand. For now, I had to focus on Voss.

I crossed the gym and entered the small suite I'd used during my mech training.

<That was intense,> Morgan said.

Just what I needed. I closed my left eye and typed on my wrist-com: "You promised me privacy."

<Sam is using you. You can't trust her.>

"Duh!"

<∞>

As promised, Sam knocked on my door at five with a clean cop-intern uniform. She handed me a cup of strong mech coffee and shoved me out the back door of the compound toward my shiny, cleaned-up cycle.

"Scan twice for tracking devices," she said, then disappeared inside.

I could have used more sleep, and much, *much* more information. Yet, I didn't feel as weary as I expected. Last night, the strong caffeine had lost the fight against exhaustion.

I swung my leg over the cycle, and didn't feel any ill effects of getting scraped-up the night before, or my Saturday arena fight with Morgan. His musky odor still lingered, along with his bristly chin on my neck, and I couldn't bring myself to hate him. That might change if I couldn't get him out of my head. *Good morning, Morgan.*

I didn't get a reply, but then I couldn't speak the words without Sam overhearing and interrogating me about him.

The cool, sticky breeze on the way into town woke me up, but I still felt myself in a nightmare. I hadn't yet completed my training, and my biggest hurdle was this mission. I didn't want either side to win. I couldn't imagine my bloated captain as a mech-warrior on a secret mission like this. She'd become too soft; perhaps the result of having her dreams dashed. Would I find myself just like her years from now?

I pulled into the cop station parking lot behind Brooks and biolocked my cycle. I didn't see another cycle, and Brooks was in her vehicle, alone. I jumped into the passenger seat of her new sedan and stretched my legs. "Let's take a ride."

"Am I working for you now?"

"Someone once said a slave with several masters is a free person."

"Careful," she said. "Sounds like something from a banned book."

"I wouldn't know. I'm not allowed to read any."

She pulled out of the lot and headed west. "What's on your mind?"

"I'm trying to fit in, but Voss and Scarlatti will never accept me."

"Can you blame them? Your high-school Harmony Director gave you such a scathing report, it was all I could do to get them to assign you to me."

"You requested me?" I turned my head to see her profile. "Why?"

"You reminded me of myself when I joined the force. Full of energy. Not well liked for being different. You didn't go home last night."

I sank into my seat. "Did you just become my mom?"

"No, but she called. She sounded worried." Brooks turned, taking us in a wide arc around the station.

"Is there something going on at the station that Voss doesn't want me knowing?"

"Where did that come from?"

"Scarlatti kept me out of yesterday's meeting." I sat up and watched for Janine. "Then Voss wouldn't let me be part of a mech-cop patrol. I'm trained and qualified on the gear. You'd think—"

"I'd stay away from that if I were you."

"Why?"

"Very hush-hush," Brooks said. "They won't even read *me* in on what's going on. That should tell you something."

"What do you think it is?"

<Yeah,> Morgan said. <I'd like to know.>

I bit my lip to keep from screaming. I needed a signal to tell him to shut up.

Brooks sighed and turned. "Most stations have one or two mech-suits, with at most three officers trained to use them. We have four suits, and counting Voss and Scarlatti, six trained officers."

I considered this. "On the way in this morning, I heard there were more protests last night. And … a big cross-border ruckus in East Knoxville. Doesn't that strike you as odd?"

"I wouldn't read much into it. Protests, kidnappings, and raids come in cycles. It's hard to predict when the next ones will come."

I checked my wrist-com for messages from Janine. None. "Yet,

Voss *has* made several captures in the past week."

"What's your question?"

"Budgets are tight from what I've heard. Yet Voss has extra equipment and resources to carry out raids. Where's the money coming from?"

"My dear protégé, I suggest you stop digging before the next rock you lift covers a fire ant colony. Now, if you don't mind, I need to get to work, before I'm put on the endangered species list." She pulled into the parking lot next to two cycles.

Janine stood by hers with fists on her hips, glaring at me. "I guess I should go home," she said when I climbed out of Brooks' car.

"Great to see you, too." I went to hug Janine.

She pulled away, climbed into the car, and rolled up the window. I followed Brooks into the station.

"What was that?" Brooks asked.

"I'm guessing she thinks I want to steal her partner."

"Do you? I might be able to arrange that."

"I'd rather have you look out for Janine. I'll manage."

"Then don't kick too many fire ant nests. They tend to sting."

THIRTEEN

The station bullpen brimmed with officers checking in and getting assignments for the day. Mine would come from Scarlatti, probably cleaning the latrine, after she finished talking to Voss behind closed doors. She pulled the blinds so I couldn't watch.

I'd been told when one door closes, another opens. I made my way up the narrow stairs. Liz Cameron sat behind her desk. She looked as if she was due any day, the product of EggFusion Fertilization with one of her two wives. This would be her second and final approved daughter.

Part of her job was to guard the captain's office from the likes of me. I hadn't found anything useful the one time I snuck into Voss' office and got caught.

No luck is better than my luck. Oh, well.

Liz drank from her thermos before looking up. She seemed determined to drown her new daughter with watered-down, decaffeinated coffee. For once, I was glad it was imitation. I could only imagine what that much caffeine would do to a newborn.

"The captain's out," Liz said. "You'd best not try anything. She warned me."

"One impulsive, juvenile mistake, and that's all you'll put on my tombstone." There I went, playing on being 16.

"You only have yourself to blame," Liz said.

Smiling, I stood over her desk and strained to read her screen upside down: a baby-clothes shopping site she wasn't to be wasting her work time with. "Since Scarlatti is with the captain, I hope you can enlighten me on my assignment for the day. Is there anything interesting?"

She eyed me with suspicion. "The usual."

"Which 'usual' will it be today?"

"I'm not at liberty to say." Liz looked down her nose at me. It didn't work on several levels. She was too sweet to pull off the image, and I was taller, standing over her.

I smiled.

"You'll need to ask Lieutenant Scarlatti."

"*Ah*, perhaps Captain Voss didn't tell you," I said, moving to the side of the desk for a better view of her shopping site.

Blushing, she blanked her screen. "I know everything that goes on at the station, but you won't trick me into telling you."

"I wouldn't pretend to do that, Ms. Cameron. I just don't want to waste the lieutenant's time. She's very busy. She doesn't have time to explain things to me."

"The captain *has* been relying on Lieutenant Scarlatti," Liz said, cradling her thermos in both hands.

"I want to be the best partner. You do want the lieutenant to have a good partner, don't you?" I couldn't believe how thick I laid it on.

"I suppose it wouldn't hurt," Liz said. "Don't tell the lieutenant I said anything, okay? There's been trouble out at the Oak Ridge Geek Institute again. Boys always stir up trouble, don't they?"

<That's where Seth is.>

I forced myself not to respond to Morgan. "Are they trying to escape?"

"Can't say." Liz shrugged. "You'll have to ask the lieutenant."

"Will we use our mech-gear—?"

"You didn't hear that from me." Liz stiffened and pushed the thermos aside.

"That gear must cost a fortune. Any idea how we found the money when budgets are tight?"

"You're trying to trick me, aren't you?"

"No, ma'am! How could you think that? I only want to learn things so I can do a good job for Lieutenant Scarlatti and the captain."

Her eyes narrowed, straining to figure me out. *Good luck.*

"I bet you scrounged the money by pinching credits from the general funds." I moved away from her desk. I didn't want her excessively nervous in her condition.

"There's nothing wrong with being frugal, but general funds are for general purchases, not equipment. The mech-uniforms were donated."

<I bet they were. In exchange for what?> Morgan asked.

"I need to get to work." Liz motioned for me to skedaddle.

<Ask about the truckloads of toilet paper that didn't make it to the station.>

I crossed my eyes and then relaxed them. *Get out of my head.*

That got me thinking. How did Morgan get such information? Could it be true?

"You need to go," Liz said. "The captain will come back soon. You don't want to be here when she does."

I headed downstairs with more questions for Morgan than for Liz. When I reached the bullpen, more officers gathered around, including the evening shift. Scarlatti's office still had the door closed and blinds down, meaning Voss was in there. I headed for the cafeteria. There was Liz, filling her canteen with more of that foul-tasting coffee substitute.

<Ask her,> Morgan said.

Before I could decide how to phrase my question, Liz saw me and scurried out of the break room. She couldn't afford for Voss to catch her away from her desk again. I had to disagree with the old wisdom. A slave with three masters was not a free person, only a hassled slave. Morgan was not my master, though he did perch inside my head.

I sat at one of the round break-room tables and closed my eyes. Since Sam could, and probably was listening, I covered my left eye with my hand, and opened my right. I typed into my wrist-com and held it up to my right eye. "Where are you going with the toilet paper?"

<With Seth's help, I hacked your station accounts,> Morgan said. <You'd have to use 20 rolls each, every day, to use what they've bought.>

My right contact filled with lists of purchases: truckloads of toilet paper, tissues, enough decaffeinated coffee to keep all Knoxville stations supplied for a month, and most bizarre of all, adult diapers.

I erased the first message and typed, "Where are all these supplies going?"

<Someone picks them up at Tenn-tucky Supply Depot across the river.>

I nodded, erased my text, and opened my eyes. I no longer heard the usual drone of activity outside. I didn't want to miss whatever was going down.

<∞>

Dozens of cops gathered at one end of the long station hall, listening to Captain Voss' high-pitched voice. The bullpen area was vacant. Scarlatti's office door remained closed, blinds now open, but lights out. Janine stood next to Brooks, her expression attentive. I headed over to join them.

Scarlatti grabbed my arm and hauled me into her office. I suppressed my mech training and didn't deck her. After she slammed the door, I bowed my head and braced for another scolding.

<She looks unpleasant,> Morgan said.

I shook my head, willing his voice to stop.

Scarlatti's squinty eyes narrowed until all that remained was darkness. "Whatever you're up to, keep it up. Give us an excuse to send you to Nashville."

I straightened up. Nashville meant the resocialization facility, where they would put me through electrical brain stimulation and intense psychological and social reconditioning. Last year, when I began the cop-intern program, they sent a friend from high school. When she returned, she no longer recognized me. They'd purged her memories and replaced them with socially correct thoughts. Despite a cheery nature, her eyes grew darker until she committed suicide. She wasn't the first.

I hung my head. "I want to be the best partner you ever had—"

"Cut the bull," Scarlatti said. "Did you think you could nose around, asking a lot of stupid questions, without that getting back to me?"

I swallowed hard. "Who said—?"

"That's not important." She sat on her desk, blocking me from viewing anything behind her.

Liz couldn't have ratted me out to the captain, who was well into her monologue. That meant Liz must have told Scarlatti. "I'm just curious," I said. "I want to learn to be a team player."

"A team player doesn't poke around."

"I thought … I mean … we both got kicked out of the mech

program. We both have reasons not to trust Sam."

"Careful," Sam said into my left implant. "You're there to observe, not to stir up trouble."

I nodded involuntarily.

Scarlatti didn't seem to notice. Her face softened and her eyes widened, showing white rims around her dark irises. "Don't think it buys you any favors just because Sam dumped on both of us. She does that: builds you up, and then uses you like toilet paper."

"Scarlatti got kicked out when Voss recruited her to betray me," Sam said.

So, if either side wins this contest, I get squashed. "I don't like being used," I said.

"No one does." Scarlatti paused. "There could be hope for you, if you toe the line."

I smiled. "I do so want to be part of your team."

<I wish I could see your poker face,> Morgan said into my right implant.

"Very well." Scarlatti moved behind her desk, pushed something into her desk drawer, and looked up. "We have few secrets here, and *none* worth your snooping around."

I was confused. The place reeked of secrets. "I only want to know about today's assignment, so I can get up to speed."

"We both know you were digging into more than today's mission," she said. "Next time you have a question, ask me. Go clean up the car, and be ready to move out in 20 minutes." She handed me her key-chip.

"And the assignment?"

"I'll brief you on the way." She ushered me out of her office, closed the door, and returned to where Voss still lectured the troops.

I was tempted to return to Scarlatti's office to "snoop around" and find whatever she didn't want me to see. But then she looked in my direction. I slipped into the common room, grabbed a bucket, and went outside to take care of her car. The trunk contained one box, covered with strapping tape and rope. It also had what looked like a tracking chip. I couldn't get it opened and refastened in time to search it. And it made no sense that anything of interest would be inside it anyway. If I wanted to hide something, I wouldn't bring it to the station.

The box was heavy. *Could be books, paper, or gold bricks.* Only fantasizing. Possession of gold meant prison. I dropped the box off in Scarlatti's office, and that gave me the chance to check the desk drawer for something that would explain Morgan's toilet paper tip. The drawers were locked. I considered breaking into them, but didn't want Sam to know I could.

"She hid something important," I whispered.

"Get back to the car before Scarlatti grows suspicious," Sam said into my implant.

I eyed Scarlatti's computer screen. Images floated onto my right contact. More ledgers of supply purchases, and a place for pickup. The dates were all Monday nights. *Tonight, maybe*—

"Get moving, soldier," Sam yelled.

FOURTEEN

I pulled Scarlatti's car into the alley and washed off a fresh layer of clay, this time not from east of town. I returned the car to the front of the station as Scarlatti descended the steps. Instead of driving, she climbed into the passenger seat and said, "Oak Ridge Institute."

While I drove, Morgan flashed images onto my right contact. I struggled to read and drive at the same time. Fortunately, there were no other cars, only a smattering of bikes and a few buses.

The lists looked like balances in a bank account. Other than large purchases of paper products and medical supplies, there wasn't anything I wouldn't find in Mama Grace's household accounts, except—

"You'd best stay where I tell you today," Scarlatti said as I turned onto the main road toward the Institute. "This is a secure facility for a reason. We'll have guards, officers from other stations, and mech units. You can't wander around asking silly-girl questions."

"And you can't stay put," Sam said into my implant. "Whatever's going down is unorthodox."

I stared at the imposing concrete wall that surrounded the Institute. "What do we know about the disturbance?"

Scarlatti turned so I couldn't see her expression. "Institute Director Margaret Devotte notified us that she discovered an escape plot."

"The director's first call should have been to us," Sam said. The heat of her anger filled my head.

I took a deep breath. "I don't recall so many escapes before."

"Underground Railroad," Scarlatti said. "They've become bolder. We have to be more diligent to shut them down."

"Do we know who's in this railroad?"

"Everyone we've caught has committed suicide before they could talk. We need to catch one alive."

I waited at a light, thinking of Nurse Wells and her helper. "You think this underground operation will help boys escape from the Institute today? Where would they go?"

Shops with apartments above lined both sides of the street. Up ahead, in the block around the Institute, the storefronts and apartments were boarded up.

"We'll catch them before they get far," Scarlatti said. "That's the point."

"I mean, they'd have to cross over 40 miles of residential neighborhoods to reach the Outland."

"Precisely. They'll terrorize the entire city looking for food, places to hide, and transportation. We don't need the entire area in a state of panic."

Even if that helps the governor in the upcoming election?

To avoid panic and spare us all these problems, we could bus the boys to the Outland, but the Institute wanted to pick their brains. Seth's brains.

When I pulled up to the Institute's main gate behind Voss, Sam stood talking with a group of women in gray attire with the Institute's insignia. Sam spotted me and turned away.

Scarlatti jumped out of the car before I could park.

"What's going on?" I whispered. "I thought—"

"Pretend we haven't spoken," Sam said in a sub-vocalized tone. "Stay close to your people."

After I parked, I joined Scarlatti and Captain Voss. The captain's round face turned red as she poked her finger toward Sam. "This has nothing to do with the Mech Corps!"

A tall, slender woman in the Institute's charcoal-gray uniform turned from Sam to Voss. "Sorry for troubling you, Captain. The commander insists this *is* a Mech Corps matter."

"Madam Devotte," Captain Voss said. She took a deep breath and smiled. "With all due respect to the commander, Oak Ridge has been part of the Knoxville jurisdiction for over a year. This is a city matter. We have things under control."

I stared at the Institute director, trying to size her up. Devotte had Sam's air of authority, something Captain Voss could never master. She was Mom's age. Her eyes gave me the impression of intelligence, or perhaps it was mastered suspiciousness.

"You two sort out your jurisdictional dispute," Devotte said to Sam and Voss. "I want those boys in custody within the hour."

"Don't you have a border to protect?" Voss said to Sam.

I wasn't sure if I should acknowledge the director or not. Her two gray-uniformed associates hung back, near the safety of the gate. The only other time I'd seen Sam and Voss together was on stage at my high school, an appearance to recruit security-tracked students like Janine and me. That was the day I first met Morgan, and almost went to prison.

Devotte held out her hand. "I don't believe we've met. I'm Margaret Devotte, director of the Institute. And you are?" It sounded more an attempt to know who was listening than to meet me.

"Annabelle Scott, Lieutenant Scarlatti's new partner." I smiled and bowed my head, while keeping my eyes fixed on the director. She had a military bearing that got me to wondering if she, too, had tried out for the Mech Corps.

"Senator Scott's daughter," Devotte said, eyes alight. "I've heard about you."

"Nothing bad, I hope—"

Scarlatti grabbed my arm and escorted me away. I wasn't supposed to meet important people, particularly ones whose attention I caught.

While Voss and the commander argued over who would get to chase down the boys, Scarlatti took me around the side of the walled facility, covered with concertina wire. External cam boxes poked out along the outside of the building, and on the sides of the surrounding wall. Those were for show. I had no doubt there were micro-cams I couldn't see. Every inch of the grounds would be imaged in visible and infrared, along with motion sensors. As with us mech recruits, the boys had tracking collars or implants, like products whose movements needed to be monitored.

"What great national-security secrets was I almost privy to?" I asked when we reached the corner and headed down another side.

Scarlatti mumbled something I couldn't understand.

<I don't think she likes you,> Morgan said.

"Duh," I said.

Scarlatti turned red. "Save your snide remarks. Jurisdictional issues don't concern you."

"We didn't get a call from Director Devotte, did we?"

"What?"

"The director wasn't expecting us," I said.

"We got a call. That's all you need to know. We're looking for two boys, around 14. They're geeks, but don't take any chances. They could be strong. They might have weapons."

My muscles twitched, recalling weeks of mech training. "You got an inside tip, didn't you?"

"Maybe."

"Someone who works for Director Devotte?"

"Drop it!" Scarlatti said.

"I want to help."

"Well, this isn't helping. Get to your post."

"Where?"

Scarlatti took me across the street from the Institute, into a deserted park. Maples lined the sides and back in a horseshoe shape. Trees and clumps of bushes dotted the middle. She parked me behind an oak I might have climbed when I was younger. I had a clear view of the concrete wall, the glistening wire, and the imposing concrete towers of the Institute inside the wall.

"Don't move from this spot," Scarlatti said. "I'll be back after I check in with the captain."

"Shouldn't I have a partner? Backup?"

"Wait here until I return, is that clear?"

"How about a weapon?"

"Use your stun gun."

"What if several boys come this way?"

"There are other officers in the area." Scarlatti hurried away before I could press the point.

I huddled down amidst the bushes and scanned the area. The wall around the Institute was an imposing hurdle for boys on the run, though it would have provided little protection to medieval armies using siege warfare.

So, Morgan, all your brother has to do is break out of whatever internal security the director has, sprint across the yard to the wall, scale the wall, avoid getting cut to ribbons by the wire, climb down the other side. Then we'll be waiting. It sounded like a great plan.

To my left, one of Sam's shiny black mech-suits stood behind a maple tree that couldn't conceal her. To my right, Brooks and Janine crouched behind a clump of bushes. I was alone, yet not alone.

<They're killing my brother in there,> Morgan said into my right implant. <They'll kill the two boys who are supposed to escape today.>

I closed my left eye and typed into my wrist-com. "Why can't you leave me some privacy? I bet you stare when I get changed."

<Help me and I'll help you.>

"I want my life back," I wrote.

<You can't turn off the sound without removing the implants,> Morgan said. <But if you remove the contacts and put them away, you can have some privacy. Neither Sam nor I can see without the contacts.>

"Or I could shut my right eye," I wrote.

<If you do that too often, Sam will know.>

I sighed. "Yeah, I'm constantly being watched."

<I'll let you know when I need your help.>

"You're nuts. There's no way out and nowhere to go."

I erased my messages and looked up. Brandy approached, wearing her shiny black mech-gear, no helmet. She looked scared beneath her auburn hair. Like Janine, she was too sweet to be in the Mech Corps, even though she'd survived the tournament and the arena.

She stopped before me. "Don't be angry with me."

"Over what?" I invited her behind my cluster of bushes, and glanced at the wall in case boys came running.

"I wish you were still in the mechs. Most of the girls do."

"Thanks." My eyes watered; I couldn't afford that.

"I mean it. You got me through training. I couldn't have done it without you. Everyone was so mean to you afterward."

"I'm not upset, Brandy. If you want the mechs, I'm happy for you."

Brandy removed her mech-glove and placed her hand on my arm. It felt heavy, the weight of mech-armor. "You know how it is. No one stands up to Dara. Except you did."

I pulled away and pointed toward the wall. "We have to keep a sharp eye out for escapees."

Brandy held out a long-range stun gun with multiple shots. "I know they don't give cop-interns decent weapons. Take it."

I laughed, took the weapon, and pointed it toward the wall. "Who's the mech with you?"

"Renee. She won't say, but I think she misses you, too."

"I doubt that."

"She calls you her most challenging pupil," Brandy said, "but with a twinkle in her eye."

"I miss you and the others, but that won't help today."

"What's going on?" Janine plopped down next to me.

Oh, you're talking to me now.

"We're commiserating over my getting kicked out of the Mech Corps," I said. "Thanks for pouring acid, lemon juice, and salt on the wound."

"Sorry," Janine said, "but I didn't bring it up. What's the plan?"

"Janine. Do I look like I have a plan? Scarlatti dumped me here and told me not to move."

"Enough reunion," Sam said into my head. "Return your attention to the job."

"Is that a boy?" Janine asked, pointing toward the wall. She looked as if she didn't know what to expect.

Despite her mech-gear, Brandy cowered next to me. I recognized the tall boy from the pharmacy, the one I had cuffed. Hank. They must have sent him to the Institute.

<Don't let him go,> Morgan said. <Something's not right. He's not the type they'd send here.>

Holding Brandy's stun gun, I jumped to my feet and sprinted to intercept Hank. I didn't want him silenced before I could ask questions. I had to be careful they were Sam's questions, not mine.

Unwilling to let me win at anything, Dara sprinted toward the boy with the power of mech-suit hydraulics. It had to be her, with that silly red-sword decal still on her helmet. She wore a special, oversized mech-suit that made her look like a charging rhinoceros.

Upon seeing her, the boy veered left and headed straight toward me. I had the uncomfortable feeling he expected to intimidate me into letting him pass. He must have read something into my hesitation at the pharmacy.

Dara closed in faster than any human without mech-gear could. She grabbed his arm, flipped him onto his stomach, and bound his arms and legs behind him. She shoved his face into the grass as he kicked and fought back. His screams came out muffled.

"Got you, you little maggot," Dara yelled.

"Let her have this one," Sam said. "Back off."

When I reached them, the boy twitched beneath Dara's knee and mech weight.

"You don't have to kill him," I said. "He could provide answers."

Dara stood up and towered over me, more so with her oversized mech-suit. She removed her helmet. "You couldn't cut it as a mech, so don't interfere in mech business." She grinned. "They gave me the tournament title, since you disqualified yourself."

Enjoy it, I thought. *We both know I beat you.*

Still holding her mech-helmet, Brandy stood back, head down. Janine approached, eyes intense, barely blinking. She stared at the boy, probably the closest she'd been to a live one. She held her stun gun in her left hand, kept her right behind her, and backed away.

Hank rolled over. His nose bled. His eyes pleaded with me. The thought jumped into my head: *What? Am I wearing a sign that says, Come on, mess up my life?*

<Don't let those friendly eyes fool you,> Morgan said.

You're jealous. I wondered where that came from. I backed away from Dara. "Look, it's your capture. I don't care, but you don't need to be brutal. He's not going anywhere."

Janine walked toward her post, along the east side of the wooded park. The outline of a pistol showed beneath the back of her cop-intern skorts, as it had at Battani Estates. *What are you up to, Janine?*

I turned away before Sam noticed the bulge.

Rita Chou marched over. She'd been Dara's cop-intern captain from East Knoxville before Dara joined the Mech Corps. A tightly muscled woman, Chou looked as if she could stand up to Sam, which made me wonder if she'd also washed out of the mechs.

"Get your commander on the line," Captain Chou said to Dara. "She'll tell you to turn the boy over to us."

Dara looked away, then toward me. "Whatever," she grunted. She approached me. "This isn't over."

"What isn't? I had nothing to do with this." I thought defeating

Dara in the tournament might end her need to best me. Evidently not. "Look, I'm sorry Sam booted me out. It's over. Let's move on. You get the win. You got him. I'm not competing with you."

Captain Chou marched the boy away. Brandy stood back.

Dara clutched her helmet and watched the retreating boy. Then she turned toward me. "This isn't right." She waved her hand in and out. "You and I could have ruled the mechs."

"Too late," I said. "Listen, do you know if your former police captain was involved in other captures?"

Dara grinned, moved closer, and lowered her voice. "Yeah, Voss and Chou are treading on our business. That boy was ours."

"Any idea why?"

"No, but I *do* know you don't want to get in the middle of this."

Too late. "What about their raids into the Outland?" I asked.

Dara shrugged and tapped her ear. "Got to go. Scarlatti caught two boys on the north side." She led Brandy toward the front of the building.

"Scarlatti?" So much for being her partner.

"Let it go," Sam said into my left auditory implant. "Captain Voss is again a hero. This wins her more support from the governor."

"And money," I whispered. I turned to head back to where Scarlatti told me to wait.

"Yes," Sam said.

"How did Voss know not only when the boys would escape, but where?"

"Good question for you to sort out."

"Voss isn't that clever."

"Never underestimate your opponent. That'll cause you to make clumsy mistakes."

I crouched down across the open park from the wall and the Institute. Brooks and Janine were gone, as were the other cops and Sam's mechs. I was alone on the southwest corner with my stun gun, waiting either for my great opportunity to capture escaped boys who eluded Scarlatti, or to find out that my partner ditched me.

It was a long walk back to the station, and I wasn't sure that if a boy did run my way, I wouldn't just help him get away. I might even be tempted to join him. Even Morgan abandoned me with his silence.

FIFTEEN

Senator Cora Scott sat in a window seat inside Tenn-tucky Bistro, sipping the most horrible mug of decaf coffee she could remember. She cupped her hand over her mouth and activated a miniature microphone that attached to a thin metal ring too loose for her slender fingers.

"Thanks for the warning," she whispered to Morgan over the tiny mike that transmitted to the earbuds he'd given her.

She stared up the street two blocks, at the formidable concrete wall of the Institute. Between the wall and the street, drama unfolded between the Mech Corps and cops fighting over who got custody of three boys they'd captured. Commander Hernandez and Captain Voss exchanged stern words, while their troops held back the media.

The senator studied the news clips on her wrist-com. Cops held human reporters and their cams back. A news cam-swarm drifted over the cops and closer to the scene, but winds dispersed the swarm before it could send images or voice. It was probably best that she'd aborted the escape assist.

Though a daytime escape was unusual, she'd received the plea for help through the usual channels. Boys would need assistance if they got outside the Institute. The request tugged at feelings of guilt over George, an ache that haunted her from the moment she'd begged Bret to take her baby to the Outland. She didn't want George to fall into one of the prisons, or perhaps one of the geek institutes if he were lucky.

"I wish we could have helped them," Morgan said through the earbuds. "This wasn't an escape: too staged, too well anticipated."

Capturing escaped boys was part of the Mech Corps charter. Yet Cora had watched Sam back away, recall her troops, and let Captain Voss take custody. That didn't feel right. There didn't appear to be any way to help these boys, at least not now.

She shed a tear for the boys, and for George, dabbed her cheek and resumed posing with her public mask. Then she flipped on the mike Morgan had supplied. "Later," she said. "Find out where they take the boys."

You can't help them all, she reminded herself. *Help those you can.*

<∞>

Scarlatti's car followed Captain Voss away from the Institute, leaving me stranded. Dara, the other mechs, and cops had left. I remained at my post in the middle of the park, across the street from the Institute's concrete walls, wondering if everyone had forgotten about me.

Brooks called. "I'm guessing you need a ride back to the station."

I ran to meet her when she pulled up at my corner. Whatever Voss and Scarlatti were up to, they didn't want me around, but I had to find a way. I wasn't against civilian control of captured boys, if we had to continue that practice. Maybe Sam should turn that over to the cops. Disband the mechs. Get rid of the force that destroyed my family.

Then I'd have to work for Voss and Scarlatti, at least until they forced me out. I climbed into the back of Brooks' car so Janine didn't accuse me of stealing her partner.

"You want to ride with us this afternoon?" Brooks asked.

Janine's face twisted into a pout.

"I'd get in the way," I said. "I'll hang around the station and wait for distress calls."

"Like last night?" Brooks asked.

I closed my eyes, with visions of the dead boy we'd found at the governor's mansion.

When we reached the station, I hopped out and waved them on. I entered the station with the intent of looking through Scarlatti's office for clues. The station was empty, with all the cops either on our stakeout or on other patrols. Pretending to have second thoughts, I walked past the lieutenant's office, empty, and tried the door: locked. Picking Scarlatti's lock would be suicide.

I climbed the worn concrete stairs to Liz Cameron's desk, outside the captain's office. If this were my office, I would put crunchy things on the stairs to alert me to visitors.

Liz scowled. "The captain's with the governor."

Best to play dumb. "Oh! For what?"

"We stopped another escape," she said, as if she'd been the one who captured the boys.

"That happens a lot these days."

She smiled. "The governor is taking notice. I wouldn't be surprised if our captain got a promotion to commissioner over all Knoxville police."

"Where would that leave you?"

She paused to consider. "I'm sure the captain would take me …" She stopped and glanced at her belly. Wincing, she stiffened and arched her back, which pushed her stomach out farther.

Liz was excitable enough without my prodding. I didn't want to send her into labor and have to deal with all those implications.

<Ask her about the toilet paper,> Morgan reminded me.

I slowly shook my head. "Capturing boys makes Captain Voss more promotable. Probably gets her more money, too."

Liz frowned. "I didn't say that."

She didn't have to. Voss wanted brownie points, money, and power. I wanted nothing better than to tie Governor Battani to a scandal, to stop her from making Mom's life difficult.

"Did the governor encourage Captain Voss to go after the boys?" I asked. "I mean, isn't that a Mech Corps issue?"

"I don't know about politics," Liz said. "But haven't the mechs let us down? We've had too many incidents over the past month, including that escape from the mech-arena." She shuddered.

"How does Captain Voss learn something's about to happen?"

Liz narrowed her eyes. "You're trying to trick me again. You know I can't discuss such matters."

"I want to be better able to serve." I smiled.

"You'd best get to work, young lady."

"I'm waiting for Lieutenant Scarlatti to return to give me instructions." I moved closer and lowered my voice. "We're low on toilet paper. Didn't we just buy a truckload?"

Liz acted fidgety. "A truckload? We have to ration toilet paper to protect our trees. Besides, we don't have space for that much paper."

Good point.

With nothing more to gain, I headed down the stairs. When I reached the station's bullpen, Lieutenant Scandia and Sergeant Montrose were leaving Scarlatti's office, dressed in their pale undercover civilian clothes. Scandia locked the door and checked it before moving on. I caught up with her.

"Great catch today," I said.

"Lucky you might say," Scandia picked up her pace.

"Why?"

Scandia sent Montrose ahead and turned toward me. "Five minutes later, and we'd have had to scour the neighborhood."

"Inside information helped, then?"

Scandia gave me her bulldog face. "Who said anything about inside information?"

"I assumed you got a tip."

"Look, I know you mean well, but leave this for the big girls." Scandia was shorter, meaning she had to be picking on my youth.

"I want to learn the ropes. You seem to know what's going on."

She brushed back her dark hair. "You have a lot to learn about investigative techniques. If you want cooperation, don't tackle people into a chokehold."

"Sometimes that works."

She laughed. "Not with those you expect to work with. No one likes being ambushed."

"Can I tag along, so I can learn? I promise to keep quiet."

"Not this time. Your job is to make Lieutenant Scarlatti look good."

"That's hard when I rarely see her and she gives me no instructions."

Scandia shrugged and walked away. "You're 16," she said over her shoulder. "Give it time."

Not seeing anyone else in the station who might help me, I headed outside into a steamy afternoon and climbed onto my cycle. I made it a block from the station before I stopped behind a bus.

"What am I doing wrong?" I said to whoever listened.

<I take it you don't have many friends on the force,> Morgan said.

I closed my left eye and typed, "Thanks for bringing that up."

Sam's voice buzzed in my head. "Lieutenant Scandia is correct. Talking to coworkers takes more finesse than you've shown."

"Thanks for the support, Sam. Pushing me for results doesn't give me time for niceties."

"Were you paying attention?" Sam asked. "Whatever your hunch about the toilet paper was, Liz confirmed that it's not coming to the station and that she doesn't know about it. Isn't she the one who would order supplies?"

"Yes."

"Lieutenant Scandia didn't deny using informants. So, how will you find out where the supplies are going and what else they're up to?"

The bus pulled away. I remained where I could watch the exit to the alley behind the station. "Why did you let Voss take the boys?"

"What could I learn by taking them, compared to watching what Voss does with them?"

"The boys could have told you who helped them," I said. "If that person double-crossed them, it could be the informant."

"What will that tell you?"

"Who helped Voss with these raids?"

"We know that," Sam said.

"The boy Dara tackled. Then why didn't you keep him?"

"A sniper would have shot him before we could get him into an armored vehicle. What's your next step?"

Spotting activity down the alley, I pulled away from the curb before I drew unwanted attention. "Since Voss is treading on mech territory, can I interview warriors?"

"I did. Besides, they're sequestered in training except for special missions."

"Can you share anything that might help me?"

"Our warriors identified several escapes over the past month that should have been handled by us," Sam said into my implant. "Voss gets the jump on us. Other than documenting each case, the only conclusion I have is that Voss wants to push me out of the way. She has informants ready to tip her off before we can respond. I'm prohibited from interrogating cops. My hands are tied."

"What do you want from me?" I asked.

"You didn't ask why, after the raid, Scandia returned to the station, when she's usually undercover."

I hesitated and thought for a moment. "They must have brought the boys here," I said. That meant I had to find a way down into lockup so I could interview them.

"I'm glad my faith in you wasn't misplaced."

SIXTEEN

It would have been nice if Sam had told me the boys were at the station before I left. Was that asking too much? I reentered the back way, by the cafeteria, where Liz was refilling her thermos again. I wanted to sneak up to Voss' office and poke around her network. She didn't have access to out-of-state prison records on my birth mother, but her files might shed light on this feud between her and Sam.

Instead, I hid until Liz headed out of the cafeteria toward the stairs. Then I eased my way down the hall toward the bullpen. The few cops at their desks had their heads down, studying files. I reached the elevator down to lockup, and considered questions to ask the boys.

The prospect of meeting boys without having to fight had my heart pumping. The weight of hours of fear preached at school of what they could do to me pressed down on my shoulders. I might have hesitated longer if I hadn't met Morgan. It felt strange how possessive I was, given how annoyed I got at how he wormed his way inside me, and not only through my contacts and audio implants.

<There's one security guard in the basement,> he said.

"How do I get past the guard?" I whispered. I wanted to ask how Morgan knew, and what that meant for police security.

Sam spoke into my implant. "Take heed of what Lieutenant Scandia said. Go in soft. Find a rationale for talking to the boys."

"Thanks for the pep talk," I whispered. "How about specifics?"

<Coffee works,> Morgan said. <At least to explain why you're there.>

I nodded, went to the cafeteria, and returned with a steaming cup of watered-down decaf. The real thing could have bought an hour with the prisoners.

While the elevator descended, eyes bored down on me, and not just Sam's and Morgan's. I glanced up, and tried not to be obvious. I didn't see the cams I knew were there—too small.

<Take a deep breath and let go of the tension. You don't want to spill the coffee or startle the guard.>

Okay, so Morgan watched me as well as my view of the world. That felt comforting, as if I had a partner of sorts. I closed my eyes, started to type into my wrist-com, and froze. If Morgan could watch from the elevator, so could others. The walls of the elevator seemed closer, confining.

<Stay calm,> Morgan said. <I'll help if I can. Then we need to talk.>

Like I need more problems.

The elevator doors opened. Sergeant Louise Proctor pointed a stun gun at me, one of the multiple-shot models I wished I had.

I almost spilled the coffee. "I … uh, thought you might want something to drink." I held out the coffee with my right hand. My left reached for my own stun gun. Instead, I raised my hand over my head.

Proctor's short, tar-black hair framed her thin face and focused eyes. "You don't have authority to be here," she said. "How did you get down here?"

<Oops,> Morgan said. <I forgot to mention I overrode the elevator's security lock.>

I forced a smile. "My partner abandoned me for the day. I haven't been near a boy except in the arena. I was curious. Are they as dangerous as I've been told?"

Proctor put her stun gun in her belt holster and took the coffee. "Thanks. My thermos is cold. If decaf is bad, cold decaf is the pits."

I laughed and wondered if she'd tried mech coffee.

She returned to her desk, which faced both the elevators and the hallway to lockup. She pointed to screen views of the cells. "These two are as docile as defanged wildcats. They look to be 12 if that. The little one sobs all the time."

<You'd sob, too, if you'd been removed from your family, pushed into an institution, and shoved into a prison cell.>

I nodded. The thin, sobbing one reminded me of Janine at night when she used to be afraid of the dark. The bigger one looked frail, as if they didn't get enough muscle-building nourishment. They didn't get Sam's mech steroids, that was for sure. The Institute only wanted their brains.

"What about the third boy?" I asked.

"I don't know anything about a third. Scandia dropped these two off a while ago. She said she'd pick them up tonight."

"Any idea where we'll send them? I doubt they'll go back to Oak Ridge."

"Scandia didn't say. I'd just as soon they dumped them all over the border. Don't quote me."

I smiled, not over the dumping part, but letting them all go. After all, how could we consider ourselves free and civilized when we enslaved others?

Both boys wore orange jumpsuits, which made them visible against the gray concrete cells.

<Go with the 'can I see them up close?' idea,> Morgan said.

"The boys are restrained," I said.

"They can't go anywhere, if that's what you mean. Unless the Underground Railroad sneaks in." Proctor's eyes narrowed at that.

"Can I meet one?" I pointed at the smaller boy, the one crying. "For the experience."

"They're in lockdown. That means no visitors."

"How can I get experience if no one gives me a chance? You can stand at the door with the stun gun and revolver. I have mech training. He can't escape."

Sergeant Proctor sighed. Her eyes looked more weary than concerned. "You get me into trouble over this, and I'll see you pay."

"I swear I won't tell anyone. I'm going nuts upstairs watching the desks grow dusty."

"Okay, but when I say leave, you leave without protest."

I nodded.

Proctor unlocked the smaller boy's cell, let me in, and shut the door. Six weeks ago, this was where Voss was sending me when Sam offered me a shot at the mechs. I struggled to breathe. My birth mother rotted in a place like this. No one would let me know where: no letters, no contact of any kind.

"Focus on what you can learn from this visit," Sam said.

I took an unsteady, deep breath and looked closely at the boy. He reminded me of Sarah, my youngest adopted sister, about the same age. I had no idea if I had any real siblings, though Mom said no.

"You got a name, boy?"

"Tommy." He looked up and dried his eyes on his orange sleeve. His nose dripped.

I handed him a tissue. "Why did you try to escape?"

He took the tissue in his delicate hand and stared at the floor. "My brain is tired all the time, ma'am. Like someone squeezes it like an orange."

The "ma'am" bit made me feel old. "Who else escaped with you?"

"Jack said he knew a way, but they were waiting."

"Who is Jack?"

Tommy dabbed his nose. "The boy I was with."

"Who else knew of your escape?"

"Jack said tell no one. I didn't. I swear." He looked up with sad eyes that tore at my heart. "Can I go back to my room?"

I took that to mean the Institute. He must have expected worse here.

<Ask how he escaped,> Morgan said.

"How did you get past Institute security?"

"Someone tunneled under the wall," Tommy said. "Jack took care of that."

"Did you see anyone else?"

Tommy shook his head.

I wanted to ask him about the boy Dara had caught, Hank, but I didn't want to give Tommy information that Scarlatti could trace to me.

"Did someone on the staff leave a door open?" I asked.

"Jack pulled the fire alarm," Tommy said. "While the others scrambled around, we snuck down to the basement."

"Did a staff member unlock doors so you could go down?"

"No, ma'am. Jack had a key-chip that opened all the doors."

I didn't want to expose escape plans Morgan might need, but if I didn't get answers, that wouldn't matter. "Where did he get the key-chip?"

"He said he made it. We make all sorts of electronic gadgets for the Institute."

"He programmed it to open the doors?"

"It's what they have us do," Tommy said. "We make things and write code, or they send us away."

I shuddered. I had my own visions of what "send away" could mean. "Away where?"

Tommy shook his head. "Someplace very bad." He sobbed and wiped his eyes.

I didn't press. "Is there anything else you can tell me about how you escaped?"

"We didn't. We're here. They tricked us so they could punish us."

"Who?"

"I don't know." He broke down again.

The door opened. "Time to go," Proctor said.

The boy hadn't given me much, but I'd grown attached to him, enough to consider how I might help him escape. I joined Proctor at the door and glanced back at him. He'd curled up onto his thin mattress.

I left before I did something else stupid. After all, I'd had more time to plan Morgan's escape. That ended in all but him captured, and two women committed suicide.

SEVENTEEN

My visit with Tommy raised more questions than answers, but I'd promised to leave without a fuss. Besides, the cell was claustrophobic. I didn't want to give Voss, the fat cow, any excuse to lock me up. Since Scarlatti still wasn't back, I headed out to my cycle.

<This is what Seth has to look forward to,> Morgan said. <I need you to find safe houses near the Institute and transport to the border. We don't want any trouble. I swear. I just want to take him where he can be free.>

I nodded gently. What place could be safe when mechs and cops would surround the area and search house by house? When I rescued Morgan the first time, I directed him to a cave by the river and put him into the trunk of Brooks' two-seater. Morgan and his brother couldn't fit into the saddlebags of my cycle.

I rode out of the station parking lot and two blocks down the road before Sam piped in: "Stop your cycle. Do a security scan."

Why bother, when traffic cams can track me? But she would know if I didn't obey.

When I reached a light, I pulled the thumb-sized unit out of my pocket and pretended to caress the cycle. I found a chip in the usual place, under the seat, and scanned again. A second device beeped inside my locked saddlebag. *That's comforting.*

I dropped both chips by the curb and turned. At the next light, I repeated the procedure and found a chip near the rear fender. I dropped that one down a storm drain and took off.

"All clear," I said.

"Where are you off to, soldier?" Sam said.

I started to explain but realized Sam hadn't been in on the discussion about the supplies, at least not the part with shipping locations. "I have a hunch. You said to follow my instincts."

I imagined Sam's eyes narrowing. "There isn't time for side trips."

The sun beat down on my black helmet. It caused me to sweat, and I wished I had mech-gear air-conditioning. As I crossed the river south of town, I raised my visor to take in a cooler breeze over the water. Then I rode to the Tenn-tucky Supply Depot Morgan had mentioned.

Nestled between two hills, the fenced-in property spread out, away from the road. The building perched at the back of the property in such a way it would be difficult to sneak in, particularly with ever-present cams. I rode past, and let my contacts scan the parking lot, the building beneath the hills, and the hills on three sides. I didn't see anything you wouldn't find at any of the dozen such supply outlets around town.

"Sam, what can you tell me about Tenn-tucky Supply Depot?"

"They're a regulated supply company. They have to keep strict records of what they buy and sell, to comply with state and federal regulations. What are you thinking?"

"How could they sell so much to Voss without leaving records?" I hid my cycle behind bushes and crept up a nearby hill for a better view of the warehouse. The building was rectangular, with outcroppings that conformed to the flat land beneath the hills.

Tenn-tucky Supply Depot ledgers projected off my right contact. I started to comment and realized they came from Morgan. The money received totaled what my station showed as paying. The items were marked as having been picked up. The purchaser was a company I didn't recognize: the Tenn-tucky Benevolent Society.

"Where are you getting your information?" Sam asked. "I don't show any records of Tenn-tucky Supply Depot selling to Voss or your station."

<Oops,> Morgan said.

My mind scrambled for answers. "Where else would Voss buy from?" I asked.

A truck with a long trailer pulled up to the building.

"Your hunch?" Sam asked. "Or do you have something you haven't shown me? Why this particular depot?"

"Can you pull up depot sales records?" I asked.

"I have them."

"Compare them to my station's purchase records."

"Wait," Sam said. "This is interesting. The payments made by your station coincide with receipts by the Depot, although the amounts are broken up differently, as if to confuse a casual viewer."

"What about the purchaser?"

"Give me a moment," Sam said.

Morgan flashed a document onto my right visual. They were playing me like some video game, Sam on my left and Morgan to the right, both inside my head. I climbed farther up the hill. Clusters of thick bushes clung to a six-foot chain-link fence and sharp concertina wire. It reminded me of the wire surrounding Morgan's school-prison, where I first saw him.

"The purchaser was something called the Tenn-tucky Benevolent Society," Sam said.

<It's a shell company. I can't pick out who owns them.>

"Sam, could Voss be buying supplies under a shell company?" I asked.

"Why would she need so much toilet paper?" Sam asked. "And adult diapers? That makes no sense."

I used the wrist-com cam to zoom in on the front of the warehouse. The image wasn't as crisp as binoculars, but my wrist-com was small and easy to wear. A steady stream of big trucks rolled in. Smaller delivery vans rolled out. I didn't know much about business, but nothing struck me as out of the ordinary.

Needing a closer look, I descended the hill and rode my cycle into the drive.

"What's your plan?" Sam asked.

Me, have a plan? You should know better. "You want answers. This is my only lead."

I removed my cop-intern badge and visual ID and tucked both into a pocket of my skorts. Then I headed into the glass-encased office that jutted out front. A sleeker, older version of Liz Cameron greeted me in the lobby. Her nametag read Carol Spinner.

I smiled and tossed my blonde hair off my face. "Ms. Spinner, I was driving by and … oh my, this place is big, much bigger than my school." It helps to be 16. Adults excuse so much of my behavior.

Spinner stared with beady, suspicious eyes. "Shouldn't you be in school?"

"They charged me to come up with a field trip. This place looks amazing."

"I assure you it isn't. What school are you with?"

"Cedar Bluff, ma'am." *Until six weeks ago.* "You get all these big trucks in, and all these little trucks go out. I bet this place runs like magic. Do you use humanoid robots?"

Spinner's face softened. "We're just a big supply warehouse. Nothing interesting."

"What are you playing at?" Sam asked.

"Could I see?" I asked. "My teammate on this project is Emily Battani. As you can imagine, I have to do all the work. Not that I'm complaining. This is a lot of fun. Please don't say anything. I don't want to get her into trouble."

Spinner rolled her eyes, but left her desk and agreed to show me around. For an instant, I felt like a kid, as I imagined Janine did when she got wrapped up in a project. I envied her that innocence.

The office was smaller than I'd expected, a small room filled with a handful of desks, surrounded by glass-lined offices. Beyond a double door lay racks spread out in all directions. Automated conveyors moved boxes in a continuous flow above us. Non-humanoid robots on our level darted in and out with boxes of all sizes, stacked on a forklift attachment in front of them. They had appendages like arms and legs, but no humanlike body.

"How do they know what to pick?" I tried to adopt Janine's energy.

"It's all electronic." Spinner pointed to electronic runners. "Orders come in with payment."

"Oh, so people pay in advance."

"We sell to companies," she said. "They pay credits with their orders. We ship on those little trucks you saw."

"Do companies ever pick up their own supplies?"

"Some companies have their own trucks. They think they save on freight, but unless they buy a truckload, we do it better."

With the facility automated, there should be electronic records. I smiled. "Ah, so if I was a company and sent you an order ... how would I pay?"

"You would send authorization for a credit transfer."

"Then I could pick up the order?"

"Not quite," Spinner said. "We have to make sure you're authorized to make these purchases. We don't want product falling into the wrong hands. Then we have to include the purchases in a report to the state regulatory commission."

"That's fascinating." I smiled, ready to puke. *How does Janine do this?*

"I'm glad you find this interesting, but I have to get to work. There isn't much to show here."

"Quite the contrary, Ms. Spinner. You've been a terrific help. Do you mind if I recommend that we visit your facility?"

Spinner shrugged, nodded, and showed me out.

<Not bad,> Morgan said. <But you gave her a way to check out your story and show you were lying. She has your image to verify your identity.>

I reached my cycle, waved at Spinner, and drove off. "Sam, did you find out anything else on the Depot?"

"Ownership of the benevolent group is classified," Sam said. "I'll have to do more digging. In the meantime, return to your station."

"What about the cop-intern who attacked Mom—?"

"I told you I'll dig into that. You concentrate on Voss and Scarlatti."

<∞>

Scarlatti closed the door to Captain Voss' office and waited for her boss to stop talking on her wrist-com. Voss severed the connection and looked glum. "Every time I turn around, that wench of a commander is there to screw up my life." She looked up, her jowls pinched. "How the hell did she get to the Institute so quickly? You told me we had a half-hour jump on her. Spies, I tell you. She has spies and informants everywhere. You can't trust anyone these days."

The captain's voice rose as she got into her monologue. Scarlatti waited. Interrupting her boss would cause the excitable captain to rewind and start over.

"If she bugged our station, I'll see she goes to prison." Voss jabbed her finger into her desk. "We need clear-cut victories. Today doesn't cut it. The whole point was to embarrass the Mech Corps. And here, one of theirs captured that boy! We need to plug the leak. We can't afford more screw-ups. The next mission has to be clean. Do you hear me?"

You had to be deaf not to hear the captain's tinny rant. Scarlatti nodded. "I have some news."

"It had better be good." Voss motioned for Scarlatti to sit.

Scarlatti remained standing. "Juicy stuff. It seems Senator Scott and the commander go way back. They knew each other socially before the war."

"I knew it," Voss said, her gloom lifting. "Tell me, tell me."

"I found records of a phone call Senator Scott made to the commander after we arrested Annabelle six weeks ago."

The captain's jowls quivered. "That explains how the wench showed up to bail the girl out with promises of a mech career. Why haven't I heard this before?"

Scarlatti grinned. *You don't want to get your hands dirty.* "Hernandez and Senator Scott have kept a low profile. I only found three other calls over a 16-year period. The others were related to requests for Mech Corps funding, which the senator supports."

"How cozy. Now that we've linked them, let's find a way to sink both of them. Come on. Sit down. You look uncomfortable."

Scarlatti sat. The captain could be temperamental, but her pending promotion promised to put Scarlatti in charge of this station. She smiled to herself. Moving up with an incompetent like Voss took pushing the right buttons. "The commander rarely leaves the base. However, the senator drives more than necessary."

"How do you mean?" Voss asked.

"Traffic cams show her making side trips. She takes the long way home, wanders out for a drive after dark. Even government officials need to conserve resources. She doesn't think that applies to her."

"Where does she go?"

"That's it," Scarlatti said. "She drives around town, nowhere in particular, and stops now and then. At first, I thought she was meeting someone. I haven't found any connections."

"Try harder. Connect her to the wench. This could be our ticket. You know what to do."

EIGHTEEN

At times like this, I wished I had more experience. Though I'd learned that people who did, tended not to act on what they knew. Experience made them cautious, afraid, and paralyzed.

While I drove away from the supply depot with sweat dripping down my neck, I considered how to spy on the place. Nothing came to mind. With no message from Scarlatti—she didn't miss me—I headed toward the East Knoxville cop station. There were few vehicles on the road, so I kept my visor up to get some air and my head tilted to avoid traffic cams.

When I reached the East Knoxville station, Sam's voice vibrated against my skull. "What are you up to, soldier? You took too many chances at the supply depot."

"Captain Chou was at the capture. I hoped she could enlighten me."

"Leave now," Sam said.

I froze on the steps of the station. My throat went dry. Sweat dripped into my eyes, blurring my vision. Captain Chou burst out of the station doors and bumped into me. I fell back, caught my balance, and held onto her arm. I let go and bowed my head. "So sorry, I didn't see you."

"Leave," Sam said.

Chou looked annoyed, too, but she shook it off. "No, my fault. I—"

"Your team did a great job today catching those boys," I said. "I hoped to bump into you … well, not like this. Could you give me some pointers on becoming a good policewoman?" Smiling, I stepped out of her way.

Chou straightened her blue dress uniform. "You're Scarlatti's new partner. Why don't you ask her, or Captain Voss?"

"We got off to a very bad start. It was my fault. I wasn't the best intern. Now that I'm full-time, I want to make it up by learning. I want to become a valuable member of the Knoxville police force."

<You *are* full of yourself, aren't you,> Morgan said.

I smiled and acted gracious. "Some of the mech trainees from your station spoke highly of you."

"Don't push it," Sam said into my skull.

"I doubt that includes Dara." Chou looked from me to a silver car at the curb. "I'm late."

I took that to mean she might talk to me. "Could I stop by later today, or tomorrow?"

"That's a negative," Sam said.

Chou moved down a step. "I've heard of your persistence."

"Please don't hold that against me."

"I defer to your captain. Nice meeting you." Chou turned and descended the steps.

I walked with her. "Did one of the boys give you the lead, or did the Institute call?"

"Persistence is one thing," Chou said. "Being a pest is another. I suggest you take this up with Lieutenant Scarlatti." She reached the car's passenger door, which opened.

"What can you tell me about the intern who attacked Senator Scott?" I rattled it off before she could disappear into the car.

Chou turned toward me, a scowl on her face. "Your mother. That's right."

"How long did the intern work here?"

The captain raised her finger as if to make a point, or tell me to buzz off. "Three months without an incident."

In my side vision, I recognized the driver from the Institute. "What was she like? Who was she friendly with?"

Chou sighed. "I appreciate your interest, but you're too close to the incident to investigate."

"I'm sorry." I hung my head. "I need answers. For me."

"She was a perfect intern. Punctual, followed instructions. Helpful. She didn't socialize. She did her job and kept to herself.

There's no crime in that. Now, if you don't mind, you're keeping me from important business. Leave this to experienced officers." Chou climbed into the car and slammed the door.

"Next time, listen when I tell you to back off," Sam hammered into my skull. "Why persist in making my life and yours more difficult?"

I climbed onto my cycle before I answered. "I wouldn't have to, if you gave me more to work with than 'Follow the money.' I have no way to access a money trail."

"Return to your station and find Scarlatti before they kick you off the force."

I headed west. My mind churned over how the money trail could lead me to Voss and Battani. The governor was the one I really wanted to embarrass.

<∞>

After she removed two tracking chips, Janine set the speed control on her cycle to the posted limit and glided toward the mech-base. Brooks had accepted her excuse that she needed to run an errand for her mom. It paid to get people to like you before asking favors. They asked far fewer questions that way.

When she reached the mech-base's concrete wall, Janine passed the guard and made her way across a well-lit-and-observed clearing to the side entrance. She hated all the secrets, yet for once, she wasn't Annabelle's shadow.

Sam greeted her at the door. "Thanks for coming on short notice."

"Have I done something wrong?"

Sam laughed, which made the scar on her face less intimidating. "No." She escorted Janine into her office and offered a cup of coffee. The real thing had Janine not liking her station's decaf.

She sipped the bitter brew, asked for another sugar, and settled into a wooden seat that faced Sam's battered metal desk, bare except for the screen and a virtual keyboard traced out on the desktop. Janine liked that the commander didn't act like some self-important official.

"I've thrown a lot of changes at you," Sam said, as if talking to herself.

Janine placed her coffee on the desk and stood. "I stand ready to deliver."

Sam grinned. "You've been avoiding your sister."

Janine's stomach tightened, and jumped as if filled with popping popcorn. "It's hard when I can't tell her what I'm doing. We confide everything. Now—"

"I know it's hard. I believe you're tougher," Sam said.

Janine couldn't help smiling. She tried to remain calm, steady, and alert. *Don't miss any details.*

"The escape of boys from the arena embarrassed the Mech Corps. It's allowed Voss to take the limelight with the recent captures."

"You think she might be involved?" Janine asked. She hated how adults danced around topics as if she were too fragile.

"I don't believe so, but Voss is exploiting the situation. What's worse, one boy remains on the loose."

Janine's throat went dry. "He could be anywhere."

"There are few places to hide. Someone has to be helping him."

"The Underground Railroad?"

Sam nodded. "He's a handsome boy who might have caught someone's eye, but he's dangerous. The sooner we take him into custody the better for everyone, including him."

"Thanks for warning me, Commander. I promise to keep my eyes open."

"When we're alone, call me Sam." She leaned forward and lowered her voice. "I need you to do more than keep your eyes open. The missing boy is Morgan, the one Annabelle fought in the arena."

"Oh, my. He was a big one. I was so afraid—"

"I need you to get close to your sister. Find out what she knows about this boy. She might not know she has information that might help us capture him."

Tightness gripped Janine's chest. "You think Annabelle's involved. No! She wouldn't." *Would she?*

"I don't like coincidences. He was her final opponent. She let him live. He's the one who remains loose."

"We were so worried about Mom … and that dreadful intern who attacked her." Janine steadied her breathing. "I can't believe Annabelle would have anything to do with a boy."

"Maybe not," Sam said. "I'm certain he'll contact her, though. He might put her into a compromising situation, where she's not comfortable telling me or you."

Janine stared at the wall behind the commander, at the picture of Sam in the Marine Corps before the war. "You mean blackmail?"

"Or worse. This could threaten her, you, and your entire family."

Tears filled Janine's eyes. She willed them away and straightened up. "You want me to spy on my sister?"

Sam leaned farther over the desk. "I should mention that if Captain Voss wins her little vendetta, it won't go well for your family. Help me find that boy before it's too late."

<∞>

<Have you found a safe house?> Morgan asked, loud enough to grate on my eardrum.

I shook my head slowly from side to side, as if watching for pedestrians. Escape didn't seem possible. I didn't make plans, at least not good ones. My big attempt had been to set him free. He still was, but it cost the lives of two women, and Sam caught the other boys. Who knows what punishment she was giving them?

<How about transport?>

I stopped at a light, and held my gaze on my saddlebag.

<Very funny,> he said.

He remained quiet until I reached the station, which was good. These one-sided monologues, where I couldn't respond, were irritating. The station parking lot was half-empty. Scarlatti's car pulled out of the alley behind the station, with Tommy's face plastered against the rear window.

<That will be my brother soon.>

When Scarlatti's car turned the corner, I followed at a distance.

"They're moving the boys to a more secure facility," Sam said, "supposedly where the Underground Railroad can't interfere. Do you have a different thought?"

"You told me to return to my partner," I said. "I'm following her."

"Don't give me attitude, soldier."

"I don't like my partner keeping me in the dark," I said, directed as much at Sam as at Scarlatti. "If this was routine, why not let me assist?"

"You weren't at the station," Sam reminded me.

I pulled over when Scarlatti's car stopped for a light. "She didn't use me as a partner when they caught the boys, either."

"Don't do anything rash."

"I'll be more careful." *Like an adult.*

<The driver isn't Scarlatti,> Morgan said. <It's the one you talked to at the station, the one who brought the boys in. You're following too close.>

"Sam, can you track the car so I don't have to follow so close?"

"I can, but I don't like this."

"You told me to find Scarlatti. That's her car."

I slowed, and let Sam direct me on the turns. I realized she could lead me anywhere. She led me across the river. Despite longing to visit the rural Outland, I didn't like the south bank. It was more remote, with more places to get lost, and more rogues from the Outland here, or so government warnings said. The sun settled below the horizon, leaving a darkened sky.

The winding road Sam directed me onto headed up into densely forested hills south of the river. I passed a sign that read "No thru traffic" and headed into a valley you had to go out of your way to find. Up ahead, amidst a wilderness of trees lay a clearing. In the middle of that was a building complex that looked like another prison. To me, anything with high walls topped with sharp wire was a prison. I couldn't see cams, though I had no doubt they were all around.

"What is this place?" I asked.

"Stop and turn around," Sam said. "It's private property. We don't have jurisdiction."

I steered off the road and pulled my cycle into the bushes.

"Leave. Now!"

"Where are they taking the boys? What could possibly be beyond your jurisdiction?" I climbed a hill and used my wrist-com's zoom to scan the compound below. The first thing I saw was concertina wire, and not only on top of the wall in the distance or above the chain-link fence on this side of the wall. Not ten yards below me were coils and twists of sharp wire, staked to poles that rose ten feet into the air in a narrow clearing like the no-man's-land that separated the Outlands.

"What *is* this place?" I asked.

"Get your butt on that cycle and leave," Sam yelled into my head, then, "No! No, stay put."

While I longed for a volume control to tone down her voice, an armored vehicle sprinted up the road. The markings on the side were runic, something from an Old Norse book Mom kept hidden.

The marking had a broken "h" followed by "l" and a strange mark a child might draw. My first thought was *secret society*.

"What's going on, Sam?"

A moment's pause, then she said, "This is a more secure facility for boys who cause trouble."

<Boys like Seth,> Morgan added. <They go in and disappear.>

"The road is clear," Sam said. "Go before they catch you hanging around."

<Sam's right. I don't want you to disappear in there.>

Thanks for everyone's concern, but I'm not ready to leave.

NINETEEN

I waited five more minutes, during which the car with the boys and the armored vehicle disappeared behind the building. Then I headed down to my cycle before I had both Sam and Morgan yelling in my head.

I scanned my cycle again for any tracking devices and headed to the one place that might give me answers, if I didn't get my brains bashed in first. I crossed the river into the western hamlets of Knoxville and headed down side roads into the country. I found the road to an abandoned plantation some ex-CEO used to own before the war, before he vanished.

I wasn't sure the place was still being used, but I counted on Dara as the creature of habit she'd been during training. Sure enough, the clearing in front of the plantation contained dozens of electric mech-cycles, despite Sam's lockdown for training. Dara didn't like to follow rules. My kind of gal, except she relished telling me what to do.

In moonlight, the outside of the plantation house looked run-down, in need of many things: paint, new windows downstairs, and shoring up the porch posts. Loud music reverberated from inside the great hall.

"What are you doing?" Sam startled me.

I wanted to pop out the contacts and plug my ears, but what fun was there in that?

"I thought you locked them down in training this week." I hid my cycle in the bushes, pointing it toward the road, away from the

129

plantation, and crept toward the clearing. I expected Sam to send her armored mech-warriors out here to round everyone up. *The night's yet young.*

"This lot hasn't returned to base since this morning," Sam said. "I'll deal with them later."

"They might have seen something this morning that could help," I said.

"That's my responsibility. Leave."

"Sam, it's not like I can hide from you. Just listen in."

The large foyer still sported a crystal chandelier, probably imitation cut glass. It sparkled in the dim mood lights. Inside the grand hall, the big amazon, Dara, danced with Capra, a smaller sandy-blonde who was part of Dara's posse. Dara broke away from her dance partner and charged toward me. I braced myself for another fight I didn't need.

"I warned you," Sam said.

"You spying on us?" Out of uniform, Dara wore jeans and a tight tee shirt, no bra and she needed one, showing off her muscles. She loved to intimidate.

"No, I miss the mechs," I said. "Besides, if I spied on you, you wouldn't see me."

Dara grumbled and narrowed her eyes. Capra and other warrior trainees gathered around. I'd defeated Dara in the tournament final, which gave the amazon pause.

I stared up at Dara's large head, sculpted cheekbones and prominent nose framed by sandy hair. "I didn't like how the cops took over mech work this morning."

"Yeah, what a cluster," Capra said.

"Load of bull, you ask me." Sally tugged on her shoulder-length cornrows.

Brandy stood behind the others, cringing.

"You're one of the cops," Margarite said to me.

"Did you see any other cops around me this morning?" I asked. I let my contacts scan the room to give Sam something else to think about besides me. She could inventory her warrior recruits.

Looking confused, Dara backed up enough so I could breathe. "You were with that Lieutenant Scarlatti who arrested us back before the Mech Corps."

"For what—the ten seconds it took for her to ditch me?"

"You're not a mech, so what brings you here?" Dara asked.

Capra took her arm. "Leave the loser. Let's dance."

"I'm sorry I let you all down," I said. "I might be a cop, but it doesn't serve anyone's interests for cops to do your jobs. We have enough other things to worry about."

"Yeah, like traffic violations," Margarite said. She looked to Dara for approval.

I didn't have Dara's leadership magnetism. Or was it just intimidation I felt? "Who contacted Voss and Scarlatti about the Institute escape?"

"Sounds like a cop issue," Capra said. "Why don't *you* go sort that out?"

"Someone must have alerted you to a problem," I said. "Sam sent you even before Voss and her team arrived."

"Yeah," Dara said. "So why call the cops?"

"Exactly," I said, "or more important, who brought the cops? Did you see anyone at the Institute who could have called Voss?"

"You think the Institute wanted to embarrass us?" Dara said.

"Who talked to Voss and Scarlatti?"

"I was in back with you. Capra, weren't you near the front?"

"How do we know she's not spying for Voss?" Capra asked.

Dara moved closer, making me uncomfortable. "Yeah, how do we?"

I backed up and turned to Capra. "I'm not spying for Voss." *If you only knew.* "Did you see who Voss and Scarlatti talked to?"

"Just Director Devotte. The commander was there."

"No one else was with Voss or Scarlatti."

"Are you deaf?" Capra said.

"Someone contacted them," I said. "What about Lieutenant Scandia and Sergeant Montrose? Did they talk to anyone?"

Capra shook her head. "Not while they were out front. They went to the north side of the building. I couldn't see them."

"How did they know which side of the building the two boys would escape by?"

"I caught one of the boys." Dara grinned.

Yeah, but he wasn't with the other two in lockdown. I filed that away for later.

"Why don't you leave?" Capra said. "We don't need losers around."

"Am I invited?"

I turned to see Janine. "Why are you here?"

"I could ask you the same thing. Can we talk?" Janine grabbed my hand and pulled me toward the foyer. She drew a figure 8 on my palm.

"Oh, great," Capra said, loud enough for me to hear. "Might as well invite all the cops."

Janine turned to face the others. "I'll have you know, I'm going to try out for the Mech Corps when I'm old enough."

"Until then, little sister," Dara said, "why don't you take out the trash?"

While I was glad to see Janine, I was annoyed to see her at one of Dara's parties. I hurried toward my cycle, to let the night mask my confusion at her sudden appearance.

"I parked next to you," she announced. "If you don't want your cycle found, hide it better."

Thanks for the sisterly advice. "Let's get you home."

"I'm not a child."

"You're only 15," I said.

"And you're only 16. Stop pretending to be my mother."

"You want to fight?"

"No. You?"

Her combativeness put me off. It was so unlike her. My actions must have disturbed her. I hadn't realized how much until then. "How did you find me?"

"I tried your usual hangouts. When you weren't there, I took a chance you'd come out here."

I couldn't question her about why she was following me, and more important, why she was out alone, without revealing things to Sam. Instead, I climbed onto my cycle and headed home. She sped ahead, stopped, and blocked the dirt road. I braked and almost ran into her.

"What's wrong?" I asked, unable to see her face in the shadows.

She climbed off her cycle. "I came all the way out here, and you don't ask why. What's wrong with you, Belle?"

"Sorry. Guess I'm not myself lately," I said. "I'm not happy being with Scarlatti." I reached for her hand.

She pulled away. "So you take it out on me. I miss you, Belle, a lot. Can't we hang out tonight?"

"Sure, we'll go home and—"

"That's not what I mean. You go places at night and leave me behind."

"Mech training until Sam kicked me out. Now I'm home." I moved closer to give her our signal about prying ears.

She moved away. "You didn't come home last night." I could imagine the pout on her face.

"It's not what you think," I said.

"That's your business. I know you were upset having to fight that boy. I saw it in your eyes. Is that why you let him live?"

"I don't want to do this now. Let's go home."

"Stop shutting me out, Belle."

"I won't kill for sport. That got me kicked out. I accepted my penalty for doing what I thought was right."

"Did you feel sorry for him?"

Sticky sweat streamed down my neck. Mosquitoes buzzed all around. How could I possibly give her a satisfactory answer with Sam listening?

"Where are you going with this?" I tried to move my cycle around her.

She held onto my handlebars. "Those boys got loose. The one you fought is still out there. I'm scared. What if he grabs me?"

<I would never hurt your sister,> Morgan said.

I forgot he was listening. I clenched my teeth. He had no idea how tenacious Janine could be in following the rules. Cops were expected to round up boys. If she caught him—I didn't want to think what would happen. "I'm sure Sam is looking for any boys she hasn't caught. That's a good reason to get you home. No telling who might be in these woods."

Even in the dark, I sensed her fear. She backed up to her cycle, climbed on and rode out. She rode slowly until I caught up. I wanted to comfort her with the truth, had often wanted to tell her everything, even about my adoption, but I had too much to lose.

<∞>

We parked our cycles next to Mom's car. I hurried into our community home. Mama Grace cleaned up in the kitchen. Mama Helen pushed her reading glasses up over her head and looked up from her e-pad, probably more medical research on her screen. The light shone under the door to Mom's office. Our seven sisters weren't there; hopefully they were in their rooms, asleep. I didn't need more drama.

133

I turned to Janine. "I'll be up after I talk to Mom."

Janine's eyes took on their worry-look. "Don't be long. We don't want to wake Sarah."

I smiled at her. As she headed for the stairs, I entered Mom's office. Mom sat, slumped over her desk. I hurried to her side. She bolted upright. It took a moment for her eyes to focus on me.

"You're late on your first full day on the police force," she said. "You okay?"

I studied the bags under her eyes, and deeper wrinkles on her forehead than I recalled. "I've been worried about you."

She nodded. Her eyes glazed over. "Politics as usual. Governor Battani is pushing for quick resolution on who has jurisdiction over escaped boys, all boys. There's a lot of backroom chatter. Nothing for you to worry about."

I wanted to know more, but not with Sam listening. I considered writing a note with my eyes closed, but Sam would get suspicious.

"You're working too hard," I said.

"So are you."

"I have to go out, Mom. I don't need Janine following me and taking risks."

"Is this necessary?"

"Stay home and get some rest," Sam said into my head.

"There's something I need to do," I said. "Can you help?"

"I'll make sure she stays upstairs," Mom said. "Be careful, Belle."

I hugged Mom, waved to Mama Grace and Mama Helen, and snuck out into the garage. I took my cycle out the side door to avoid the garage door's hum. Then I walked my cycle down the street so Janine's sharp ears couldn't pick up the quiet whine of the electric motor.

"Your mother was too easy on her 16-year-old daughter going out late," Sam said.

TWENTY

When I reached the community gate, I checked that no one followed me. "I want to check out the supply depot again," I said for Sam's benefit.

"Be careful," she said. "You don't have backup. Check the toolbox in the back of the U-Store unit. I arranged for a pistol and an automatic stun gun. Don't ride in like the Wild West."

"Wild West?" I pretended I didn't know about cowboys and Indians and other banned topics.

"Never mind."

Covering my face, I entered the storage unit, tucked the automatic stun gun and pistol into my saddlebag and locked it. I set the speed governor at four miles over the speed limit and headed across the river.

The night was muggy. Sweat beaded on my brow and neck. Even with the helmet's visor up, I didn't feel much breeze. It would have been grand to have mech-suit air-conditioning.

At the supply depot, I pulled off the road and hiked the cycle farther up the hill. I left the sweaty helmet with the cycle, and climbed up until I reached a clearing with a view of the front of the supply depot. I spotted a tractor-trailer and three boxy utility vans.

I zoomed in using my wrist-com's cam. Scarlatti stood with Scandia and Montrose. A warehouse utility robot transferred boxes from the tractor-trailer directly to the three utility vans. The zoom didn't pan in enough to read the sides of the boxes. I saw no supply depot employees, only the utility robot that did the heavy

135

lifting. Scandia and Montrose loaded the bot, which then scurried into one of the vans to deposit the load. These boxes weren't the same as the clearly marked ones I'd seen inside the warehouse.

"Sam, you see this?" I showed her views from my wrist-com. "The station paid for toilet paper. Those aren't toilet paper boxes. Too small, too heavy."

"They've paid off someone at the supply depot," Sam said.

"Bribing, you mean. Why would Voss—?"

"Scarlatti and her friends," Sam said. "We don't have anything that connects Voss."

Is Voss the Boss that clever, or is this all the lieutenant?

"Scarlatti must be paying for phony supplies," I said, "so the supply depot staff will look the other way and allow Scarlatti to use their robot. Why?"

"Scarlatti must want a quiet place for this type of transaction."

I scanned the area for anyone else. I couldn't see drivers in the vans, too dark. The truck driver, on the other hand, sat in his cab playing something on a lit display. "Given the amount of money in the ledgers, this has to be big. I'm going down for a better look."

"No!" Sam said. "Scarlatti could arrest you on the spot for trespassing. I have no jurisdiction to help you if she does—"

"They're doing something illegal. If I could open the boxes—"

"You won't get that chance," Sam said. "Stand down. That's an order. This time, you'd best obey."

I crept downhill to get closer to the trucks. Something bit my finger. I fell back onto a rock and used my wrist-com backlight. All around were coils of concertina wire. The bundles disappeared to the right and left, another barrier I hadn't noticed before. I licked my finger and tasted blood. The cut didn't want to stop bleeding.

Concerned I might have made a sound, I put pressure on the cut while I hid my wrist-com, which left me in darkness. I squinted at the scene below and couldn't see any change. I crawled uphill. Surrounded by hills, this spot made sense for taking a secret delivery. No one, including me, could get close enough to be sure what they were doing.

Red lights flashed to my right. I got to my feet and scrambled down to my cycle. I pulled on my helmet, and rode off with lights out. After turning a corner around the next hill, I eased off the road and waited. My breathing was heavy, taking in too much dust.

<You do live dangerously,> Morgan said.

Intent on listening, I ignored him. There were no sirens. No cops came. The silence unnerved me. Buses didn't run this late south of the river. With no cars on the road, I imagined myself in the Outland, quiet and peaceful, except my heart raced. Sweat trickled down my neck. The night air cooled, a damp cool.

Beyond the hills to my right, a halo of light hung over the west end of Knoxville, not enough to see the wooded hills all around me. Twigs snapped nearby. I moved farther into shadows.

<It's not worth it,> Morgan said. <I need your help to free Seth before they move him. Snap your fingers if you'll try.>

The last thing I needed was to make more noise out here. I gently shook my head and pretended to scan my surroundings.

<Okay, nod if you'll consider helping.>

For the sake of quiet in my head, I nodded.

"Did you see something?" Sam asked.

"No, just making sure I stay awake and alert."

"Go home and get some rest. You've done enough for one day. You've confirmed my suspicions about your police station. You can pick up in the morning."

<I know you don't believe we can do this,> Morgan said. <We can. It'll be much easier to get Seth out of the Institute we know than out of the facility you saw this afternoon. You should go. If you get busted, you won't be able to help anyone.>

I closed my eyes and kept my breathing slow, steady, and quiet.

"Annabelle," Sam said. "Put those contacts in and go home."

<Your commander is quite agitated. You should listen to her.>

I opened my eyes so Sam could see I still had the contacts. Then I closed my left eye and typed into my wrist-com: "I need privacy. Go figure how to get past security."

<Already have. See you in the morning.>

"You won't even give me privacy to take a shower?" I wrote.

<I promise not to watch, but you can't be sure who else does. You shouldn't look at anything you don't want others to see. There are other hackers.>

I didn't need that news. "Thanks for the tip." How could I look at myself in the mirror in the morning? Not a pretty sight.

I cleared the texts and put my wrist-com away so it gave off no light. It was midnight. Sam was right: I needed sleep. As I walked my cycle out from behind the bushes, the guttural electric hum of utility trucks broke the silence. I withdrew into the shadows just as all three utility trucks rumbled down the road. I saw only one figure per truck, but it was too dark to see faces. Instead of crossing the bridge into town, they veered left. Headlights shone on a cop car up by the next turn.

I glanced at the road toward the supply depot. That way would add a half-hour to my travel time home. The shadows already spooked me. I could take my chances up and over the hill to my right. That residential community would report me for sure.

The cop car followed the three trucks up the hill, a winding road given how the first set of headlights weaved.

In the green glow of my wrist-com's zoom and night-vision, the four vehicles disappeared behind a wilderness of trees. The plates on the cop car matched Voss' sedan. The road was the one I'd been on earlier, when I followed Scandia and Montrose to deliver the two boys.

"The boys and supplies are linked," I said.

"I see," Sam said into my implant. "Good job."

"I'm going to investigate."

"No! Not without backup. Not at night."

"I'd be less visible at night."

"That's an order, soldier. Go home. Get some rest. You've had a good day. Don't ruin it."

I looked up at the gloomy, winding road, darkness all around. Even the moon drifted behind clouds. To my left and behind me were spotty hints of civilization, their glow against a cloudy sky. All around was quiet, desolate, beautiful—evidence of the governor's ban on construction south of the river. Oh, how I longed to visit the Great Smoky Mountains on the other side of the Outland border.

Out of curiosity, I checked my wrist-com for newsfeeds on the two escaped boys. There were no posts after their capture at the Institute, no pictures, no evidence of where the cops took them, or even if the boys were still alive. There should have been vid reports, cam swarms, something. Voss didn't want to give the Underground a heads up.

I eased my cycle onto the road with lights out. My wrist-com night-vision showed where the road was. When I reached the bridge, I turned on my lights and sped across. I was in no hurry to get home despite weariness that set in after the adrenaline of the hunt wore off, but when I reached Pleasant Acres, I was ready to crash for a week.

"Don't forget to drop your weapons off at the U-Store before you go home," Sam said into my implant. "I don't need you triggering alarms."

When I finally reached home, the downstairs nightlight remained on. The hushed purr of the refrigerator broke the silence. I considered crashing on the sofa rather than risk waking Janine or Sarah, but then Mama Grace would wake me early as she prepared the kitchen for breakfast.

Up in my bedroom, the chainsaw—Sarah—snored away. I couldn't imagine how she didn't wake herself up. I removed my contacts and slipped out of my cop skorts and blouse in the dark. Holding Dot's furry calico body, I climbed under the covers, reminding myself I'd have to take my morning shower without the contacts.

When I let Dot go and rolled over to face the dark closet, Janine tucked herself next to me. She wasn't the usual furnace. Her hand was clammy. Her pinky dug into my palm, a figure 8 to say we needed to talk without sound, our secret code. It seemed pointless with Sarah snoring nearby. Till I reminded myself that Sam and Morgan could still hear.

Using finger codes against my stomach, Janine wrote, "Where were U? It's late."

I took a deep breath, and used the back of her hand to reply, "Had work. Go to sleep."

"RU helping that boy?"

I rolled over to face her: too dark to see. "No!" I marked on her hand.

"I know UR in trouble. Talk to me."

"I'm fine. Now sleep."

"Not till U talk to me," she wrote.

I turned toward the dark closet. Anything I told her would make things worse. The mechs were doing it again, tearing me from those I loved.

"Be that way," she wrote, and moved away from me.

<∞>

To avoid more conflict, I skipped breakfast and snuck out before anyone else woke. I slipped out the front door and around the side of the garage to avoid Mama Grace, who was preparing eggs and fruit in the kitchen. The cool morning air was damp, hinting at another muggy day where temperatures could hit 100. You might figure I'd get used to this, but every year, it seemed to get warmer. At least that was what the morning weather posts said.

When I reached the station, I parked my cycle in an empty parking lot, grabbed a stale soy donut at Union Bakery, and sat outside Scarlatti's office. I must have dozed off. The next thing I knew she unlocked her office door, her blue uniform not as pressed as usual.

It was time to toady up to my boss. "What do you have for me today?" I asked as cheerfully as I could.

Scarlatti opened her door, hesitated, and gave me a twice-over. "Where did you disappear to yesterday?"

"Looking for police work," I said, not entirely a lie. "You were busy." I smiled and followed her into her office. "I'm ready for work."

She unlocked a drawer behind her desk and dropped in a package. Then she motioned for me to close the door and sit. When I did, she stood over me, and looked down. It seemed peculiar to me how hung up some women got about size, like Dara acting as if she had to be the biggest and most important person in the room. Real women let their spirits define their stature, not a few inches here or there.

I scanned her office for anything of interest. Only the usual trophies scattered across her desk. "Is there any police work I could do today?"

"You're acting like a guilty child who got caught."

Am I? My face flushed. Prickly heat stabbed me all over. "I wanted to help yesterday. You didn't take me with you."

"Help? Is that what you call it? Why in God's name did you talk to our prisoner? Did you think I wouldn't find out?"

"I want to learn good police work and how to interrogate." I stared at a governor's award plaque on the wall behind the desk. "I've never been close to boys, except in the arena. I wanted to learn how they escaped, so I could be on the lookout."

"You got Sergeant Proctor in trouble. She had express instructions to let nobody see the prisoners."

"I'm sorry for everything I've done to make you and Captain Voss hate me. Blame it on youthful ignorance. I want to do better, if you'll let me."

Scarlatti hovered over me. "Yet you continue to irritate. No one wants to work with you."

I wanted to mention Brooks, but I didn't want Janine to lose the best partner in the station. It surprised me that Scarlatti didn't ask if I'd learned anything from my prison visit. I suppose she could study the jail's ever-present security cams for that.

"Why did you interrogate Liz and Lieutenant Scandia?"

"I wasn't interro—"

"I need a partner who's discreet, who does what I need done, and doesn't make more work for me."

"I'm sorry," I said. "I'm trying to learn. You were gone all day."

"You disappeared yesterday afternoon. Captain Chou didn't appreciate you ambushing her, either. I'm putting you on report. One more mark, and your mech performance won't save you from being sent away. Is that clear?"

"Please, don't. Just tell me what to do." I should have counted on the surveillance, yet how could I get answers without network access and the ability to talk to anyone? Was I supposed to make stuff up?

"I'm not surprised by your behavior," Scarlatti said. "Like mother like daughter."

"What do you mean?" I bit my tongue.

Scarlatti grinned. "She's being interrogated over last Saturday's escape."

"Why?"

"It's need to know, and you don't. Go clean out and wash my car while you ponder that." She opened the door and waited for me to leave.

I held my tongue as I headed outside to wash her car. I was too much in shock to say more. *Mom, don't let them take you away.*

Morgan's bass voice boomed in my right ear. <How did you get her so ticked off at you?>

"Long story."

"What was that?" Sam asked.

"I ... just thought this would make a long story."

"Scarlatti can be tough. You can handle her," Sam said. "Think Dara, without the bulk."

I laughed at the idea of a skinny, shorter Dara.

<I know you have enough going on,> Morgan said. <Any ideas on a safe house for Seth and me?>

TWENTY-ONE

Senator Cora Scott received her guest, closed the door, and returned to her seat. Instead of sitting, she stared out her office window at the plaza below. She couldn't decide what unsettled her most: the beefed-up security around the Senate Building, the distress she saw in her daughters' eyes since Belle got kicked out of the mechs, or that Commander Sam Hernandez broke protocol to pay her a personal visit.

Sam took the seat across from Cora's desk. "Nothing escapes our ubiquitous media attention, Senator."

Cora turned to face Sam. "You said this was urgent. My girls are out of the Mech Corps. What else?"

"I never got a chance to express my regrets and sympathy over the attempt on your life."

"You could have called me for that."

"Have we become such strangers?" Sam said. "Forgive me. This hasn't been easy. There's been a lot of anxiety over Saturday's escape. And embarrassment."

Cora sat uneasily in her seat. "I was sorry to hear that." Not about the breakout, but how two women she cared about died helping those boys escape. She poured the commander some weak caffeinated coffee from an instant machine on her credenza. "What have you done to my girls? I hardly recognize them anymore."

"I was preparing them for the rigors of surviving in our world."

Cora handed Sam her coffee and returned to her chair. "They've become strangers to each other."

"I'm sure it's just growing pains," Sam said. "Janine looked up to Annabelle as a successful warrior, and then—"

"You dropped her from the program. Was that fair?"

Sam looked uncomfortable for a split second. "Warriors can't question orders in the heat of battle, Cora. Hesitation kills."

"I won't pretend to tell you your business," the senator said, "but I miss the bond my girls used to have."

Sam stood and moved to the side of the desk. "You have more pressing issues." She hesitated. "Don't force me to arrest you."

"For what?"

"I have reason to believe the boy Annabelle fought and let live will contact her, or you, for help." Sam let that hang.

"You think I'd risk everything by helping him," Cora said, wondering how much the commander knew. "I just want our lives back."

"This isn't a social call, Cora. I'm serious. I'll take my investigation wherever it leads."

"I expect nothing less. And I assure you, there's no way to hide a boy in a household of 12 females."

Sam laughed. "I suspect not, but don't push me. I'll catch the boy, and whoever helps him."

<∞>

After I scraped the mud off Scarlatti's car, she took off with Scandia and Montrose. I wanted to follow, but I had bigger worries.

I reached the Senate Office Building just as Sam drove away in an armored vehicle. Other than the Institute capture, I hadn't seen her off base since she offered me the mech "lifeline" as an alternative to resocialization in Nashville or prison. It seemed strange for her to mingle with civilians.

Inside the State Senate Building, a line funneled visitors through a security checkpoint. Two older state security agents eyed those who entered. A large sign said to drop all electronic items into a bin on a conveyor that contained a sniffer. I considered leaving, but the agents would search me for acting suspicious.

I dropped my wrist-com and single-shot stun gun into the bin. Then I rejoined the line.

<When you enter the scanner,> Morgan said, <close your eyes. Seth says lack of data prevents your contacts from transmitting.>

I closed my eyes and walked through the scanner. On the other side, the agent looked me over and secured my stun gun in a locked cabinet. I smiled, picked up my wrist-com, and moved on. I made my way through wide, tiled corridors to Mom's office. I knocked, opened the door, and waited for her to look up. She sat behind her worn oak desk with eyes closed.

"Are you just going to stand there?" she asked.

I closed the door, passed my usual seat, and stood by the window. More guards milled about below, in response to all the escapes and assassination attempts. I was proud of Mom for going back to work after the attack on her life. Yet, I worried.

"What's on your mind?" Mom asked.

I pointed my contacts out the window, while keeping Mom in my peripheral vision. "I heard a report that they were interrogating you over the escapes."

"A particular escape," Mom said. "What's your question?"

"They can't possibly think you'd help a boy escape." I hoped this was a good performance for Sam, and whatever office cams were recording us.

"You didn't come all this way to tell me that, did you?"

I bent over and hugged her, lingering, as I must have when they ripped me away from my birth mother. "I've been so worried since that horrid intern tried to—tried to …"

"Kill me. It's okay. Say it."

"I can't, Mom." I saw the corner of a written note on her desk and looked away. It looked like one I had seen before, a call to help boys. *I can't lose you, too.*

It was crazy to visit Mom when we couldn't talk, but maybe that was why I did. She once told me she suspected someone had bugged her office. At home, we had our cone of silence, where Mom relaxed and told me more than a mother should. I couldn't afford that now.

"Can I buy you lunch, Mom? One of those tasty turkey burgers from the Bistro?"

Mom checked her wrist-com and nodded. "It'll have to be quick. I have a legislative session at one."

After she locked her office door, I held her hands and studied her eyes. They looked hollow, filled with sorrow. Yet now and then, a spark flashed.

She smiled. "What is it, Belle?"

"Are you sure you're okay after Saturday?"

"I'm fine." She nudged me down the wide corridor. "How are you adjusting to civilian life?"

I laughed. "I miss you, Mom."

"Janine misses you, too. She's the one you need to worry about."

"Why?"

"She's becoming withdrawn and secretive. Like a flower that lost its bloom."

"Because of me?"

"I … don't know. She had her heart set on following you into the Mech Corps. Now she seems confused."

Me too.

When we reached the lobby, the security guard smiled and returned my stun gun. Mom and I stepped outside into sweltering heat. We would need a blast of arctic air to cool that down.

The cafeteria in the Senate Office Building would have been nice, but it offered no privacy. Tenn-tucky Bistro was down the street, beyond the security barrier. We were early. Foot traffic was light, a few office workers in pastel dresses out to grab an early lunch.

"We'll find something else for Janine." I waved to a security guard I saw on the way in.

"She acts brave to be like you," Mom said. "But she's fragile. She looks up to you."

"I'm not sure how, after Saturday's humiliation."

We crossed the street toward the Bistro. A faint electric hum caught my ear. I turned to see a cop-intern on a cycle, wearing the regulation beige blouse of cop-wannabes like me. The helmet masked the face.

Janine, are you following me again?

I hurried Mom across the street as a silver limousine pulled away from the Senate Building. The cycle stopped. A second cycle with a cop-intern rode in behind the first. The first intern raised her arm and pointed a pistol. I shoved Mom behind the limousine and spun toward the cyclist with evasive moves I'd learned in mech training. The cyclist fired twice, and turned to flee. I grabbed her arm. I still couldn't make out the face behind the helmet.

We crashed in front of the limo and spun into a tangle of arms, legs, and cycles. The gun fired once, twice, a third time. I didn't feel any pain or heat, but I'd never been shot before and didn't know what to expect.

I grabbed the gun-holding wrist and banged it against the curb until the gun fell away. Then I released the helmet's safety clips. The helmet fell away. Sweat-soaked black hair covered the face of an intern I'd seen at the East Knoxville station. The other cyclist removed her helmet: Janine.

"Check Mom," I yelled as I pushed the gun into the shooter's neck.

Janine slipped the pistol she shouldn't have had behind her back and moved away.

The shooter wrestled to get free. "Long live Harmony!"

"This is Harmony?" I said. "Who sent you? Who do you work for?"

The shooter spit in my face. "Go to hell."

She reminded me of animal rage in the arena, the desire to obliterate an opponent. I pinned one of her arms under my knee and twisted her other wrist so she couldn't fight back. Then I pressed the barrel of the gun to her eye. "Tell me who—"

"Don't kill her," Sam said. "We need her alive."

"Did Captain Chou send you?" I asked.

"Die, you traitorous bitch," the shooter said.

"Do you work for Voss? Scarlatti? The governor?"

"Careful," Sam said. "That's not how to interrogate."

Several city cops sprinted toward us, along with two Senate Building guards. I had seconds before I might not get another chance. I squeezed the attacker's neck. "Who do you work for?"

"For Harmony!"

I fired her gun into her right shoulder. "Talk."

"Damn, bitch, that hurts." She looked like a frightened child.

"Who sent you?" I pressed the gun to her left shoulder.

"No, please. I had no choice. I—"

Her head exploded. Blood and brains splattered the curb, and my right arm. Her eyes rolled back; she stopped panting. I could barely breathe, let alone move. I'd never watched someone die before, not this close. Dark thunderclouds fogged my mind. I forced myself to look at my gun, her bloody shoulder, and what was left of her face. I couldn't have done that.

I fell away from the body and looked for shooters. My eyes

blurred. Everyone moved away, including the cops and guards who had sprinted my way. Two cops trained their guns on me.

"Sam, what's going on?" I whispered.

"You shouldn't have shot the intern."

Janine took the gun from me and returned to Mom. Blood covered my right hand and arm up to my elbow. Unable to see Mom, I looked up at Janine.

"Mom's fine," she said. "You saved her." She said that with the same pride I felt when she saved Mom on Saturday. Two attempts in less than a week. My mind twisted back on itself like an overloaded circuit. *Mom's safe. Assassin's dead. Who is doing this?*

Brooks helped me to my feet. "We have to take you to the station. Routine procedure. I'm sorry this happened again." She opened the back of her car so I could climb in. Then she shut me in.

I was glad it was Brooks, not Scarlatti. She must have followed Janine, who was checking up on me.

"I can't get answers from behind bars," I said for Sam's benefit.

Brooks and Janine mounted my cycle on the back of Brooks' new car, while I sat in the back. At least Brooks hadn't slapped cuffs on me or a maroon criminal collar. She'd watched me save Mom. But what if she was the only one who knew what happened?

"Sam," I whispered.

"Not another word," Sam said into my implant. "I'm very sorry about your Mom. She appears shaken but unharmed, thanks to you. You did great, but you shouldn't have shot the intern—"

"I only shot her once. In the shoulder. Someone else killed her. I didn't see. It had to be a sniper."

"I'll check the cams."

"She wasn't working alone."

"Say nothing until we get you an attorney."

"Is that necessary?"

While I waited, I checked my wrist-com. Already there were newsfeeds of me shooting the intern in the shoulder. Of course, no one thought to look up and capture the sniper.

Brooks drove me to the station. "The captain and someone from internal affairs will question you," she said, her voice softer than usual. "We need to document what happened. I'm sorry to put you through this, but it's standard procedure. Good news, I believe your mom is okay. I wish I'd gotten there sooner."

"Why were you downtown?" I asked.

"I said to say nothing," Sam said. "You want to do this on your own, but you need to trust me."

I smiled through the wire mesh that separated me from Brooks.

"Now that your sister has her own cycle," Brooks said, "she's been taking advantage of her freedom. You might talk to her about what it means to be a good partner."

"I'll do that." *If I get the chance.*

"Janine hasn't gotten herself into trouble, has she?" I asked.

"No, but she's adopting some of your bad habits. It's lucky for your mom that you were downtown."

"Becky, is all this necessary? Couldn't you just take me home? After all, I acted as a police officer."

"Until you shot the woman," Brooks said.

"One more time," Sam's sharp voice rang in my ear. "Not another word!"

For someone used to holding so many secrets, you might think that would come easy, but I wanted to get my story out before Scarlatti twisted it into something ugly.

When we reached the station, Voss and a stern-faced woman I took to be internal affairs greeted us. Janine pulled her cycle alongside Brooks' car. Scarlatti held my sister back.

"You can't help," Brooks said to Janine.

"But I saw the whole thing."

Scarlatti grinned and grabbed my arm. "I'd have bet you'd last longer than two days."

"Thanks for your concern over an assassination attempt," I said.

"Stop *talking*," Sam said.

Scarlatti's grin faded. She led me into an interrogation room across from the elevators that led down to lockup. The small room was empty except for a plain metal table and two wood chairs. I stared at the mirror on one wall, and wondered who was on the other side. It didn't matter. With all the cams, a much larger crowd could study me. After all, a senator's daughter killed a cop-intern who tried to kill that state senator. Those who manipulate facts would have a field day.

TWENTY-TWO

Scarlatti introduced the serious woman as Katarina Pavlov from internal affairs, and stood by the door, a scowl on her narrow face. The official, a thirtyish well-tanned blonde with coal-black eyebrows, sat across from me.

"Can you walk me through what happened?" Pavlov asked.

"I wish to see an attorney." I fought to keep my eyes from tearing up over someone attacking Mom.

"It's not that type of investigation."

Really? Then why is Scarlatti enjoying herself?

"A police intern was shot and killed," Pavlov said. "I know this is tough because of the attack on your mom, but we need to document the facts while they're still fresh."

Why are you bothering me? There must be a dozen cams that show what happened. Haven't you heard? Eyewitness testimony is unreliable. An example presented during mech training was Abraham Lincoln's assassination. Officials questioned everyone who witnessed the event. They didn't get consistent answers as to what Booth wore, what he said when he jumped onto the stage, or even what he'd done. That was within hours of a devastating event.

"Annabelle, you aren't helping your case," Pavlov said.

"So I *am* a case."

"Shut up," Sam yelled into the base of my skull. The words reverberated around my brain, sparking a headache.

"If you don't cooperate, you look guilty," Pavlov said.

Voss and Scarlatti would see me as guilty no matter what. "Why aren't you out looking for who ordered two hits on the senator?" I asked.

"You're digging your own grave," Sam said.

"Let *us* worry about that," Pavlov said. "You need to cooperate right now. Tell us what you saw."

There was a knock at the door. Scarlatti opened it for a petite woman with a South Asian complexion. The woman shook hands with Scarlatti and Pavlov. Then she took mine in her soft, delicate hand.

"I'm Fatima Patel, here to render assistance since this is your first time wading through internal affairs."

My last, I prayed.

"Give her the benefit of the doubt," Sam said. "She's very good at what she does."

Pavlov closed the door and faced Patel. "It's not necessary to have an attorney for these proceedings."

Patel bowed her head and stepped behind me. "With all due respect, I beg to disagree. I reviewed the cam feeds on the way over. They were quite revealing. Someone with high police clearance erased all the footage of the incident, including citizen feeds through the towers. How convenient."

"What?" The internal affairs woman turned pale. "That's impossible."

"I suggest you check it out before you further trouble my client. I received footage of the incident from another source. It shows the cop-intern riding in on a police cycle and approaching my client and Senator Scott. The attacker raised her gun and fired two shots before my client could subdue her."

Pavlov turned to me. "Is that what happened?"

"Say nothing," Sam repeated.

I remained as still as I could, and held my breath, which didn't help because I was already having trouble breathing.

Patel pulled out an old stylus and twirled it as she spoke. "The assassin wrestled with my client and tried to shoot my client when another cycle officer rammed the assassin. My client prevented the attacker from shooting her targets, and tried to gain control of the gun. The attacker wrestled with my client, while yelling that she wanted my client to die. In the scuffle, the gun went off and hit the assassin in the shoulder.

"Ballistics will show only one bullet from this gun struck the assassin. Ballistics will also show that the shot to the assassin's head came from a 60-caliber sniper rifle intended to make a mess and reduce the risk that the assassin could tell my client who hired her. If we are through here, my client has been through quite a shock."

Pavlov stared at me in disbelief. "Do you have anything to add?"

I shook my head. The footage Patel had recited must have come from my contacts, with a little embellishment on how the attacker received the shoulder wound.

"You're free to go," Pavlov said. "I'd tell you not to leave town, but your travel restrictions have been recorded in your police chip. We might have more questions. Ms. Patel, can I have a word?"

<∞>

<I'm sorry about your Mom,> Morgan said as I walked out of the interrogation room. <I'm glad she's okay.>

I leaned against the wall, closed my left eye and typed into my wrist-com, "Thanks, but I need privacy."

<I truly am sorry, but we're out of time. Find me a safe house and transportation. Then I'll shut this down.>

I gently nodded my head and erased the wrist-com before opening my left eye.

"There you are," Janine said. "I've been waiting. Let's go." She took my wrist and tugged me along.

I followed her through the bullpen as if I were her puppet now. Brooks sat at her desk, looking glum. I pulled away and stopped there. "Thanks," I whispered.

"For what," Brooks said. "Giving up my partner for the afternoon?"

"That's not necessary." I turned to Janine. "I don't want you in trouble."

"Oh, go ahead, you two," Brooks said. "I'll manage. Go comfort your mom. She's been through a lot."

Janine pulled me toward the exit. I tried to explain that I needed to be alone, but I couldn't connect my thoughts and my tongue.

"Mom's okay," Janine said when she got me outside. "Thanks for asking. I'm fine, too. I'm glad they didn't lock you up."

"Don't be so sure they won't." I inhaled the muggy air and choked.

Janine steadied me. "You okay?"

I nodded but then shook my head.

"Anyhow, you're free right now. I'll race you down to the river."

I halted at the curb. "Janine! What's gotten into you? You always obey the rules."

"I miss you."

I was having trouble getting my eyes to focus and decided I'd best focus on her. "Are you still juggling school and cop-internship?"

She shrugged.

"You can't quit because I screwed up. You'd best make things right with Brooks."

"Things haven't been right between you and me since Saturday. What do you want to do this afternoon?"

Find out who wants Mom dead. "Don't get into trouble."

"Thanks for your concern, sis." Janine walked toward her cycle and stopped. "Do you have any idea how hard it is to be your sister?"

"I'm sorry I'm such a disappointment."

"Don't apologize, Belle. You've made me stronger." She pulled me toward the cycles. "I want to help. Let me in, Belle." She stopped and faced me. "You don't have to go through this on your own. Tell me what you're feeling. Tell me what's been going on. You know I won't quit until you let me help. Does your avoiding me have to do with that boy?"

"No!" I sighed. She was getting me even more mixed up, as if she were crawling into my skull with everyone else. "I want to get whoever's trying to hurt Mom."

"Then let me help."

"It's too dangerous. I don't want you hurt."

"Is that what you've been hiding from me?" Janine asked.

I nodded. My eyes watered. I wiped them, but couldn't prevent the new tears. I needed her to stop, but I couldn't push her away again.

She wrapped her arms around me. "I'm sorry. I've been so insensitive. Here you've been through one shock after another, and all I can think of is how you're pulling away from me." She let go and looked deep into my eyes, staring for the longest time. "You know you can count on me."

"Thanks for helping today but … I couldn't live with myself if anything happened to you."

Janine climbed onto her cycle and turned toward me. "Today's assassin worked for the East Knoxville police station until a week ago. They suspended her for erratic behavior and disobeying orders. She got into a fight."

"Where did you get this?" I asked. That meant both attackers came from Captain Chou's police station.

"I did some digging."

I got onto my cycle, not sure where to go first. I felt drained, numb. "I don't suppose you found evidence of who the intern worked for."

"Evidence points to her working alone," Janine said.

I tried to steady my breathing and concentrate on anything but the grief I felt over Mom. "The intern's last words were that someone forced her—"

Janine held my hand on my handlebars. "It's okay, Belle. We don't have to do this now."

I took a deep breath, closed my eyes, and felt stillness all around. It didn't last. "I'm okay," I lied.

Janine let go. "So, the attacker had a partner."

I nodded and tried to get my mind to think clearly.

<Your assassin received a tidy sum of money a week ago,> Morgan said.

I caught myself before I said anything, and moved my head up slightly, then down, hoping he'd catch my signal and continue.

"Belle, you look like you saw a ghost," Janine said.

"I'm worried about all these assassins. They could be watching us."

"Then let's get moving."

<Whoever paid the assassin, took the money back. They cleaned out the assassin's accounts, took everything. There might have been earlier payments …. Ah, there it is.>

"Don't let the attacks sidetrack you," Sam said. "Focus on learning more about Voss and Scarlatti. Let me dig into the assassins."

"If she worked with a partner, there should be calls, texts, meetings," I said. "How do we find out?" I hoped either Sam or Morgan would check.

Sam sighed into my ear. "Send your sister to look into the assassin's partner, while you get your butt to the mech-base. I can't have you thrashing about."

153

I clenched my fists over the handlebars and wished I had gas instead of electric so I could really rev the engine. I was a puppet on a string. Several sets. Sam pulled me one way. Morgan wanted help. Voss and Scarlatti hungered for me to screw up again. I would take that bet. Now, Janine wouldn't let me alone.

"I could use your help," I said to Janine. "We could cover more ground if we split up."

TWENTY-THREE

I felt as if I were ditching Janine. The look on her face when I sent her back into the station was of disappointment, suspicion, and more secrets. She'd tried to make things right between us and I pushed her away.

I took the roundabout way on side roads to the base to make sure no one tailed me. When I passed a cop along the empty road to the base, I realized how foolish this was. Sam tracked my implant. City cams tracked me from cam to cam. In a world without privacy, how could a group of assassins work together unless they had the governor's blessing?

Sam greeted me at the back door. *Yup, you know where I am.* She escorted me to her private gym, where I paced, waiting for the lecture.

She reached into her locker. "Suit up." She handed me a haptic suit.

"I can't do this now."

"Now is exactly when you most need this. Take the suit."

I grabbed my training outfit. "You're not going to lecture me on how I handled the attacker."

"I thought I did." Sam stripped out of her dress blues and pulled on her body-hugging haptic suit, with all its built-in electronic sensors. "Do you need more?"

I tugged on my suit. "I have to know who's trying to hurt Mom."

"Leave me to get to the bottom of that."

"I wanted answers before the cops took over."

"Did you get any?" She moved onto the mat.

I joined her. "Only that she wasn't alone. She was afraid of whoever got her into this."

"For good reason." Sam attacked with boxing moves, and switched at the last minute to kung fu. She smacked me hard, and sent me sprawling onto the mat. It cushioned my fall, not by much.

I got to my feet, prepared for another attack, yet how do you prepare when your opponent is so versatile? "Why for good reason?"

"High-powered rifles are hard to come by," Sam said. "We've accounted for all of ours. The police don't have them. Regular army has a handful of snipers. Air command has them mounted on choppers. This was a professional hit, intended as a warning to others not to talk."

"What makes you say that?"

"We found the sniper. Dead. Single shot to the back of her head at close range."

"So any investigation will lead to a dead end."

Sam launched a second attack. This time she feigned kickboxing, shifted to karate and landed a blow to my stomach that sent me flying onto the mat. "You need to concentrate."

I stood, doubled over in pain, then moved back to keep her in view. My stomach was already in knots over what had happened. The hit had me ready to throw up what little I'd eaten today. "It's hard to, with everyone pounding on you."

"That's when you're most vulnerable. As mechs, we fight surrounded and under fire. Come on. You need to step up your game."

To stall, I asked her about a news report I'd heard on the way over, a cautionary tale not to wander out of designated areas. "A newsfeed mentioned a girl found out here the other night, with a cycle."

Sam launched a karate attack, feigned a switch to boxing, and swept at my feet. "Is there a question?"

I dodged, jumped, and stayed on my feet. I feigned a counterattack, and pulled away at the last moment before she could clobber me. "Who was she?"

"Not your concern."

"I'm making it my concern." I faked an attack to prod for

weaknesses, didn't see any. "That could have been me."

Sam grabbed and spun me onto my back on the mat. "Very well. She was a victim of an Outland raid. We got the perps after they killed her. I staged her so cops would stop hunting for you. It's not helpful that I have to keep cleaning up your messes."

As I absorbed the lesson, I struggled to breathe. "I can't do this spying bit, Sam."

She held out her hand and helped me to my feet. "You want to complete your training first. There isn't time. You need to act now, or there won't be a Mech Corps for you to train with."

Sam assumed a boxer's stance. "You still believe you can handle things on your own. Lone heroes look glamorous from a distance. In reality, they rarely work alone. The sooner you learn to work with others, the better your chances."

I struggled to fight and think at the same time. I backed up. "You told me I had to keep this a secret."

She launched a kick. When I grabbed her foot, she swept me off balance and landed on top of me. "You do. You also need to work through other people. Give them what they need in order to help you." She stood and stepped back.

"Like you do with me." I rolled over and pretended to get to my feet. Instead, I swept her legs, sending her to the mat. "Sorry." I scrambled to my feet, prepared for her counterattack.

Sam stood and grinned. "Good one. Don't apologize, and don't make me regret my faith in you."

"Why did you send Dara and the other trainees to the Institute, instead of trained warriors? They were supposed to be locked down in training." I braced myself for another punishing attack.

Sam moved closer, her body limber. She stared into my eyes. "Why do you think?"

I hated how she distracted me with mind games before she attacked. I pulled a punch and fell back. "If things didn't work out, as it didn't, you wouldn't lose as much face?"

"You're learning the politics." She zeroed in on me like a laser, or a cat stalking its prey.

I kicked and moved back, beyond her reach. "I don't think Captain Voss is smart enough to pull off such a complicated exercise."

"Never underestimate your opponent." Sam sprang at me, caught me before I could move aside, and dropped me to the mat.

I cushioned my head on the way down.

Rolling, I got to my feet before she dropped on top and pinned me. "I'm convinced the governor is behind this. She wants to keep people scared so they'll vote for her in the upcoming election."

"You think this is a political move."

I nodded and kept my eyes on her in case she attacked again. "The governor has—"

Sam rushed, took advantage of my distraction, and threw me onto the mat. "Are you trying to connect the dots you wish were there, or the ones right before you?" she asked.

I regained my footing. "Voss could do the money thing, but only the governor has the power to move the boys."

"It doesn't matter what you think or what you believe you know." Sam approached me. "All that matters is what you can prove. You believe the governor is connected. Show me proof. Your gut doesn't count."

Every part of my body ached. I forced my attention on Sam. *Never let your guard down.* "I can't concentrate on what Voss is up to until I know who's after Mom, until I know she's safe."

"She won't be if you keep inserting yourself."

"I'll do what I have to, to protect Mom."

"Don't be a fool," Sam said. "Anything you touch on that case will make matters worse. Trust me to look into that. You focus on Voss, those supplies, and the money trail. Now clean up and meet me in my office."

<∞>

By the time I coaxed my muscles to pull on my police skorts and blouse, Sam was gone. I followed the short khaki-colored corridors. The light was on in her office, but she wasn't there. With no personal effects, it looked austere for the commander of the elite Mech Corps. I closed the door and paced.

The windows some ten feet above were dark. The overhead lights bleached out whatever stars might have been visible. The desk was clear, except for the screen and the projection of a virtual keyboard. The panel behind the desk to her tiny control room remained closed. No light shone around the floor. Either the panel was sealed, or the lights were out.

I inched closer to her desk, to where I'd almost looked for records on my birth mother.

A single green light blinked on a gray setting. Faint lines of a floor plan for the complex hovered in the background. The light shone in the box for Sam's office. She tracked me at all times, including now. I made sure Morgan saw this. At my touch, the image panned back to reveal blinking lights clustered toward the back of the complex, the mech-gym. Each light tracked a mech-warrior or recruit and carried a code, like tracking boxes at that supply warehouse.

When the image panned again, it showed the entire Knoxville metropolitan area, with several lights scattered about, none near my police station, or home. I brushed that screen to the background and pulled up a search tool. I typed in "prison escapes over the past 20 years."

What I'd learned before my mech fiasco was that records showed my birth mother had escaped from various prisons before they shipped her out west. As I scanned down the list of breakouts, Dorothy Montgomery's name never came up. I noticed few prison breaks until two months ago. Then they occurred weekly, sometimes several in a week.

I suspected the reports of Dorothy's escape were a smokescreen so they could send her away. The files that appeared on Sam's screen showed she had access to out-of-state data. I reached for the keyboard projected onto Sam's desk.

<What are you looking for?> Morgan asked. <Maybe I can help.>

I pulled up the background of the compound that showed Sam tracking me and other mech recruits. *Even if Morgan could help, how can I ask without divulging too much?*

"Find anything useful?" Sam asked. She emerged from the small control room behind me.

I pointed to the screen. "Why do you have a trainee downtown?"

"Who said it's a trainee?"

"A spy like me?"

"What do you want with prison files?" Sam scooted me away from her desk.

"The pattern started two months ago," I said.

Sam nodded. "I know you feel you're in over your head and can't handle this. I'm confident you can, confident enough that I have a lot at stake with you. You're right to believe there's an elaborate plan. I don't know what it is, just suspicions. I need facts,

facts I can't pursue myself, or through proper channels. That's where you come in."

"I could do more if you gave me more clues."

"In good time. Ponder this: every plan has a weakness."

"You can't trust me with your suspicions?"

"They could endanger you as much as me. Consider that whoever is behind this has weaknesses. One is a need to work with agents who could expose her, agents she must eliminate. The more people who share a secret, the less private it becomes." Sam nudged me toward her door. "I have business to tend to. Remember what I said, and make sure no one sees you coming or going from the mech-base."

She ushered me out of her office to the back door of the mech complex, and left me in the passageway to the gate. In the dark, I rode my cycle toward town, convinced Sam had left me alone in her office as another test. Had I passed, or dug a deeper hole for myself?

It ticked me off that I'd been maybe a few keystrokes away from learning more about my birth mother, and hadn't been able to without Sam knowing. For that, she would have been compelled to send me away, just like Dorothy Montgomery, only not to the same prison. They wouldn't do that for me.

When I reached the end of the mech road, Sam's voice startled me. "Get off the main road. People are coming. I can't have anyone see you out here."

TWENTY-FOUR

Janine made sure to obey every speed limit, stop sign, and light on her way to the mech-base, as the obedient model citizen everyone assumed her to be. She didn't act re-*Belle*-y-ous because she saw how futile that was for her older sister.

She hated how Sam sat inside her head and knew everything she did. Not that Janine had done anything to shame her family. She needed Belle to explain this grief that threatened to consume her, grief Janine felt like Sam's voice in her head, grief that grew worse after Sam kicked Belle out. And it had gotten worse with the attacks on Mom, but it'd percolated long before their mech training. Janine hated the secrets Sam expected her to keep from Belle, and the ones she felt Belle kept from her.

Among moonlit shadows, she saw movement along the side of the road to the mech-base. She sped up.

"Don't worry," Sam reassured her. "They're warriors returning from patrol. They'll leave you alone. Proceed slowly."

Janine didn't mind doing secret, important work for Sam. She didn't like doing it alone. After she became a mech-warrior, sister warriors would look out for her. She would never be alone. That gave her comfort, like living with three moms and eight sisters did, a sense of belonging, of being part of something larger than herself. It gave meaning to life to do things for the family, for the mechs, and for the nation.

If you keep repeating that, you'll start to believe it.

She walked her cycle toward the side door to the mech

compound. Shadows had her jumpy, ready to flee. She might have left if Sam hadn't opened the door. Janine sprinted into the safety of the mech building.

"Are you okay?" Sam asked. She closed the door and followed Janine to her office.

Janine's body quivered with jitters she wished would fade so she didn't appear weak in front of Sam. "I'm not used to riding out this way at night alone. I'm fine." Her stomach wrestled with butterflies and wormy things that made her feel fragile.

Sam closed the office door and offered Janine a seat. "I was with you the whole time."

I'm sure you were. Janine smiled and tightened her stomach muscles. It seemed to help.

Sam sat behind her desk and whisked away the screen so she could peer at Janine. She smiled and assumed a relaxed pose that made Janine feel self-conscious. "I want to cover a few things with you in person," Sam said. "We'll fit in some training afterwards."

Janine nodded. "I'm ready, Commander." She decided her jitters were worry over the attack on Mom, and how Belle wasn't handling it well. That thought didn't help.

Sam leaned forward. "I want you to see if that boy tries to contact Annabelle. I know it's hard for you to keep secrets from her, but I believe that boy could hurt her and your family."

"I understand, Commander." Janine couldn't imagine Belle hooking up with a boy, but she couldn't be sure after the way Belle had been acting.

"You don't need to act so formal here," Sam said. "Save that for training and around other warriors."

"I tried to get her to talk." Janine shifted on the wooden seat. "I don't think she knows anything."

"Either way, stay alert. The reason I called you in is I want you to look into the two attempts on your mother. I know this goes against protocol, since you're so close to the case."

Janine fought shallow breaths to fill her lungs. The jitters now had her shaking all over as if she had chills. During Belle's arena contest, Sam had alerted her to the first assassin. For the second, she'd followed Belle downtown. When that cop-intern raised a gun, Sam urged Janine to act and she had, saving Belle and Mom.

"It's okay," Sam said. "You've had a tough day. This is important."

Janine straightened up. "Can Annabelle help me? I won't tell her I'm working for you. She wants to find who's behind this as much as I do. It'll give me time to see if that boy contacts her. Besides, she's much better at interrogating people."

Sam laughed. "I doubt that. Annabelle damaged herself today in how she handled the attacker. She'd be a liability in the investigation and could compromise the case."

"I'm sure she wanted to kill the attacker. I did. Belle showed restraint. Can't she help?"

Sam came over behind Janine and massaged her shoulders. "While she's under investigation for how she handled the attacker, she needs to stay as far from the case as possible. To keep her from getting involved, you need to convince her you'll investigate, so she won't feel the need."

Janine shrugged and tried to relax. Doing so put her more on alert. "What do you want me to do?"

"Find out what enemies might want to harm your mom."

Those words came as a blow to the stomach. "Who could hate Mom that much?" Then she took a deep breath. "I'm sure as a public figure there are many who might disagree with her."

"This is more personal. Let's get you some training."

<∞>

Senator Scott let one of the Senate Building guards walk her to her car. The guard checked beneath and around the vehicle before letting her climb in. While the senator pulled away, she scanned the well-lit streets for cop-interns and anyone who looked like an assassin. Though why would she think a cop-intern would be?

She didn't like how cautious the two attempts on her life had made her. She hoped whatever troublemakers were out there had grown tired of waiting. After all, both attempts had been during the day. On the other hand, the night brought out unsavory types.

"I see more scratches on the trunk lid," she said, glancing through the rearview mirror at the well-lit Senate Building. "I trust you're comfortable."

"Not really." Morgan's muffled voice came from the trunk.

"I was clear. Don't put my family in danger." She drove slowly, remaining vigilant for cop-interns.

"I'm out of options."

"You relish taking unnecessary risks," she said. "I'm being watched by people who would delight in catching us together."

"I need your help."

"You should have gone to the Outlands when you had your chance."

"And get caught?" Morgan asked.

"There are spies everywhere, and cams. You can't be sure you weren't seen. I don't appreciate you endangering my family by involving me."

"I need to rescue my brother from the Oak Ridge Institute. Can you find a safe house and transport after I get him out?"

"Are you crazy? It would be hard enough to get him out if they *weren't* looking for you."

"Will you help?"

"I don't know what I can do. Right now, I need to move you before we both get caught."

"Drop me off by the river. I'll contact you when I'm ready. We haven't much time."

<∞>

After conditioning and fight training that left Janine exhausted, Sam brought her to the office, and sat her in a corner with a virtual keyboard and projected screen. "Here's everything I have on the two assassins, the cops they worked with, their families, friends, connections. I want you to familiarize yourself with these two. Look for patterns."

"A puzzle, then."

Sam smiled. "A puzzle. I want you to check out anyone who might have been angry enough and had access to these two interns. When you have that, return here so you can dig into their backgrounds. Don't use any net access from home or the cop station. Those are all monitored, and could be traced back to you."

"This one isn't?"

"It's more secure. I can't impress upon you enough how important it is to unravel this puzzle quickly."

"I understand, Commander. I won't let you down."

While Janine rode home in the dark, her mind played tricks. She imagined that large redheaded boy popping out from the bushes along the road. It made no sense that Belle would help him: too dangerous. Janine was sure she knew Belle better than that. Yet, Belle had been acting strange.

Janine returned her attention to the road and her other puzzle: *Who would hire assassins to kill Mom?*

164

TWENTY-FIVE

I slowed my cycle and took my time. Sam wanted me to gather information for her vendetta with Voss. She didn't want me to talk to anyone, dig into electronic files, or in any other way expose myself to information that could help. I was ready to explode. I was ready to turn around and take my chances in the Outland. Except I couldn't do that to Mom or Janine.

"Are you watching me 24 hours a day?" I asked as I rode toward town. "Do you ever give me privacy?" It was a burst of frustration, and a test to find out who listened.

"Focus on your job, soldier," Sam said into my left implant. "I record you 24-7. I try to respond to your verbal communications in case it's an emergency, so stay off the channel unless you have something important."

<You're not adjusting well to constant surveillance,> Morgan said. <Welcome to my world. We need to talk.>

That answered my question. No privacy.

<Face-to-face.>

I scanned dimly lit roads side to side, as I shook my head.

<There's an abandoned warehouse north of Farragut.>

I wanted to scream for Sam to pick up Morgan. My training demanded that. My throat went dry. I was hemmed in with nowhere to run. *Leave me alone.*

<To avoid surveillance,> Morgan said, <I put in your saddlebag a hoodie with aluminum polymer shielding. It stops transmissions to and from your contacts and implant. It has a

special transceiver so we can talk. When you're ready to enter the gate to your community, put the shield on under your helmet. I'll tell you where to go.>

I set the cycle's governor at the speed limit. I didn't know what scared me more, seeing Morgan, or what Sam and Voss would do to me if they found out. It troubled me that Morgan knew me so well. I gave that away by helping him three or four times already.

When I reached the woods that separated my community from the river, I turned off my lights. It was tricky to unlock my saddlebags without looking. I rummaged around until my fingers caught unfamiliar material. It was flexible, yet stiff.

I drove into the U-Store facility and ducked into my storage unit. After pushing the old cycle aside, I traded stun guns, taking the automatic, in case. Then I removed my contacts. "Private time."

When no one replied, I removed my helmet and slipped the crinkly hood over my head. Other than stiffness, it gave no hint of being metallic. The aluminum must have been embedded in the material itself. The night was too warm and muggy for the hood, but if meeting Morgan got him to stop bugging me, what the heck.

"There's a second hood that fits over your cycle helmet," Morgan said in a tinny voice above my ear.

The second hood was all the way at the bottom of my saddlebag. After I put on my helmet, I slipped the black covering over the helmet and rode off. I wondered how long before Sam yelled in my ear to fix whatever went wrong—a long time if this hood actually worked. This was crazy stupid. If Morgan kidnapped me, no one would know where to look.

Using side streets with less-frequent cams, I followed the directions Morgan provided. I watched for escaped boys, and for mechs hunting boys. Was I leading them to Morgan, or was this a trap to send me to prison? I imagined my birth mother when she helped my dad over the border. Was I doing this because of them?

The dark didn't frighten me, which I must have acquired from comforting Janine at night. Now, every shadow jumped; every odd whine of my cycle or snapped twig made me cringe. Mostly it was the hum of the electric grid, an excited, high-pitched background noise that was most noticeable whenever I returned from being outside Knoxville, such as out at the base.

When I reached the warehouse, I circled the chain-link fence and studied it in the glow of my cycle's headlight. No barbed wire, low security. Probably nothing left worth taking.

"Do I have to climb the fence?" I whispered.

"There's a gate around back that's unlocked," Morgan's voice said from the speaker above my head. It gave me some comfort that Sam couldn't hear.

I found it. There was still time to back out, to ride home, or call Sam. This was insane. I could face unspeakable punishments, not to mention what they might do to Janine and Mom. I took a deep breath, turned out my lights, and opened the gate.

Might as well get this over.

By moonlight, I walked my cycle behind a utility shed. I used my wrist-com's infrared to find Morgan. It didn't show anything larger than a rat. *Yuck.*

"From the shed, turn left and take ten paces to a door," Morgan said.

I scanned the area with night-vision: lots of unclaimed debris, abandoned when the business closed. I found the door and entered complete blackness. My wrist-com gave a ghostly green glow of wide-open space and nothing more. I could have used some of Janine's caution, some of her DNA. My instincts warned me of a trap: Voss lying in wait. After all, how did I know the mechanical voice was Morgan? Maybe all boys sounded alike over the waves with their bass tones.

"Walk straight back from the door twenty paces. You'll find another door," Morgan said. His voice sounded more comforting, nearer.

While I walked, I recalled cautionary tales my school had taught me. My outstretched hand touched something flat and dull. Night-vision didn't help. I found a doorknob. This was it.

<∞>

I pushed the door open to more blackness. After I entered, the door closed behind me. Wrist-com night-vision showed a single large human form, just before lights blinded me.

"Welcome to my temporary home." No longer in my head or the tinny speaker, Morgan's voice sounded clear and warm.

I blinked until my eyes adjusted. The tuft of red hair hung over his ears. He'd shaved his facial hair. He looked larger, and yet not as huge as in the arena. He stepped back to give me space. My body tensed into fighter mode. My eyes scanned dusty desks and piles of broken clutter.

"You're in what's called a Faraday cage," he said. "You can remove your helmet now. Your implant and contacts can't transmit here."

I took off my head coverings layer by layer: the black outer cloth, my cycle helmet, and the stiff inner hood. I placed them on a cluttered desk to my right and looked up. The room was a small bullpen, with metal desks along two walls. It smelled of dust and decay, probably of rats. I pointed to my mouth.

"It's okay to talk," Morgan said. "I've tested the shields."

"Good. I've wanted to give you a piece of my mind for some time. How dare you worm your way into my head?" I shoved him against a desk, sending a box of supplies crashing onto the stained tile floor.

He held up his hands, but didn't fight back.

"Leave me alone." I hit his shoulder. "Stop bothering me. Stop putting my family at risk. Stop driving me crazy. It's bad enough I've got Sam in my head. What have you seen? Did you see me naked?"

He pulled away. "I swear. It's not that way. I really like you."

"I bet you do." I shoved him. "Stay away from me. I can't help you. Sam and Voss see everything. Sam wants you. She'll stop at nothing to catch you. Voss wants me dead. You're giving her ammunition to destroy my life. I can't even talk to my own sister!"

Morgan grabbed my arms and moved them to my side. "I don't want to hurt you. You should be more concerned that Sam watches you constantly. You might ask yourself: if I can hack into your contacts, who else can?"

I pulled free and shoved him. "Oh, so it's okay for you to be a jerk because others are?"

"Please, Annabelle. All I want is to free Seth. Then I'll leave you alone. I promise."

Exhausted, I fell back against one of the wobbly desks. "I told you. Sam sees everything. This will destroy my family. I won't do it."

"What if I found a way?"

I wiped sweat from my forehead and neck. I took a deep breath of dusty air, coughed, and sneezed. Inside was warmer than outside, despite a fan blowing in the corner. "It doesn't matter. There's no way to break your brother out of the Oak Ridge facility."

"With your help, there is."

I glared at him. He was bigger than me, well muscled, strong, which I had witnessed in the arena when he almost choked me to death. Yet, even with my life hanging, I couldn't bring myself to hate him, to want him dead. I looked around. The room brimmed with junk, heaps of bins and old electronics. He had arranged a cot for himself in the corner. "How did you find this place with everyone looking for you?"

Morgan laughed. The muscles in his face softened. "I created this cage before they sent me to that prison across from your school. Luckily, they caught me while I was hunting for supplies. It doesn't look like they found this place."

I cleared my throat. I'd helped Morgan before. I told myself it was because Mom raised me on tales of her son, George. Helping Morgan was like helping George and Mom. I couldn't deny the attraction, but this boy was poison to my family and me. I closed my eyes and took a deep cleansing breath, then sneezed.

"They're going to move Seth in the next couple of days," Morgan said. "Then it'll be harder if not impossible to reach him." His shoulders sagged.

Even I felt the weight. "Why did you spare me in the arena, when you could have won?"

Morgan shook his head. "I couldn't hurt you after you helped me escape."

"At risk to your life?"

"The mechs wouldn't let me go." He turned away. "I felt suicidal. Sorry for myself."

"Because of Seth?"

He slumped onto his cot. "There was no point winning if I couldn't help him. It was my own version of hell."

"Then why yield to me?"

He stood, took a step toward me, and stopped. He hung his head like a guilty child. "I didn't want my death on your conscience. You hesitated. It bothered you more than the other girls."

"So you wouldn't have hesitated to kill Dara?"

He looked up at me with sad-doggy eyes. "Someone needs to put that ... uh ... that one down."

I nodded. I'd been on the receiving end of Dara's wrath.

"I hoped you might help me again," Morgan said. "And you did."

"How presumptuous." I used a dusty rag to wipe off a corner of a desk, and sat. "The others got caught. Two good women died."

"I'm sorry for them," Morgan said. "Right now, all I want is to free Seth. I want him to breathe fresh air, and know something other than the four walls of his prison. All he did to deserve this was be born with a Y chromosome. How sick is that?"

"It's all wrong, but I can't help." Despite the heat, I shivered. I stared at the door, my escape.

Morgan held out a picture of a scrawny boy with light hair and a thin face. "He's only 14. He watched cops take our mom away for hiding us. You have a sister. You know what it means to look out for family. I'm sure you'd do anything for Janine."

I would, yet she was in danger every moment I stayed with Morgan. "I could turn you in and be a hero."

"That wouldn't make you a real hero." He reached out, touched my hand, and withdrew. "That's not what you want, or why you came here."

I pulled away. "What if I came to entrap you? Cops are outside, waiting for my signal."

"I don't think so." He sat on a desk across from me. "Besides, this room is shielded. You couldn't signal if you wanted to, unless you step outside that door." He pointed and made no gesture to stop me.

TWENTY-SIX

I mopped my forehead with a damp handkerchief and studied the redhead across from me. His eyebrows were thick, but light, his jaw square and strong. His eyes held that sad-puppy look that tugged at me. A hint of a smile crossed his lips.

"Are you going to threaten me to get me to help you?" I asked.

"I need your help, Annabelle. I can't rely on that if I coerce you." Morgan got up, held out his hand, and approached. "My mom said to treat a girl like a lady, and she'll treat you well in return."

"She did, did she?"

"I've never had a girlfriend." His face turned bright red, punctuating his freckles. He looked away. "My mom kept us hidden. Then I was in that prison across from your school." He returned his gaze to me, more composed. "If I did have a girlfriend, I'd want one just like you."

"Like me," I said.

"I do, a lot. You have a passionate belief in ideas that clash with our society. You wrestle with doing the right thing. You have an inner strength others don't see. You're beautiful."

I shifted farther back on the desk. "Now I know you're laying it on thick."

He hung his head. "I have no experience with girls. You're the prettiest girl I've seen, and smart enough to figure out how to help us escape the mech-base."

"Stop reminding me of my failures."

"I'm free because of you," Morgan touched my hand. "Thanks for that. Seth has a chance now."

That tiny contact sparked a mild electric shock. The hairs on my arm lifted. I didn't let go. When I didn't resist, he pulled me up off the desk.

I expected him to kiss me. When he didn't, I pushed him away. "This is crazy. You know very well there's no way to get your brother out of the Institute. Several boys have tried. They were caught before they left the grounds."

Morgan held his soft green eyes on me. "Their escapes had no chance of success."

"You have a better idea? Remember what happened to mine."

"Yours failed when someone alerted the mechs to place patrols by the border. Your escape worked fine until then."

"The only reason you didn't get caught is they were too busy catching the others," I said.

"Precisely."

"Meaning what?"

Morgan smiled. "Two escapes: a decoy and a real one."

"How?"

"You heard about a tunnel dug by Institute inmates a while back."

I nodded.

"The administrators closed off the entry from the Institute side. They didn't fill in the tunnel. It's still there. We can open it and let boys escape."

"The decoy," I said.

"Institute staff, cops, and mechs expect that," he said. "They'll be waiting. Seth will take a utility tunnel. Institute staff use that to supply the Institute without letting the trucks enter the gates. It opens up across the street, in an abandoned warehouse."

I stood and absorbed his words. Could we really pull this off? More important, should I risk everything for this boy? "The moment they escape, the staff will shut down that tunnel. Cops and mechs will swarm every building and hideaway around the Institute."

Morgan held my hand. "They'll try, but we'll surprise them."

"How? Never mind. What about all the boys who get caught? They'll be punished."

"I can't help everyone. The Institute will look for the escape leaders. They'll be with us. The Institute will have to keep most of the boys. Otherwise they'll have to shut down."

"Too many cops and mechs." I pulled away. "Too much surveillance."

"They'll be blinded by an electric disturbance."

"You're counting on a lightning strike. You're nuts."

Morgan nodded. "Man-made."

"That would hurt a lot of people."

"It shouldn't, but it will disrupt all of their surveillance long enough for us to escape."

"How would you do that?" I asked.

He drew a rough map in the dust on one of the desks. "The Institute runs its own electrical system, independent of the city grid. They want a power structure that'll never go down. They have special transformers to make sure they have a lot of power for their data and security systems."

I stood next to him like a co-conspirator. "How?"

"We'll overload the Institute's system in such a way as to create an electronic pulse."

"EMPs. I've heard of those."

"It'll fry all non-shielded electronics for thousands of feet around the Institute. We'll sneak the boys through their blind spots."

"You really do have everything figured out," I said. "Why do you need me?"

He faced me and grinned. "I need you to take a surveillance ride around the Institute, so I can check one last time before I give Seth a go signal."

"Do you have his brain tapped, like mine?"

"The opposite," Morgan said. "He tapped into me so I could talk to him and into you so I could reach you. He's lonely. Most of the time they keep him isolated from the other boys. He gets a few hours a day on their network to work on systems problems. During that time, he talks to me."

"All you need from me is to ride around the Institute?"

"I'll direct you as to what to look at, yes."

"If I do that, you'll leave me alone?"

He sighed and hung his head. "I need you on the day of the escape. I'd like you to position yourself behind the warehouse across from the Institute, the one they use as a supply station."

"To do what?"

"Make sure the coast is clear. Then direct the boys across the alley to what I hope will be a safe place."

"You know they'll search every building. This is hopeless."

A smile grew across his lips. "They'll check every building, but not every garbage truck."

"You can't be serious. This can't work."

"It can, if you help." He took my hand.

I had to talk him out of this. "Who will drive the garbage truck?"

"Me. I can't let anyone else risk it."

"You're joking." I withdrew my hand. "The moment you leave this place, they'll pick you up."

"Have a little faith in yourself and in others, Annabelle."

That, from a boy they hunted like a wild bear. He still believed. My faith was in Mom and Janine. I took an unsteady deep breath and stepped back.

"Don't laugh. I've got it covered." Morgan opened a cabinet and pulled out a long, pastel green dress. He held it up to his neck.

"You look ridiculous." I shook my head. "You'll never pass."

He put on a muddy brown wig and bookish glasses, and then held up the dress. I couldn't bear to look at him.

"That's a natural reaction," he said. "People look away so they don't have to see unattractive souls."

"Unattractive doesn't begin to describe it."

"Maybe that's part of Dara's problem. She's tall and big. People stare, then look away. That has to leave scars."

I wasn't in the mood to feel sorry for Dara. "Put it up again. Let me look at you." This definitely wasn't how I envisioned Morgan. I didn't recognize him. "You're flat, and no hips."

"You want to see the full effect?"

I shuddered at that visual. "I'll take your word for it. You're serious about this?"

"I am. Can I count on you?"

"Put that away before I get nightmares." I closed my eyes and saw the picture of George at age three, the last one Mom had of him. He would be grown up now, handsome in my dreams, independent, and a great one to help me sort out my dilemma. He wasn't here.

After he put the dress away, Morgan returned to me, looking

shaky and uncertain. "Something else you should know. That facility where they took the two boys …"

I nodded.

"They receive shipments of bioagents."

"For what?" I asked.

"Biological substrates, gene-splicers, and bits of some kind of biologically experimental goo."

I winced. "They're experimenting on the boys?"

"Seth couldn't hack their secure data. Boys go in and don't come out, that's all we know. And they want to take Seth."

I cringed at what might be going on at that facility. Yet I had my own problems. "You said Seth can hack into my contacts and stuff." I took a deep breath. "Can he help me find someone?"

Morgan nodded. "That depends on how well hidden." He put the wig away.

"Prison out west."

"Who?"

I closed my eyes and said the name with reverence, a secret held so close that Mom was the only other soul who knew. "Dorothy Montgomery."

"Who is she to you?"

I glared at him. "That's not your concern. You want my help, then help me."

"Your mother? That's it. You're adopted. That explains why you don't look like Janine or the woman you call Mom."

"How dare you?" I launched myself at him, throwing him first against a desk and then onto the tile floor. I pinned his arms over his head beneath a desk. He offered no resistance.

"Yes, I'm adopted," I said. "Happy?"

"You don't have to go crazy over it. You aren't alone."

When I released his hands, he caressed my cheek. I scrambled to my feet and leaned against a desk, feeling flushed and embarrassed. It felt good to get physical, yet also confusing. If mechs hadn't taken my birth mother and forced George to flee to the Outlands, I would have grown up with George as what, my best friend? My boyfriend? He'd been part of my life every night, yet I'd never met him. With Morgan, I felt some of the same attraction. I didn't trust this. I was betraying George.

"I've got to go." I reached for the door.

"Don't."

"Why not?"

"For one," Morgan said, "the moment you leave, your commander will know where you are."

"Oh." I leaned the back of my head against the wall. "Where will you go? The Outlands?"

He approached. "It's the only place I can take Seth. I'd ask you to come with me, but it's too dangerous for you over there, and they'd punish your family."

I looked up at Morgan. He could be my escape from a world that fit me like an undersized leather glove, a wet one at that. "There's someone you should look for when you get there. George Shaw. He's about our age, and lives east of here."

"Boyfriend?"

I laughed. "I've never met him. I doubt he knows I exist."

Morgan nodded. "Then we'll head north to what used to be West Virginia. It's beautiful country, easy to get lost in." He took my hand. "Will you help us?"

I didn't pull away. "Get me information on Dorothy Montgomery. Help me find out who attacked my mom, and I'll help."

Morgan closed his eyes. After a moment, he nodded. "Seth says he'll do what he can. He thanks you."

"You're talking to him right now?"

"I want him comfortable with the plan."

"You said this place was shielded."

"I have a transceiver node outside the cage that bypasses the cage shielding."

"So that's why you wanted me here at a particular time."

Morgan nodded. I said, "I also need your help to nab Captain Voss."

"You ask too much."

"If I can catch Voss, my commander might overlook that I don't catch you."

"Ah …" Morgan let go. He seemed to be listening to Seth.

"Plus," I said, "it'll remove the cops who are trying to capture boys."

"There's not enough time," Morgan said.

"Tell Seth I'm in my own prison, caught between Voss, Sam, and you."

"You just did. He says he can't promise anything, but he'll work on it." Morgan raised my hand to his lips and kissed it. I stood up straight, leaned toward him, and closed my eyes. I was within his control without any of my earlier angst.

His lips touched mine, gently, like a spring breeze. Tingling spread across my cheeks, down my neck and out along my body and arms like a shot of adrenaline, only better.

He pulled away. "I shouldn't have done that."

The moment of longing faded. I took a deep breath and steeled my nerve. Did he do that to get me to help him? I'd already decided I would. Did he want me to stay? I didn't want to leave a place that cushioned me from Sam and Voss. I wanted another kiss, and didn't trust it.

Morgan's eyes saddened. "My lady, you should go before Sam suspects and comes looking for you."

"Is that what you want?"

He shook his head. "I can only offer you misery. Go, before I change my mind."

TWENTY-SEVEN

On the ride home from Morgan's Faraday cage, I couldn't believe what I had committed myself to. I didn't want to leave. I felt comfortable with him. It was more than that. I wanted to be with Morgan to my very core. He touched me in ways no one had before. Heck, he got me to consider risky things. I couldn't refuse him, or Seth.

My contacts rested in their case so they couldn't communicate with Sam. The double-shielded helmet caused me to sweat, and I wished I had the mech-gear water system to rehydrate. At such a late hour, the streets were empty, even of city-buses. I glanced up at each cam and rode at the speed limit. If only Sam knew, she would send me to a worse place than my birth mother.

I felt light and free. I'd helped Morgan escape the arena, something no one had done before. There was a slim chance to help him and his brother reach a freedom they hadn't known, one I hungered for. I tried to clear my mind before I did something more stupid.

Before I'd left, Morgan supplied me with a jamming device. "I suggest you use it until you get close to home," he'd said. "After the pulse takes out electricity, no one will be surprised that your links don't work."

"Won't the pulse take out the jammer?"

"It's shielded. After the escape, dispose of the jammer so they can't connect it to you."

New questions popped up. What if Sam anticipated something

178

like this? She was good at that. What if we couldn't get anything on Voss? In the end, Morgan turned out the lights and nudged me out the door.

Instead of going home, I left my cycle, helmet, and aluminum-cloth shields in the storage unit. Using the jammer to shield my signal, I ran into the woods. I lay down in a clearing and stared up at the starry sky, bleached out by city-lights. Then, I put in my contacts and turned off the jammer.

"Where the hell have you been?" Sam yelled into my skull.

I opened my eyes so she could see the night sky. "I needed privacy."

"Have you been jamming my signal?"

"How would I do that?"

"Never mind. I've gotten a whiff that Voss is up to something tomorrow. I need you on alert, and close to Scarlatti."

"Do I have any allies in this?" I asked.

"Not that you can rely on. I'll have some mech trainees on alert. You can't let them know you're working on this, though. I'll be with you most of the day, *if* you don't lose signal again."

"I'll stay away from the woods unless Voss leads me here."

"You should have gone home," Sam said.

"No privacy at home."

"Make sure you have your pistol for tomorrow. Then go home and sleep. That's an order."

The last thing I needed was Sam ordering me home. With her and Morgan in my head, home offered no comfort or escape. She expected me to do things most adults couldn't do. I'd wanted out of high school so people would treat me as an adult. Now I wanted my old life back, such as it was, a pinch of my girlhood.

Think of the consequences.

The penalty for helping Morgan as a civilian was prison; as a mech trainee, it could be treason, punishable by death. I hated how he permeated more than my visual and auditory senses. I couldn't stop thinking about him, and not just about his escape plan.

I took my cycle home, to our duplex. It was impossible to sneak anywhere with such a large family. This late, I only hoped my sisters were in bed and asleep.

When I entered the great room, Mama Helen wasn't downstairs, which meant either she got a call to the hospital or she was in bed. Mom's light was on in her office. *I miss you, Mom.*

Mama Grace grabbed me before I made it to the stairs. "Good," she whispered. She hugged me as if she hadn't seen me in weeks. "Everyone's home and safe." She kissed my cheek.

"Tell Mom I'm too tired to talk," I whispered.

Mama Grace nodded with sad eyes that betrayed worry about Mom. Concerns over mortality tended to bring out Mom's pensive mood. She kept those thoughts to herself, though when we were alone, she could talk for hours about George, her husband Bret, and how much she missed them.

I tiptoed upstairs and into my bedroom, and nearly tripped over Dot. I picked her up, stroked her fur, and set her down. Sarah snored in an angry growl. I removed my contacts, slipped under the covers in my clothes, and bumped into Janine. She tended to sleep on my bed when I was away, poor thing. I scooted around to her bed, which was in the middle, up against mine. There she was, as if she'd grown large enough to occupy both queen beds. Either that, or another sister had taken my place. I returned to my side and pushed Janine out of the way.

I faced the dark closet, and began to sort out what to do. Lieutenant Scarlatti would have stuff for me to do in the morning, something mundane to keep me away from the real activities. Sam wanted me involved, which meant Captain Voss didn't. Morgan wanted me to ride around the Institute.

Janine dug her fingernail into my side. I pushed her hand away. She pinched my thumb hard enough I wanted to yell at her. I didn't; Sam could hear over Sarah's snoring. Janine pushed my hand away. With her fingernail, she made a figure 8 on my stomach to signal silent talk.

"IM dying here," Janine marked out on my stomach.

I turned to say something. She put her hand over my mouth and continued writing with her finger, "IM ready to explode if I don't tell U."

"What?" I marked on the back of her hand.

"Sam's digging into U & Mom. She wants to destroy R family. She's in my head."

I cringed as that sank in. Sam was using Janine, the straight arrow, by-the-book, love-the-New Harmony sister of mine.

"Sam watches everything I see & hear," Janine wrote. "She has me watch U & Mom. She thinks U helped that boy. Tell me U didn't. I couldn't bear to lose U."

I took a deep breath and took my time. "It took guts to tell me. Does that mean Sam's training U?"

"Don't be mad."

"IM impressed," I wrote. "She's in my head, training me. You can't let her or anyone else know."

"I knew it," Janine wrote. "I knew Sam couldn't kick U out. Promise U won't help that boy. Sam says he'll contact U & make U do something terrible."

I should have known I couldn't get anything past Sam. "I promise not to lie to U about this."

"Have U heard from him?" Janine wrote. "U have to help me catch him so Sam will leave us alone. We can do this together, like playing basketball. We just need new signals."

Janine's enthusiasm could be contagious, but not tonight. "It's best U don't know certain things right now, Babe."

"U mean like that big dark secret U won't share with me."

"Get some sleep. We'll talk soon."

"How can he hide with everyone looking for him?" Janine wrote. "U haven't brought him home, have you?"

"For heaven's sake, no!"

"Then where is he?"

"Go to sleep."

I wanted to tell her more, but despite how she still looked up to me, I couldn't be sure she wouldn't tell Sam, in the belief that it would help the family. It wouldn't. Sam had another set of eyes now, and I couldn't rely on Janine.

<∞>

Next morning, to get a jump on my day before Sam or Scarlatti sucked me into whatever they might come up with, I headed on my cycle toward the Oak Ridge Geek Institute. The warm morning promised another muggy day.

To me, Oak Ridge conjured up the Manhattan Project. I couldn't decide if "Geek" was attractive to geeky boys, to make them complacent, or if they saw it as an insult. I would; I didn't like labels.

Janine relished being a geek as a badge of merit—too smart for my good. That contrasted with her athletic ability and basketball prowess. She was better than I was at everything. Yet she didn't make me envious. If anything, I felt proud to introduce her to things she excelled at in order to impress me. She didn't rub my nose in her successes. She was into doing things together. That made it hard for me to exclude her from my mech assignment, or my promise to help Morgan free his brother. He was right; I wouldn't hesitate to do anything for Janine.

I left the house while she showered, confident she wouldn't chase after me dripping wet, though she'd done that before. The moment I veered from a direct path to my cop station, voices in stereo reverberated in my skull.

"Why aren't you heading to your station?" Sam wanted to know.

<Are you ready to scope out the Institute?> Morgan asked.

"I need you on-task today."

<Let's see the side streets first.>

"It bugs me how those boys got out of the Institute," I said, "and where they could have imagined going after they escaped. If they had access to the upper floors, they'd only see homes and businesses all around."

"Get your butt over to the station and check in," Sam said.

"It's early. I doubt Voss or Scarlatti are even out of bed. I'll be at the station before nine."

I rode my cycle along the main road up a hill. Beyond a shallow valley rose a smaller hill. Perched on top was the reinforced concrete wall that surrounded the Oak Ridge Institute. The full name was Oak Ridge Institute for Quantum Informatics, whatever that meant. Most people called it the Geek Institute, or just the Institute. They kept very smart boys doing classified work the public wasn't to know about.

To me, "Institute" sounded like school or prison, which negated any attractive aspects of "Geek." The other suggestion was of a medical institute, where they did horrible experiments on boys to test drug reactions and diseases. That rumor, I believed.

"Do you want me to kick you out of the mech program for good?" Sam asked.

"No, Commander. But if Scarlatti refuses to teach me, I have to learn on my own. You taught me to use my initiative."

"Not today. Make sure you're at the station before they start whatever it is they're up to."

When I reached the street that surrounded the Institute, the massive wall stood before me, imposing and intimidating. It reminded me of pictures of medieval castles, with ladders placed against them during a siege. I spotted cam locations all around, on both sides of the street, although I couldn't see the cams themselves, too small.

Across the street from the Institute, a guard station inside what had been a storefront watched the front gate. On either side of the station were stores, abandoned because of location. Who wanted to shop across the street from dangerous boys behind a twelve-foot wall lined with concertina wire and guard towers? Upstairs from the abandoned shops were boarded-up apartment windows. Yet, along the street that led away from the Institute, stores remained open. Upstairs windows sported pastel drapes.

I rode the streets that surrounded the Institute, more wall and wire to my left, empty buildings to my right. On the southwest corner was the wooded park where Scarlatti had stationed me and Dara had captured that boy. The Institute wall on this side stood as imposing, with an open field the boy had to cross in order to escape. Like a medieval castle with a moat, there was no easy way in or out, not to speak of the top-level security systems inside. Out front, guardhouses stood on both sides of the gated entryway.

<There's no way over the wall,> Morgan said, reading my thoughts. <Move out in concentric circles. Let's see the surrounding area.>

"Okay," Sam said. "You've had your little joyride. Get over to the station."

<She is testy this morning.>

I swerved to avoid a bicycle and swung my cycle out to the alleys that ran behind the empty stores. They looked like other alleys in the old town, with empty garages built for a time when the government allowed private cars. The ever-present smell of garbage percolated in the sizzling heat of the cloudless day.

I was partway around the Institute when Morgan chimed in. <The warehouse is on your left. This is where I need you to do lookout.>

Garbage littered the alley. Since the buildings were empty, would city garbage trucks still service this place? I looked to the right for possible safe houses. Nothing looked promising. I kept moving so Sam wouldn't focus on this place.

After I completed that round, I moved out to the next circle of streets, with residences and less tension in the air. Women had begun to stir. A few headed off to work. No way could boys escape the Institute and find shelter unless someone here helped, at grave risk to her wellbeing and that of her family. Escape made no sense, except as desperate acts. It made no sense for conditions to be that bad inside the Institute, when they wanted the boys to help with sensitive high-tech problems.

<Good job,> Morgan said. <Everything looks as I remembered it. But we need to move today, before they send Seth to another facility.>

Instead of heading to my station, I returned to the huge gate in front of the Institute. Beyond the gate stood stark, sterile gray-concrete buildings with limited windows on the lower levels. My heart ached for the boys kept behind these walls. As angry as I'd been over what the Federal Union had done to my parents, I was lucky. Mom took me in and gave me a good home. I could go outside to the woods and down by the river.

<This place is killing Seth. Please don't get cold feet.>

I shook my head slowly side to side, while I took in the view of the empty street. The guard eyed me from inside the gate.

An administrator's car drove up. A tall, lean woman in a crisp gray Institute uniform stepped out. Director Devotte.

You caught me.

"I got a call someone was prowling around." Her eyes narrowed like laser beams.

I should have gotten used to the scrutiny. I looked down, decided that looked guilty, and returned her gaze. "I want to learn to be a good cop. My partner … Lieutenant Scarlatti … she's too busy to train me. I was trying to figure out how those boys could get past these impressive walls." I climbed off my cycle and smiled, hoping it wasn't a stupid grin.

"Is that so?"

"I see multiple cam locations." I pointed them out, though I couldn't see the cams. "The wall and wire don't show any damage. I'd say the boys didn't go over or through the wall."

"Astute observation."

"There's nowhere for them to go after they get out."

"The facility is secure," Director Devotte said. "If I give you a quick tour, will you leave quietly? Our security gets nervous when anyone hangs around."

"I promise. I just want to be sure it can't happen again."

<Nice touch,> Morgan said. <Make sure to look around. I've never seen the inside.>

I expected Sam to chime in, though I imagined she'd relish a look inside the secure facility as well.

I followed the director's car through the gate and biolocked my cycle. A drive led up to the front door. A small parking lot held three cars and about two dozen cycles. Two hundred feet of grass separated the wire-topped wall from the building. Tiny cam boxes on the building and the concrete wall made sneaking out impossible. They crisscrossed, so even if most didn't work, Institute personnel had complete coverage.

"As you can see, the exterior is secure," Devotte said.

"Then how did the boys get out?"

"We're still looking into that." She led me into a room like Sam's command center, with dozens of screens that scanned from cam to cam around the facility. Two twentyish women sat at adjacent desks, screens before them, while Devotte pointed to screens behind them.

"We have complete coverage of the outside of the building and the surrounding wall." Devotte sighed and lowered her voice. "Last year, there was an attack from outside intended to capture the boys. We caught all the boys and the culprits."

The place was a fortress. I spotted patrols in gray uniforms, security tracked girls like me. They walked the halls inside the Institute with multi-shot stun guns, the version Scarlatti wouldn't let me have.

<Turn right,> Morgan said. <I want a closer look at the inside cams.>

"What about these?" I said to Devotte while I studied another wall of screens. They showed cells, each with a young boy on a bed or seated at a desk with screens full of fancy graphics.

<Don't linger, but Seth is three from the left and down two.>

I glanced at the scrawny boy I recognized from Morgan's photograph. He looked much younger than his 14 years, though Mom told me boys matured later and tended to be smaller at that age.

"They have nice, clean rooms," I said. "Are they dangerous?"

"They're better off here than outside, if that's what you're asking," Devotte replied.

<Don't believe that.>

"If they can't go over the wall or through it, they must have gone under," I said.

<Don't ask too many questions, or she'll become suspicious.>

"Underground passages." Devotte nodded to the opposite wall and took me there. "Here, we have surveillance belowground. We rarely use this section. Somehow, the boys made it down there and found a passage. Our surveillance team tracked them. That's how we caught them so quickly, with the help of the Knoxville police."

What about the mechs? I wanted to ask. I didn't get the chance.

"It's time for you to leave as promised." Devotte hurried me out of the control room toward the front door. She seemed like a cross between Sam and Voss, sharp as my commander, yet suspicious like my captain. She wasn't someone whose path I wanted to cross.

As she led me out of her facility, it felt like a prison with well-lit corridors, cams, and tiny windows to discourage escape attempts. When we reached the parking lot, I took a deep breath of steamy air that burned my lungs.

"Thanks for the tour," I said. "It looks very secure." I bit off my words, smiled, and hurried off before I said something I'd regret.

I couldn't imagine any way to get Morgan's brother out of a place this well guarded. I also knew he wouldn't leave me alone until his brother was free. I wanted to take another ride around the facility, to impress upon Morgan the futility of his efforts, but I needed to get back to the station before Scarlatti and Voss made their next move.

TWENTY-EIGHT

<Great job in there,> Morgan said as I mounted my cycle. <Seth looks healthy enough for what we need to do. It's one thing for him to tell me, another to see it myself.>

"That was helpful," Sam said. "Now hustle back to the station. I need you to stick close to Scarlatti. Get her to let you partner with her for the day. Be helpful."

<Don't let the security display change your mind,> Morgan said. <When they lose electricity, that center goes blind.>

While I sped toward the station, I didn't have time to process the Institute visit with what Morgan wanted and Sam demanded. They kept hammering me. "You'll never be alone," was the motto of the New Harmony, with its community-living arrangements. I was living the next step: Big Sister in your head.

Just before I reached the station, I moved Morgan's hood from the saddlebags to my backpack without looking. In my fumbling around, I almost hit a bus that cut me off. When I pulled into the station parking lot, Janine stood there.

She shoved me against a light post. "You ditched me again. Fess up. Where did you go? What are you hiding from me?"

"Janine—"

She jabbed my side and marked a figure 8. Then I remembered; she was also performing for an audience. "I don't want excuses. I want answers. You owe me that." Her eyes narrowed.

"We have to get inside." I pulled her toward the entrance. "You don't want to be late."

"You promised not to keep secrets from me."

"I had an errand, and you were in the shower."

"Don't give me that. If you can't be honest, then we're through." She hurried into the cafeteria to clock in.

I steadied my breathing. If I held too many secrets before, now I could barely keep track. I was in over my head, unable to turn back. My first instinct was that Janine was back, but she wanted Morgan caught. We weren't on the same side. Sam had shoved a wedge between us.

Yet Sam said I needed allies. As I glanced across the bullpen at Brooks, Scarlatti, Montrose, and others, all I could think was: *Who can I trust?*

"Trust your instincts," Sam said, as if she'd read my thoughts. "I didn't want you wasting time out there, but you did great at the Institute. For now, pay attention to Scarlatti. Whatever Voss is up to, she's putting her players into motion today."

"This isn't a game," I whispered as I skirted the outer wall toward the cafeteria and common room.

"No, it isn't. You need to become more flexible. Take what you learned during basketball and mech training. Put it to good use. The first lesson you've forgotten is you can't do it all by yourself. You still imagine you need to be strong for Janine, and don't need anyone else. That won't work for this mission."

"But—"

"No buts."

I reached the common room. Janine took one look at me and slipped out the other door. After I made sure Janine had checked me in, I headed out the back door.

"Now what?" Sam asked.

I waited until I was outside. "You say I can't do this alone. Yet, there's no one I can trust."

"Calm down and think."

"I am calm, Sam." Denial was pointless, of course. My pulse and blood pressure had to be off the charts. She could read those stats off my implant.

"Let's start with basics. Do you trust me?"

"The right answer is yes, but you keep withholding information."

"Honest answer, at least," Sam said. "Assume I could win your trust. Could you trust me to deliver the Mech Corps when needed?"

I nodded. "I suppose, but Dara—"

"Will follow orders. What about your sister?"

"Leave her out of this."

"What about Brooks?"

"When she isn't around Voss and Scarlatti."

"That's a start. You need to dig deep on this assignment, very deep. Who can help you get close to Voss?"

"Scarlatti."

"How do you get close to her?"

I took a deep breath. "Not by washing the mud off her car."

"Who can get you closer to Scarlatti?"

"I don't know ... Sergeant Montrose."

"Find her and appeal to her team spirit."

<∞>

I didn't find Montrose anywhere inside the station. She would typically be out on undercover work, but not if Voss was working on something big. I headed out back.

Montrose was in the alley with Lieutenant Scandia, having a quiet talk. Dot Montrose was taller, lean, with short brown hair tight to her face. She looked attractive in short hair. Terry Scandia was rounder, though not like Captain Voss, more big-boned. She had a bulldog face and was sensitive about the dog analogy, or so I'd heard.

Scandia left the moment she saw me: no point hanging around the intern with a social disease. Except, I was no longer an intern.

I brought a cup of decaf as a peace offering and handed it to Montrose. "Hi, Dot ... Sergeant."

She took the cup, sipped the bitter liquid, and stared down the alley at her retreating partner.

"Sergeant, I know I had a bad attitude as an intern. I'm trying now, but Lieutenant Scarlatti is too busy. Could I hang out with you and Lieutenant Scandia to learn the ropes?"

"You'll have to speak with her," Montrose said. She headed inside. "Thanks for the coffee."

"You're welcome. Could I ride with you today?"

"In the back?"

"I wouldn't mind," I said.

189

Montrose studied me. "I'll talk to Scandia."

"That would be great. I'll try not to get in the way."

"Better," Sam said into my implant. "Now find Scarlatti. See what you can learn."

When I returned to the bullpen, Janine was with Brooks. She cast me an odd glance. If that was a signal, I missed it. Scarlatti was in her office with Voss. When the captain looked my way, I hid behind a post.

<∞>

Scarlatti was going through her mental checklist for tonight's escape-and-capture plan when Captain Voss entered her office and closed the door.

"We need to take care of that troublesome Scott girl," Voss said in a muted voice. "She was out questioning the director this morning." She glowered at her wrist-com and shook her head. "Just now, she asked Montrose to let her ride with them."

Scarlatti shook her head. She checked her desk-screen's cam shots of the station interior, and located Annabelle wandering about like a lost child. While Scarlatti merely didn't want the troublemaker, she sensed Voss carried personal venom for this girl.

Voss winced as she sat in a padded seat. "Find a way to destroy her, and that mother of hers."

"We can connect the senator to the commander, and show they've gotten cozy."

"That'll take too long."

Scarlatti put down a carved wooden elephant she'd collected in a raid and looked up. "What do you have in mind? We could lure her—"

"She wants in on today's stakeout." Voss grinned. "Perhaps we should grant her persistent wish."

"I don't trust the girl. She's trouble."

"I'm counting on it. She let that boy live in the arena. The boy escaped. What poetic justice that she gets caught helping his brother escape the Institute."

"His brother?" Scarlatti asked.

"He's the boy we need to pick up today. What better way to disgrace her family than to catch her red-handed."

"She can't be that stupid."

"Don't be so sure," Voss said. "I've had suspicions about the senator's sympathies for some time. The fruit won't fall far from that tree."

"I'm not comfortable working with the girl." Scarlatti pushed her screen away and considered her options. "Do you think she'll take the bait?"

"She's a sympathizer. She likes boys. We can use that against her. If all she does is hesitate, that could be enough."

"She's unpredictable," Scarlatti said.

"She's a child," Voss said, "a wounded bird. She's hungry for your attention. Give her a little." Voss pushed herself up out of the seat. "This could be a triple win for us. Capture Morgan, which the mechs failed to do. Deliver his brother. And catch Annabelle for helping them."

<∞>

When the door to Scarlatti's office opened, I expected Voss to head upstairs so I could talk to Scarlatti.

"Annabelle Scott, stop lurking in the shadows," Voss said in her high-pitched whine. "Get your obstreperous derriere into the lieutenant's office. Now!"

I wished I could have listened in on their dialogue, to have some hint as to what to expect. I braced myself.

Voss closed the door behind us and pushed me into a hard seat facing the desk. I imagined a grin on her face.

"What in God's name were you doing interrogating the Institute's director?" Voss asked.

"I wasn't interr—"

"Don't interrupt. The director is an important official. You're barely out of the intern program. What possessed you?"

I waited and took steady breaths, thankful Sam didn't give me her "I told you so."

"Nothing to say for yourself?"

"I didn't want to interrupt, Captain. I had a pleasant talk with the director. She invited me in for a tour."

"What did you learn?"

"There should be no way for boys to escape that facility."

"Careful," Sam said into my implant. "She's baiting you."

In the Middle Ages, they would have locked me up as insane or burned me at the stake as a witch for hearing voices in my head. Or, they might have ordained me as a saint if I led some army into victory, though saints tended to be dead.

I took a deep breath and tried to take comfort that Sam was with me. That was hard when she wanted to destroy my family over Morgan.

"Boys did escape. We caught them," Voss said. Her voice carried a twinge of pride.

"I want to learn how to help," I said. "I want to be the best partner Lieutenant Scarlatti has ever had."

<Don't lay it on too thick,> Morgan said. <Otherwise she won't believe you.>

Voss circled around and stared down at me. Her chubby cheeks sagged. Up close, she looked as if she might have high cheekbones beneath layers of plump flesh. "You want to do your part to make our department look good, don't you?"

"I do," I said. "This is my life now. No more fanciful dreams."

"Then maybe you did learn something from mech training." Voss sat on the desk, which sagged under her weight. "Very well. We have another stakeout tonight. If you promise to do exactly what Lieutenant Scarlatti tells you, nothing more or less, you can partner with her for this assignment. But ... I will only say this once ... your future depends on how you handle yourself."

"I won't let you down, Captain."

"Good," Scarlatti said. "Go wash my car and clean up around the station. Be ready to leave when I give the word." She dismissed me and closed the door.

TWENTY-NINE

I watched Brooks take Janine out on patrol. Voss took Scarlatti
upstairs. Unable to find Montrose or Scandia, I washed Scarlatti's
car again. More mud. Could it be from that facility in the hills
across the river? I needed to go back and check that out.

Soaked from cleaning, I returned to the bullpen. Scarlatti stood
with Lieutenant Scandia and Sergeant Montrose behind the closed
door of her office. I wanted more information about today's role,
but Sam said not to irritate. Well, I was irritated. How could I do
my job without directions? I could ask the same of Sam.

I cleaned the cafeteria and checked from time to time. Scarlatti's
door remained closed. Other interns rushed in for decaf and rolls.
They left more for me to clean. You could only do so much before
you wore out the cheap tabletops and cleaning tools.

Complete silence in my head was unnerving. I imagined Sam
pacing her office, impatient for me to do something. I couldn't
win. If I barged in, Scarlatti would toss me out of the station.
Without results, Sam wouldn't keep me in the mechs, which meant
they could ship me to a place worse than Seth's Institute. Could
Morgan's brother really provide information on my birth mother,
and on who attacked Mom? If not, was I prepared to help Morgan
anyway?

Scarlatti's door opened. After Scandia left with Montrose, I
entered. "Excuse me." I stood by the door, ready for a quick exit.
"How can I help? I've washed your car, cleaned the cafeteria and
common areas. Can I help prepare for the mission?"

Scarlatti looked up from her screen, stared at me for a moment, and mumbled something I didn't understand.

"What have you done to turn these people so hostile?" Sam asked. "Never mind. Just show me persistence."

<I'm waiting to hear from Seth,> Morgan said. <He's late. Be patient.>

Now everyone chimes in. Be persistent, be patient, don't irritate.

Scarlatti raised her index finger to tell me to wait. She cupped her hand over her mouth and whispered, "Don't let me down."

Pretending not to hear, I studied the reflection of Scarlatti's screen in the glass of a boring cityscape on the wall behind her. I moved for a clearer picture, but the image was too fuzzy.

Scarlatti removed her hand from her mouth and looked up. "Can't you see I'm busy?"

I smiled. "I just want to help while we wait."

"Have you washed my car?"

Weren't you listening? "Yes."

"Cleaned the common area."

"Done." I smiled.

She eyed me as Mama Grace did when I hadn't done a good-enough job on the bathrooms. "The best you can do is be ready to roll. Close the door on your way out." She waved for me to leave.

Nothing was worse than having to stand around and wait. If I had gone on patrol with Brooks and Janine, at least I'd have company. I looked for Montrose: gone. The voices in my head fell silent. To fight my nervous energy, I retired to the gym and pressed weights.

During mech training, I got into a rhythm of repetitions that burned off my frustrations over the fights and having to put up with Dara. Workouts usually shut down my worry neurons. It wasn't working now. Sam didn't bug me to get in there. That wasn't like her, as if she was distracted.

Janine! Sam was using her. If I didn't deliver, the commander would make my sister do my dirty work.

I climbed off the equipment and took a quick rinse in the shower without looking at anything I didn't want Morgan to see. Then I changed into my cop-intern uniform and camped out near Scarlatti's office. From there, I could keep an eye on the bullpen, Brooks' desk and the entrance in case Janine returned.

In all our time growing up, I'd never had so little contact with my sister. She usually sent me messages to cheer me up or make plans to go somewhere. Now she remained as silent as the voices in my head. I'd have traded theirs for hers in an instant.

Scarlatti opened her office door, grabbed me by the arm, and headed outside to her car without a word. The streets thronged with evening commuters catching city-buses home. I'd wasted the entire day hanging around the station.

"What can you tell me about the assignment?" I asked as Scarlatti drove us out of the parking lot.

She headed west. "We got a tip about another escape."

"How can I make contacts to get tips like that?" I fingered the multi-shot stun gun she provided me and double-checked how to trigger a single shot and quickly reset. Then I realized I might have to use this on Scarlatti. *Control yourself. Patience. You don't want prison.*

"Don't point that in my direction," Scarlatti said, as if she'd read my thoughts. Her voice softened. "It takes years of solid police work to develop connections who trust you enough to pass on information."

A potent threat can work as well, I didn't say. "Catching boys is the most important work we do. I want to help. What's the target?"

"The Oak Ridge Institute."

"Again?" I tried to act surprised.

<They're going to move Seth tonight,> Morgan said. <We have to hurry.>

I clutched the stun gun and shifted the position of my pistol, which dug into my side. Scarlatti would confiscate it if she knew.

"Someone is helping the boys," Scarlatti said. "It's critical tonight that we capture not only the boys, but also the Underground supporters." She looked my way.

<She's trying to rattle you. You'll know we're on when the Institute lights go out. I'll try to warn you. Shield your head and your wrist-com. If shielded, it should still work, but no signal. Then turn on the jammer and come to my location.>

I nodded. "Do we have any idea who this Underground is?"

Scarlatti shook her head and turned onto the street up to the Institute. The gray concrete wall loomed ahead, surrounding the Gothic twelve-story concrete prison. The sunset provided a halo around the Institute. *Except it's not heaven.*

"Get Scarlatti to talk without getting her defensive," Sam said. "We need details of the operation."

<Take a deep breath and stay calm.>

How could I, with two voices pinging around inside my head?

"How many officers will we have on this stakeout?" I asked.

"Most of our station," Scarlatti said. "East Knoxville offered 20 officers and detectives. You just focus on doing what I ask. I don't have time for your attitude."

"I've changed. I want to help."

"We'll see."

"Where will you be?" I asked. "In case I find something?"

Scarlatti parked behind Voss, a block from the Institute. "See that building?" She pointed to a rundown brick storefront on the corner with boarded-up windows. "It used to be a hardware store. Now it's vacant. With help from the outside, boys dug a tunnel under the Institute that connected to its basement. You're to park yourself there and wait until I tell you different."

"Why didn't the Institute seal the tunnel so they couldn't use it again?" In the side mirror, I watched Scandia pull up, and then Brooks with Janine.

Without answering, Scarlatti got out of the car and approached Lieutenant Scandia.

<They aren't interested in fewer escapes,> Morgan said. <Escapes provide a cover to move boys to their special facility. Whoever Voss works for wants these boys.>

I got out of Scarlatti's car. "Why?" I asked.

<Medical experiments, or secret computer work. I suspect both.>

"Why what?" Sam asked.

I caught myself—too many voices. "Why not seal off the tunnel to reduce escapes?"

"They're staging this to catch the Underground Railroad."

Mom, tell me you aren't out there. I looked around.

While Scarlatti talked with Scandia, a mech crawled out of the back of Scandia's car. It had to be Montrose. That should have been me.

Janine joined me, with Brooks right behind. "This is exciting," Janine said, eyes wide. "We get to do important stuff tonight."

"Not as much as if we captured border jumpers," I said, referring to desperate Outlanders who managed to cross into our lands.

Janine cringed, but then brightened again. "Maybe we'll catch the Underground people tonight."

You wouldn't be so cheerful if you knew Mom might be one of them.

<∞>

I stood at the back of the hardware store and watched other cops arrive and spread out along the well-lit streets and alleys, and between the old buildings surrounding the Institute. It was overkill: all this effort, to capture a few boys. This couldn't be the full story. I looked for the warehouse Morgan wanted me to watch. It was a quarter of the way around the Institute, with dozens of cops in between. All the streetlights and power-generated floodlights made it hard to tell the sun had set.

Janine nudged me. "Earth to Belle. What's going on?"

"Wish I knew. Scarlatti wants me to stand here and wait. How about you?"

Brooks patted my shoulder. "It's like the military. Lots of standing around and preparation for a brief mission. Still, groundwork is important. Janine and I will be at the other end of this alley in case any of the boys get that far."

Janine's face lit up. "You think we'll find some?" She turned my way and studied me, as when she wanted to figure out what I thought or felt.

"All right, everyone," Scarlatti said. "Gather around."

I adjusted my backpack, made sure my pistol was still hidden, and tried to act cheerful. Looking super-serious and grim, Voss joined Scarlatti. The mech-cop sauntered down the alley. Other cops from our station joined us.

Voss' chubby jowls curled up in a smile. Victory filled her face, like the time she arrested me and tried to send me to resocialization in Nashville.

"We have a chance tonight to catch this Underground and crush them for good," she said. "There's been movement in the area. They think they're clever, but we have some secrets of our own. Captain Chou will have her forces on the northwest corner. We have the rest of the Institute cordoned off. No one gets in or out without my knowing. I received a call from Director Devotte. Boys are on the move. This is real, ladies. This will happen tonight."

"Stay in position," Sam said into my skull. "Be my ears and eyes up close. I have three teams in the area. Your trainer, Renee, is in charge. Trainees you've worked with include Dara, Margarite, and Brandy, as a team. They'll stand back and watch for now. You need to keep moving around so I know what's happening."

Mom, I pray you're not part of this.

"Take your positions. Let's do this," Voss said. She took Scarlatti aside as the other cops headed to their posts.

Janine squeezed my shoulder. "Wouldn't it be great if you and I caught the boys together? I'll be right over there."

"This isn't a game, Janine. These boys are desperate. You don't know who might be helping them. I don't want you hurt. Stay close to Brooks. Do as she says."

Somber-faced, she nodded and followed Brooks down the alley. I scanned the street to my right, the side with boarded-up storefronts, to allow Sam and Morgan to see the number and arrangement of cops.

Twilight settled in over the rest of Knoxville, but lights around the alley added heat to the muggy evening. I couldn't just stand and wait in one spot like this. I hurried to the street that surrounded the Institute and looked around. The Institute and wall looked ominous in the long shadows from Institute lights. The idea came that with everyone looking for the boys to use the tunnel, it might be easier to climb the wall.

A hand grabbed my shoulder and spun me around. "This is why I can't work with you," Scarlatti said in a low growl. "You're out of position." She headed up the street.

I ran after her. "You were with the captain. I wanted one last look at the Institute. It seems to me it would be easier to climb the wall than to dig a tunnel."

Scarlatti stopped and studied the front of the Institute. "Good point." She spoke into her wrist-com. "I want one cop on each corner facing the Institute, in case the boys try something different."

Good, that's several fewer cops watching the alleys.

Cop cars blocked the road toward Knoxville. Newsfeeds on my wrist-com showed all the roads blocked, which meant no vehicles could get in or out. So much for Morgan's garbage truck idea. I lingered so he could see this. The buildings surrounding the Institute appeared to be vacant when I rode through before. Now the homes and buildings beyond the alley were closed and shuttered.

Cam-swarms buzzed above our heads, feeding more vids for newscasts. A southerly breeze scattered a swarm across the alley, sending the little critters crashing into a brick wall. The swarm reformed, minus a few dozen that remained sprinkled across the ground. As it moved out along the street, the news vid quality grew fuzzier. Another swarm became the primary feed, showing the well-lit Institute surrounded by cops.

"Knoxville's finest are taking the latest threat seriously," the newscaster reported.

The escape was a trap, too well anticipated and staged. Morgan had to be desperate, as I would be if Janine were in danger. I looked her way; she waved.

When I reached the back door to the hardware store, I shuddered at what tools the boys might find. I only had my stun gun, and the pistol I didn't want to use. Sam could see any activity and bring in her mech-warriors, but they were blocks away. I hated these politics between Sam and Voss. Each wanted to capture these boys and be the public hero. Despite Morgan's plans, the boys, including Seth, were merely pawns.

<I'm in position,> Morgan said. <After the pulse, get to the warehouse.>

My head swayed from left to right. At one end of the alley, Scandia crouched with the mech-cop. At the other end, Janine stood, too eager to bring down the Underground Railroad and punish boys. How could I get past either of them to get to the warehouse? Then what? It would be easier to turn Morgan in. I'd be the hero. And a skunk.

Janine ran toward me. "You're not alone, Belle. I'm here for you. Just give me a signal. Any signal."

"Thanks, Babe, but when this goes down, you need to stay with Brooks. Now go."

Janine shuffled back to her post.

I checked both ends of the alley. Across from me were boarded-up back doors to homes that faced the next street. There was no way off this alley except past Scandia or Brooks. I hoped Morgan could see the situation and call this off before it was too late.

The doorknob behind me turned easily. The door slid open. "Shouldn't we wait at the tunnel opening?" I whispered.

"This looks extraordinarily well orchestrated," Sam said. "They've got reporter cams on each street and two reporter cam-swarms in the air. They're expecting a public spectacle. You need to stay in position. Keep looking around."

"I could scope out the tunnel—"

"No! Scarlatti's heading your way."

Scarlatti turned the corner to my right, talking to Scandia. Janine looked up the alley from the other direction, Sam's other set of eyes. *Poor Babe, you have no idea what Sam expects of you.*

"Step away from the door and keep your eyes on Scarlatti," Sam said. "Any idea where Voss is?"

Captain Voss. Another wild card in tonight's activities. I opened the hardware store's back door and glanced inside. Dark. I took infrared images on my wrist-com and closed the door. The pictures showed more than I expected, due to the Institute lights shining through gaps in the boarded-up front windows. The hardware store was empty. Boards blocked any escape out the front. At least there was no evidence of tools the boys could use

"Stay outside," Sam yelled into my head.

A headache crept in behind my left eye. Janine inched away from her post, toward me. I felt like a prisoner. Or the bait. I wanted to return to my world, even high school, if I had to.

At any moment, boys could pour out of this door. My reaction might betray me. I had to leave.

<Stay calm,> Morgan said. <It's time.>

Would I turn Morgan in to save Janine? I stepped aside, and scanned the alley. Janine moved behind the corner with Brooks. Down the next block, other cops took up positions. At the other end of the alley, Scandia crouched next to Scarlatti.

"I can't see Voss," I whispered to Sam.

"She's behind Scarlatti. She never was one to put her life on the line. Dara's team has eyes on them from the other side. Do you hear anything from inside the hardware store?"

"No. Could this be a false alarm?"

"Captain Voss wouldn't embarrass herself," Sam said. "Every time she's mobilized, they've caught boys. One more success and I fear they'll name her commissioner of police over the entire Knoxville metropolitan area."

For the first time, I sensed fear in Sam's voice.

<After the pulse,> Morgan said, <I won't be able to talk to you. Turn on the jammer and find your way to the warehouse.>

There was no way past Brooks or Scarlatti, no way out the front of the hardware store. *Sorry, Morgan.*

But what was there to be sorry for? Seth hadn't provided me evidence against Voss, information on my birth mother, or names of who called the attack on Mom.

"Sam, what do you want me to do?" I asked.

"Stay where you are. Keep looking around. Prepare to move."

I nodded. I was used to relying on my own wits. Other people let you down. Now I had three partners who gave me so little to work with, they were of no help. Yet, for the first time, I couldn't act on my own.

Janine gave a slight nod. I had a fourth partner, if I could noodle a plan with her without letting Sam know. But she wanted to capture Morgan.

THIRTY

The Trojan horse works because the enemy brings it within their secure walls, Seth thought with a grin. *Like bringing me into their secure Institute.*

He triggered his program, stood up, and hurried away from his work screen, as he often did when he waited too long to use the toilet. The timer allowed him five minutes to catch up with Mole, the name the strange boy called himself. Seth had just unlocked every door on the dorm floors. When the fire alarms blared, all the boys would head downstairs.

Seth didn't like crowds. He didn't want to be trampled by frightened boys who didn't understand. He rushed down narrow, puke-colored Institute corridors, as if the alarms already blasted his ears. Women staff stared as they scooted out of his way. One advantage of being labeled high-functioning autistic was that people left him alone unless they wanted something, such as having him find glitches in their complicated software. Otherwise, they didn't expect much. He walked faster.

Counting down in his head, he played out what must be happening, what *was* happening. The Institute's technology was predictable despite its bugs. In a crisis, so were people, to a point. At least Morgan liked to say so.

Seth made another turn and passed two staff women in gray uniforms running to check out the emergency. He winced as alarms sounded their annoying pulses intended to wake up all but the dead. By now, the boys upstairs would have flooded the corridors. Afraid of all the boys, staff women would run for cover and call security. That took time.

It seemed like chaos, but there was a rhythm, like water rushing through a hose. Boys would enter the stairwells. In their control room, Institute staff would try to seal off all the exits. Seth had disconnected their access. Others would pass out those stun guns he hated, the ones that scrambled his brains. It took days to recover from the shock, and left him wondering what he might have lost.

Around the next corner, Seth bumped into a plump gray staff woman with fear blazing from her round head. He dropped to the floor as if blinded by the glow.

"So sorry," the woman said and helped him to his feet.

Seth hurried on. Past the next doorway, he entered a stairwell and found Mole, whose real name was Hank, a big boy with a gray, cloudy face. Three boys from Seth's floor ran down the stairs and stopped. He knew them only by sight. The staff didn't want him talking to other boys. That was fine with Seth. He didn't need to talk to know they were happy to be out of their rooms. He could see their cheery yellow glow on top of the fearful sparks.

"Fire," the biggest of the three said in a monotone. "We must go to the basement."

Hank glared at Seth. Swirling dark clouds grew thicker across his face. "I'm only taking you." He jabbed his finger at Seth.

Seth smiled. That was usually enough for people to decide not to reason with him.

Hank shook his hands as if they held a thermos of lemonade before he headed down the stairs. By then, dozens of other boys stacked up behind Seth's three floor-mates. He checked the time on his bracelet, the one that told him when to get up, when to go to sleep, when he could eat, and when he needed to work on their programs. He hurried after Hank. Five more minutes before the next part of his program shut off all the lights. Seth didn't like the dark.

For security, the Institute disconnected from the city grid. They had four separate sets of generators. Each had backups with separate transformers for redundancy. By now, the power in each had kicked up so high that in a few minutes, overloads would hit all four transformers. Electricity would back up into the generators until sparks bypassed the override switches. Four pulses would converge at lightning speed into a single, coordinated blast and a single high-energy pulse. If Seth's calculations were correct, that would take out all the Institute's electricity and fry unshielded electronics, including communications nodes near the Institute.

It would become dark and scary. Surveillance would be dead. Their stun guns wouldn't work. Their infrared sensors would be blind.

When Hank first told Seth he could get them out, Seth thought Morgan had sent him. Morgan said no. After that, Seth didn't want to go with the gloomy Mole. Too many dark clouds followed him, like Charlie Brown's cartoon friend. Morgan said Hank's involvement could help even though Hank was a snitch, a different kind of mole. Saying yes cleared the cloud on Hank's face for a while, though the next time Seth saw him, the cloud returned, darker than before.

Standard Institute drill called for boys to go to the basement in case of fire, since staff didn't allow them outside. The few staff women he saw stepped aside to let them pass. A big concrete room stood in the middle of the basement. Director Devotte said they would be safe there until firefighters rescued them. It had sprinklers like in the data center. Seth didn't believe Halon gas was friendly to organic life forms that needed oxygen.

The electric surge was rising. The hairs on Seth's arm stood at attention as he entered the dank basement and followed Hank toward the big hall with its Halon sprinklers. Mole's face looked stormy, worse than ever. Seth spotted the corridor to the tunnel, now sealed, that boys had used to escape the Institute. They never returned. Seth didn't think they got away. Otherwise, there would have been more chatter about catching them.

Hank insisted that while the tunnel was sealed on the inside, there was only a thin layer of plaster they would have to break through. Then they would be on their way to freedom.

Seth pressed himself against the corridor wall to let a stream of boys push ahead of him.

"It's okay," Hank said, his face gray with gloom. "Nothing to worry about."

<∞>

I ached to escape this well-lit alley and find some passage where no one could watch me. That wasn't going to happen. I checked my wrist-com. News flashes showed cops blocking the streets around the Institute. Trust citizen reporters to hype another escape attempt. That would give frightened voters another reason to support Governor Battani's tough controls.

I glanced down the alley and caught the mirror of my anxiety in Janine's face. I took a deep breath. I had to remain calm for her. The sky was black, yet seemed to reflect the lights from the Institute, the streets, and the alley. In other words, it was like a bright, cloudy day.

"What do you see?" Sam demanded.

I scanned the alley. No change. "I don't like this. When boys rush out, they'll run me over before I can respond." I hoped that sounded convincing. "We should go in after them."

"Attempted escape doesn't carry the same penalty as actual escape," Sam reminded me.

<Things are in motion,> Morgan said. <Seth can no longer communicate. It'll happen within minutes. Please don't back out on us now.>

I scanned the alley, first toward Janine at one end, then at Scarlatti and Scandia at the other. I stared at the boarded-up doors across from me. Morgan wanted me to move to his warehouse the moment the lights went out. Scarlatti would have me sent to the Nashville Resocialization Facility if I moved from this spot.

<I get it. You're surrounded. Please find a way. The pulse will come any instant. Take advantage of the chaos.>

I squatted beside the door, closed my eyes, and placed Morgan's stiff shield over my head. It blocked out the bright lights. I stuffed my wrist-com in for good measure.

"What—" Sam began. The shield cut her off.

A high-pitched whine morphed into a squeal like truck emergency brakes, coming from the Institute. It sounded as if the sky had split open. In that instant, a flash seemed to penetrate my shield and glow all around me. Blackness followed, like inside a cave.

I removed my wrist-com from the shielded hood and activated. "No signal," the tinny voice said. I activated the jammer Morgan provided, removed the shield, and tucked it back into my backpack. Surrounding blackness reminded me of no-man's-land and the ghostly reflection of lights farther east. Lights in the alley, street, and around the Institute were out, leaving a dark hole in the clouds above.

Shouts came from Scarlatti's end of the alley. "What the—!"

"Where are the lights?" "What happened?"

My wrist-com reported no connections, no newsfeeds. "Is anyone there?" I whispered. No response.

An arm touched mine. I jumped, and then recognized Janine's touch. I could barely see her in the darkness. I slipped my wrist-com into my skorts pocket.

"You okay?" Janine's voice wavered.

"I'm fine. We need to find out what happened."

"I'm sticking with you, Belle."

Nice. The one time I needed her to let me go.

"None of my links work, Belle. I'm worried." Meaning she couldn't hear Sam.

"It'll be fine." I turned away and aimed my wrist-com infrared at Brooks. She stood at the end of the alley with two other cops. I turned toward Scarlatti. Four cops paced nearby. I had to move. "If we don't have electronics, we'll have to settle for something else."

The sky remained lit toward Knoxville, giving some reflected light when my eyes adjusted. I concealed my wrist-com. At least I didn't have two voices screaming inside my head.

Scarlatti joined us. "Janine, I need you to run communications down the line. Check in with Captain Chou."

A runner came from Brooks' direction, a cop-intern from night shift. "What happened? What do we do? Our communications are dead."

"This proves the boys had outside help," Scarlatti said. "This is the night we end these escapes. Return to your post, keep your eyes open, and use runners to communicate."

The night-shift intern nodded and left.

Scarlatti handed Janine a written note, on real paper. "Deliver this to Captain Chou. Tell each post the escape is on, and to use runners. After you meet with Captain Chou, bring back any messages."

"Janine's an intern," I said. "It's too dangerous for her on her own on a night like this."

Janine started to protest. I grabbed her hand and traced a figure 8.

"I need you here," Scarlatti said. "This is your post."

I picked out eight cops standing around Scandia. Voss must have called in other stations. Likely there would be dozens of cops between the warehouse and me.

"Let Janine stand watch," I said. "I'll do the run myself."

"It's not safe," Janine said. "I'll go with you." Her eyes were wide, anxious, frightened.

"Janine will be fine," Scarlatti said.

"Not with boys able to climb over the walls in the dark," I said. "I'll find someone else."

"I'm fast. I'm trained. I'll do it."

"You're too eager."

"The boys are on the move, Lieutenant." I took the message from Janine and ran toward Brooks. I heard footsteps behind me.

"Janine, get back here," Scarlatti said.

"Do what the lieutenant says," I called over my shoulder.

"Let her go," Brooks said. "I'll be fine."

"I'm sticking with you on a night like this," Janine whispered from right behind me. "We're going to catch that boy tonight, aren't we?"

"Janine, concentrate on not getting hurt."

I had to get to Morgan without her hanging around, while Sam was counting on her to make sure I didn't.

At the first street, I looked left at the gaping darkness of the Institute, as if it had been erased. To my right the night-shift intern relayed the message from Scarlatti to Brooks. I kept going. I didn't need Janine *solving* me tonight.

At the next street, a lieutenant and six other cops greeted me. I relayed the message from Scarlatti.

Up the street, toward Knoxville, it was dark for three blocks. Then streetlights shone up to the top of the next hill. I looked for mechs, didn't see any.

Nearby, a mech-cop removed her gear. She cursed.

"Shouldn't she stay in her mech-suit?" I asked the lieutenant. "The boys are on the move."

"Damned electronics," the mech-cop said. "It's like being in a body cast. The helmet is fried. The hydraulics froze up. The suit's useless. Even flashlights are dead."

The pulse worked! I couldn't see a thing from the direction of the Institute. "We need to get eyes on that wall," I said. "Boys could climb over any minute."

The lieutenant nodded. I hurried down the alley.

"This is bad," Janine said, her voice shaky. "What if we run into those boys?"

"You'll be fine," I assured her. I wanted to tell her about Morgan, but she wouldn't understand, and there wasn't time to try to explain.

"My wrist-com doesn't work and … and Sam is no longer in my head."

That's a good thing.

The alley turned sharp left behind buildings that faced the north side of the Institute. To my left was the back door to the warehouse. To my right, barely visible in the dark, a big garbage truck faced the street. Seeing it sent shivers down my spine.

I stopped and bent over to catch my breath. I spotted two cops in the alley by the next street. I suspected there were others along the sidewalk.

"You okay, Belle?"

"I'm fine. Hurry to the next post. Give the lieutenant-in-charge the message. Make sure to mention she should watch for boys coming over the wall. Go! I'll catch up."

While Janine ran to the street, I checked using my wrist-com's infrared. There were four cops near the corner, and no mech-cop. I leaned against the wall behind a utility shed.

What are you doing, Belle?

On my wrist-com's infrared, I made out several figures inside the warehouse. During my brief time with Morgan I'd grown comfortable around him. The thought of being with several boys had me on edge.

Janine reached the corner and talked with one of the cops. She pointed my way, and then down the alley toward Captain Chou. I tried the door to the warehouse. It opened. I pushed my way into total darkness.

THIRTY-ONE

Something struck me on the back of the head. I fell. In the dark, my fall seemed like slow motion. My senses played out details. Whatever had hit me smelled of dust, and oil. My body sought out targets as I clutched for something to hold onto. I collapsed onto the floor. My hand hit concrete and eased my knee down. Dust filled my sinuses along with the scent of fear, sweat, and musky odor I recalled from the arena.

In the dark, I kicked and punched, hit air. I scrambled to my feet and felt around.

Lights came on, a flash beam. I squinted at rows of empty warehouse shelves. Little Seth sat in the corner, as if he didn't have a care in the world. Next to him were three boys about his age. One cried. Beside them, Morgan sat against the wall, blood on his forehead, arms behind his back. Then I saw the gun, attached to a muscular arm: the boy I almost helped at the pharmacy.

"Hands where I can see them," the boy said. His dark eyes looked sad. They tugged at me as they had before. "Let the little one tie up your wrists. You're under arrest."

"Under whose authority?" I asked.

"Lieutenant Scarlatti."

Impossible. "You have no authority," I said, inching backward. "You're under arrest for escaping."

"I have the gun."

I looked for an opportunity to disarm the boy or reach my

209

pistol without him shooting me. "What happened?" I asked Morgan.

"Boy's name is Hank. This was all a setup to transfer Seth and catch you. I'm sorry. Most of the boys escaped the way they expected. Your cops are rounding them up—"

"Shut up." Hank pointed his gun at Morgan.

I moved to grab my gun. Hank aimed his at my head. "Would you rather I shot you?"

"That'll get you the death penalty."

"That's better than what waits for you. Now sit down and let the little boy tie you up."

"Why are you doing this?" I asked. "Why not help these boys escape?"

Hank backed up next to a support pillar and tried to use his wrist-com. He looked confused. I slipped mine into the pocket of my skorts and looked for a way to attack.

The back door creaked; Hank turned.

Janine!

Instincts fine-tuned by mech training took over. I kicked Hank's gun hand and rammed his wrist into the support pillar. He cried out and dropped his weapon but kicked out, caught my thigh. *Damn that hurts.*

Off balance, I spun into a kick. He grabbed my ankle and threw me onto the floor. As I fell, he looked up to see Janine holding her pistol. "I work for Captain Voss and Lieutenant Scarlatti," Hank said. "I've been trying to reach them. This girl was helping these boys escape."

Janine's eyes narrowed. "This girl is my sister." She pointed her gun at him.

His eyes grew wide. He rushed Janine and grabbed her gun wrist. I leaped to my feet and slammed my fist into his throat. Janine pulled free and fell back. He swung at me while he gasped for breath. I blocked, kicked, and swept his feet out from under him. He slammed onto the concrete floor. He got to his knees and came at me, as if his size would intimidate me. He was big, though not steroid-enhanced as Morgan had been in the arena.

Hank grabbed for my ankle. I jumped and kicked him in the face, connected with his forehead. He tumbled, rolled away, and lunged for Janine. She pointed the gun in his face and stared him down. He hesitated.

She looked paralyzed by shock or fear or both. I jumped him before she could shoot and bring every cop in the area. I tackled him to the concrete. He muscled his way on top. I slammed my fist into his ribs; something cracked. He screamed and grabbed my neck. I rammed my other fist into his throat and shoved him off me.

Gasping for air, he got behind me and grabbed my neck. I pulled away. Unable to release his grip, I rammed him in the groin with my heel and stomped on his instep. He pulled away. I rammed his knee, got behind him, and grabbed him in a chokehold.

"Do you really want to do this?" I asked. I glanced at Morgan who looked concerned ... and amused.

Hank pushed up and tried to roll over on top of me.

I pulled away and got to my feet. "Before you attempt round two, let me warn you. I have mech training. I fought in the arena against stronger and better fighters than you. I won the last mech tournament."

He attacked. I moved aside, swept his feet from under him, and dropped him face-first onto the concrete floor. Then I wedged his arms under an empty shelving rack. "Anyone have some rope?"

"Just kill me," Hank moaned. "Don't let them take me prisoner."

The littlest boy, sporting a tuft of sandy hair, brought rope. Janine aimed her gun at the boys along the wall but glared at me while I bound Hank's wrists. After I finished, I took her wrist and drew a figure 8: *later*.

I tightened the rope on Hank's wrists and ankles, and pulled him into a sitting position against the wall next to Morgan. Then I checked to make sure my electronic jammer worked and remained out of sight.

Janine removed her contacts and put them into their case. Then she looked up at me, her head cocked. "We're going to arrest these boys, aren't we?"

I dabbed the blood on Morgan's forehead. "Are you okay?" I began to untie the rope around his wrists.

"You can't untie him," Janine whispered, holding up her gun. "He's dangerous. He almost killed you—"

"Hush." I finished freeing Morgan's wrists and stepped back. The other boys sat in the corner next to Seth, who stared at the floor.

"What are you thinking, Belle?" Janine whispered.

"That you shouldn't be here."

"Yeah," Hank said. "Guess she forgot to tell you she's helping those boys."

When Morgan stood up, he towered over Janine. She pointed her gun up at him. "Is that true?"

He held his hands out at his sides. "Why does Annabelle call you Babe?"

Janine kept her eyes on me. "Belle?" She returned her attention and the gun toward Morgan. "I'm her baby sister. When we were little, that was her name for me."

Morgan smiled. "The boy in the corner is my brother, Seth. They were hurting him."

I approached Hank and activated the recorder on my wrist-com. "What shall we do with you?"

"You should have killed me," he said as he tried to wiggle free of my knots.

"No, thanks."

"When Captain Voss and Lieutenant Scarlatti get here, you'll wish you had."

"You admit they paid you to entrap boys, like at the pharmacy." I wanted his confession, though it wouldn't be admissible in court.

Hank squirmed, tightened his muscles, and relaxed. He hung his head. "They promised to leave my family alone if I helped. After we catch the Underground Railroad—you—they'll let me go."

"Go where? The Outland? People over there will know what you did."

"They'll destroy your family for helping those boys," Hank said. The defiance in his voice sounded shaky.

"What I do to you … that depends on whether you tell me everything you know. You're not geek material, so you didn't belong at the Institute, did you?"

"No."

"Who was your main contact, Voss or Scarlatti?"

"Scarlatti." Hank's dark eyes grew sadder with each question.

"She sent you to the pharmacy to trap me?"

He nodded.

"Why?"

"She said you let that boy go in the arena. She said you'd try to help me escape. If I trapped you, she'd let me go to the Outland with my dad."

"Don't believe that," Morgan said. "He's a professional spy for Lieutenant Scarlatti."

"Who else worked with you?" I asked.

"I work alone, less chance for mistakes," Hank said. "Scarlatti mentioned a Captain Voss a few times. I saw her with a big woman who might be your captain. She was with another cop. I didn't hear her name." He swallowed hard before continuing. "They used me. They took my mom, and said I'd never see her or my dad again unless I helped."

I hated how he was playing on my sympathy. I could attest that they would never let him see his parents again.

"Scarlatti said you helped the Underground Railroad," Hank said.

Janine glared at me. I cupped my hands in a figure 8 and stared back.

"She said they'd flush out the Underground tonight," he said.

Morgan pulled the other boys to their feet. "We need to go."

I expected her to shout for help, but Janine hovered nearby with her pistol, looking confused and scared.

"What was your plan?" I asked Hank.

"Get Seth to escape, since he was Morgan's brother," Hank said. "Use the old tunnel to the hardware store. In the dark, Seth brought us here instead."

"That explains why they didn't seal the tunnel," I said. Also why Voss and Scarlatti wanted me outside the hardware store.

"We have to go." Morgan pulled his brother toward the back door.

Janine stood between Morgan and me. I could almost see her puzzler sorting things out.

She said, "Belle, unless you want to share separate cells in some far-off prison, we need to arrest these boys."

I stood over Hank, feeling sorry for him. I couldn't afford pity right now. "Where were they taking Seth?"

"I don't know."

I kicked his foot. "Pay attention. You don't have many friends."

"Neither do you."

Seth pulled away from his brother. He took my right hand with his left and looked up at me. His soft brown eyes were those of a child much younger than his age, yet filled with warmth that surprised me. I'd assumed he was a high-functioning autistic like other Institute boys, but now I wasn't so sure. He pulled me away from Hank and clasped his right hand to mine, dropped something smooth and hard into my hand, and let go.

He pointed to Hank and said in a mechanical monotone, "He bad, very bad. Lock him up."

I clutched two chips in my hand; one was labeled "SAM," the other "AMS." Annabelle Montgomery Scott.

My breath caught. Could this be? I tucked the chips into an inner pocket of my skorts and smiled at him. "Thanks, Seth. You're a very brave and clever boy."

He stared at the floor and whispered, "Hank help Scarlatti find assassin to kill your mom, twice." Seth nodded toward my pocket.

"But the pulse—"

"Shielded," Seth said. "Scarlatti got Hank to escape with me. They want to take me to Biogenetech Informatics Hospital south of river. Scarlatti tried to kill Commander Hernandez." He glanced at Janine and smiled. "You pretty." He headed for the door.

<∞>

"What do we do with Hank?" I asked Morgan. "Can you take him with you?"

He closed his eyes, which sagged with deep circles. "Get us across the alley. I'll take him. If he causes trouble we'll castrate him, cut out his tongue, and then do some real damage."

I didn't think Morgan would do that. I untied the rope around Hank's ankles and pulled him to his feet. I was tempted to leave him for Scarlatti, but he knew too much.

"After the trouble you've caused, I should kill you," I said to Hank. "Instead, I'll leave you with this. You might think you're doing this for your family, but everyone you hurt is someone's parent, child, sibling, or loved one."

"You won't get away with helping them."

"If I don't, you won't live to see that day. Just think. You'll get to see the Outland."

Morgan put the rope around Hank's neck and turned out the flashlight.

Janine grabbed my hand, traced a frantic 8, and pulled me out the back door. "We have to arrest them," she whispered. "We have to. Please."

"If we do, Hank will say I helped them escape. Voss will send me away, or worse. I wish you hadn't seen this. I never wanted you involved."

"If you're involved, so am I. I-I don't know you, Belle."

"Focus on making sure no one is in the alley, so we can be done with this."

When Janine turned to scan the alley, I fished out my wristcom. Still no connection. In infrared, I saw the boys behind us, no one to the right, or around the corner. To the left, I saw a single cop. "You'll need to distract her."

"Belle? We need to—"

"The older boy is Morgan, the one I fought in the arena. He saved my life. I owe him. He begged me to help his brother. I'd do anything to free *you* from such a prison."

"He's a boy," Janine said. "They're dangerous."

"No more than I'd be under the circumstances. He's had plenty of chances to hurt me. He hasn't. I can't do to him what I wouldn't allow anyone to do to you. Now go, before that cop hears or sees something and alerts others."

I waited until the cop at the corner looked away, and then pushed Janine toward her. I remained in the shadows, and prayed Janine didn't develop pangs of conscience, or convince herself she could help me by turning the boys in.

I scanned the buildings across from the warehouse, down the alley, and beside the warehouse. The only heat signatures I saw were Janine, the cop, and the boys.

After Janine drew the cop's attention away, I opened the door. Seth came out first, with black cloth covering the left side of his body. He led the three younger boys, who looked like ducklings waddling after their mother. Like he was the one they looked up to, the one who would protect them and keep them safe. He was only 14. How could I ever turn these boys in?

The four boys climbed into the back of the garbage truck. *Yuck.* Morgan pulled Hank outside. "You cause any trouble, and this knife will rearrange your spine." He winked at me and pushed Hank across the alley.

I followed. Janine stared my way. In the reflection of a

flashlight, I saw questions in her expression, her eyes. She would pummel me with those later.

"They'll check the back of the truck," I said to Morgan.

"We've got that covered," he replied. "We'll be behind the shovel."

He helped Hank up into the truck and climbed in after him. He was gone several minutes, during which I scanned the alley in infrared. When she didn't hear back, Scarlatti would send more runners.

I looked toward Janine. I needed to go, but I lingered for Morgan.

He returned. "He's secured and gagged. He shouldn't cause any more problems tonight. Thanks for everything."

"I … I wish I could go with you."

"No, you don't. It's no good for you over there. Besides, you have Voss to deal with. Guard that chip Seth gave you. It should have all you need to take her down."

"I know it sounds school-girlish," I said, "but I've always wanted to see the Outland, the Great Smoky Mountains."

"Your sister is already angry with me. She looks up to you. Otherwise, this place would be swarming with cops. If you don't return, she might change her mind."

"She's confused."

"Aren't we all? I've never met anyone like you. Now go, before I change my mind, before you get caught. Thank your mom for the truck."

"Mom? You involved her?"

"I am sorry." Morgan patted my shoulder and withdrew. "Seth said he found something on your birth mother. Good luck. Now go."

He'd just reminded me of a major reason I couldn't go with him, no matter how much I wanted to. "Will I ever see you again?"

"Unlikely. But you'll be in my dreams and prayers, and who knows?"

Silence fell between us. And was there really anything more to say? I watched as Morgan climbed into the truck, into darkness.

THIRTY-TWO

I waited to leave the garbage truck until Janine had the cop looking the other way. Infrared showed two other cops walking along the side of the warehouse. I hurried to the warehouse door and ran toward Janine. Before I reached her, I used my wrist-com to check behind me. The two cops approached the corner as I reached Janine.

"Where have you been?" I asked Janine. I cupped my hands in a figure 8 to signal for her to go with this.

"You said to meet here," Janine said.

"Is there a problem?" the sergeant she was talking to asked.

"Boys escaped. I'm sorry I wasn't clear, Janine. Have you passed on the message?"

Janine nodded.

"Then we have to go see Captain Chou." I grabbed her hand and pulled her down the next alley.

I wanted to look back to check on what those cops in the alley were doing. They had to be near the garbage truck. I ached to see Morgan once more before he was gone for good, but I couldn't put Janine in any more danger.

"I can't believe you did that," she whispered. "What's gotten into you? Do you like that boy?"

"No! I feel bad for how they treated his brother."

"Do you know how many laws you've broken?"

"It's wrong what the Institute does to those boys. Let it go. Someday we'll talk about it."

"I want to understand. Why did we just put our lives in jeopardy?" Janine's voice sounded tentative and shaky.

"Not now. Do this for me, and for Mom. Don't give her more heartache by turning me in."

Janine grabbed my arm and pulled me to a stop. "Every thought compels me to turn them in, but my heart … it's breaking. I-I don't understand."

Mine ached as well, to tell her about my adoption and getting closer to finding my birth mother. I couldn't. I needed her to believe in our blood connection so she wouldn't turn me in.

"We have to go, Janine. We have things to do. It's a dangerous night." I tugged her along.

She pulled back. "How deep have you gotten yourself?"

"I don't have time to explain. My assignment is very deep. I need you to trust me."

"Did it involve helping those boys?"

"No," I said.

"I didn't think so. I'm drowning, Belle."

I grabbed hold of her. "You're strong, Babe, stronger than me. Sam tried to tell me that and I didn't listen. You can do this. Just follow my lead." I pulled her at a jog down the alley.

At the next street, Captain Chou talked with the lieutenant-in-charge. She paused, held her flashlight beam on me, and looked me over. It made me wonder if I had bloodstains from fighting Hank. My hair had to be a mess. I straightened my blouse.

"Do you have word from Captain Voss?" Chou asked.

I handed her the written message and gave her the verbal one about managing without electronic aids. "It sounds as if boys have broken out," I said. "It's hard to tell in the dark."

"We'll have floodlights soon. Then we'll canvas the area."

"Do you have any message for me to run back?"

"Tell Captain Voss we alerted Commander Hernandez to send backup," Captain Chou said.

I nodded and rushed away before Chou opened the written message. I was afraid it might read, "Arrest that girl."

"What if those boys hurt someone?" Janine asked while we ran along the alley on the west side of the Institute. "That will be on our heads."

"Come on, Janine. Do the little ones look like a threat?"

"No, but the big one gave you trouble in the arena."

I laughed. "Didn't you see him get me in a terminal chokehold? He let me live."

"He did? I thought you reversed on him."

"His grip was too strong."

Janine ran close to me in the dark, bumping me now and then, as if to reassure herself she wasn't alone.

We paused at each street crossing to relay Scarlatti's message to the lieutenant-in-charge, and moved on. As we ran along the southern alley, my stomach tightened. I hadn't thought through what to do about Voss. I had Seth's chips, and no way to read them. I couldn't let them fall into the wrong hands.

At the last street before Scarlatti's post, I saw a figure dart out of the shadows, a profile I recognized before it disappeared. *Mom? Get as far from here as you can.*

I took Janine to the right, away from the Institute, in the direction of the shadow, and streetlights. I stopped when we came upon a black swarm scattered in the middle of the street. It looked like an ant colony, but none of the swarm-bots moved. The pulse must have taken them out.

"What now?" Janine asked.

<∞>

Out of breath, Scarlatti found Captain Voss in a makeshift office in the back of a van, three blocks from the Institute. It had been a chaotic night. Nothing had gone according to plan. That would take a lot of explaining later, but there were still things she needed to do.

The captain looked up and scowled, which did not improve the appearance of her bloated face. "Where the hell have you been? Do you know how hard it was to find a vehicle with lights? I haven't had a good cup of coffee since the lights went out."

Scarlatti shook her head and wished she had real coffee. There was no point stopping the monologue. The captain would only restart her rant, from the beginning.

"While you were partying, we caught 89 boys. Your mech friends caught another 41. That wasn't supposed to happen. We still have no sign of the boy. Where did all those animals come from? Hank was only supposed to bring the one. Director Devotte is furious. She blames us for this fiasco. What tools did you give Hank?"

"The key-chip to the stairwells and basement. That's all."

"Well, it's done," Captain Voss said. "The director reported 140 boys escaped. That means 10 are still on the loose. This was supposed to be a straightforward police matter. You assured me you had it under control. Now we have to share glory with the mechs. Do you know what you've done?"

"I've caught the boy and four others," Scarlatti said.

The captain took a deep breath and smiled. "No kidding. Where?" She stood up, banged her head on the van's roof and dropped down, rocking the vehicle.

Scarlatti continued, "Three blocks up. Scandia and Montrose will transport them. Not only that, Hank confirmed that Annabelle and her sister helped them escape. We finally got her."

Voss sat in stony silence for a moment. "We have her, really? Where is she?"

Scarlatti sighed. "I don't know. I had to secure the boys first. We'll find her. Don't worry. She can't go far. Now that we've connected her mother with Commander Hernandez, the only link we're missing is how to connect her mother to the Underground Railroad, and to this escape."

"Then we can eliminate the mother, the daughter, and Commander Hernandez. How—?"

"Hank might be able to make that connection, but he wants assurances that he and his dad can go to the Outland."

"Promise him anything." Voss waved her hand to dismiss Scarlatti.

THIRTY-THREE

I was tempted to hunt for Mom, to warn her. But I couldn't be sure no one was following. I pointed toward the Institute, now lit by floodlights. Frightened boys sat in small groups along the curb. Cops scurried back and forth, watching the boys or running messages. No cops stood near the corner of the street and alley.

"We should help." Janine tugged at my arm.

"We are. Follow my lead and forget what happened back there." I headed away from the Institute.

"How can I? None of it makes any sense, Belle. I can't believe—"

"Don't say it."

"When Scarlatti asks why it took so long—"

"Leave that to me." I turned at the next street, spotted a boy hiding in the bushes, and broke into a jog. I pulled Janine along. "We should get back before Scarlatti gets too suspicious."

"What about Sam?" Janine stopped. "Belle, what if she finds out?"

"I'll handle her." That gave me an idea.

"My audio implant doesn't work."

"Can you trust me?" I asked.

Janine shrugged, and then nodded.

"Put your contacts in and follow my lead."

After she had her contacts in, I turned off the jamming device and ran down the street parallel to the Institute. We crossed the next street and entered an alley. I slipped the jammer into a Dumpster and pushed Janine to keep up.

We were in the lit zone, on the city-grid. I stopped, pulled out my wrist-com and froze. News vids from shaky swarms showed the police barricade around the Institute. The swarm crossed the line and scanned police positions. Then the feed went to black. I realized I was watching the feeds prior to the blackout.

"And that's all we have until just a moment ago," the reporter said. "This just in, our brave police have captured most of the boys."

"The blast fried my wrist-com," Janine said.

"For some reason mine works," I said. "Now quiet." I made the call.

"Annabelle, what's going on out there?" Sam asked.

"The blast took out communications. My wrist-com works, just not in the blackout zone."

"Where are you?" Sam asked.

"I'm at the southeast corner of the Institute, heading east on foot. I need your help. Voss was right about the boys escaping through the hardware store. She knew in advance when and where."

"As we suspected."

"There's more," I said. "She arranged this escape and the last one, so she could kidnap boys to deliver them to that secure facility. This is all a cover so no one asks questions."

"Except you."

"She had a boy working as a snitch. He—" I caught myself before divulging too much. "He tried to trap me a few nights ago at the pharmacy. Voss thought I would let him go, but I arrested him. Voss got the assassins to attack my mom."

"I suppose you have evidence this time."

"I do."

"Find Dara," Sam said. "She's three blocks east of Scarlatti. I'm deputizing you to help on this assignment."

"And Janine," I said, her ear next to mine.

There was a pause on the line. "Is she with you?"

"Yes. I figured out that you were training her to assist me."

Sam sighed. "I suppose you'd best work together, then, before you get yourselves tangled in your underwear. Janine has proven herself very resourceful."

Janine started to reply, no doubt to thank the commander. I gave her a figure 8 and smiled. What I'd done went against everything Janine was taught to believe in.

I ended the connection and headed east. At the next street, a garbage truck rolled by. I recognized the markings as the one Morgan was in. I smiled and kept going. *Way to go.*

We met Dara in a well-lit alley behind an old residential street. I recognized her by the oversized mech-helmet with a red sword painted on. She removed her helmet. There were Dumpsters up and down the alley, but no garbage trucks, not at this time of night. Well, there was one.

"Sam says she deputized you for a special assignment." Dara's face made it look like a question.

"Captain Voss is up to her eyeballs in corruption," I said. "We need to confront her with authority outside working for her. I don't know what cops I can count on."

"I see you brought your little sister." Dara winked at Janine.

Janine stood shoulder-to-shoulder with me, as if to say she wasn't intimidated. I felt her tremble.

"Give me one good reason why I should stick my neck out when you washed out of the program," Dara said.

"You mean aside from Sam asking you to," I said.

"Ordering, you mean." Dara didn't like taking orders, even in the mechs.

"I'll give you the arrest. I just want Voss to pay for what she's done."

Dara nodded, took off her glove, and shook my hand. "Pity you're out of the program. We could have had some real fun together."

A green armored mech-vehicle pulled up. Sam climbed out of the back. Dressed in her navy blues, she looked small next to the massive Dara in mech-gear. Two black-shielded mechs stood guard at the other end of the alley.

"Captain Voss and Scarlatti are holed up in a van outside a drugstore on the corner," Sam said. "I need eyes and ears on them, but they're being tight-lipped. Why don't you step into my office?" Sam moved aside to let Janine and me in.

The van was more spacious inside than outward appearances would indicate. Two pairs of cushioned seats faced each other with a table between. Embedded in the table were screen displays that showed the surrounding area. Eight green dots glowed on the table: Dara, the two mechs down the alley, another group of three mechs, Janine, and me. So, Sam *had* been able to track my movements after the pulse.

I sat facing backward. Janine sat next to me. The dots moved as we did. Sam closed the door and sat across from us. She brought up a map of the area on the tabletop. I saw the van Sam had mentioned. Red dots scattered around the southeast corner of the Institute: the boys. The pulse hadn't blinded Sam *or* the implants. What I didn't see were dots for Morgan, Seth, and the other boys. Morgan's aluminum shields must have blocked their signals.

"Before we start, roll up your sleeves," Sam said. She pulled out a small version of her injector gun.

Janine followed orders. I took my time. "What are you giving us this time?"

Sam's eyes narrowed. "I've tracked your movements, young lady. The pulse knocked out electronics, but not the tiny implants, except for Janine's and yours. Your implants went dark the moment you left your post at the hardware store until you returned to this end of the Institute."

"I—"

"Save it. I have new implants that won't be so easy to mask."

Janine's body stiffened. She grabbed my hand and traced a figure 8.

Sam pulled up my sleeve and injected something into my arm. My pride hurt more than my arm. I felt invaded by her tiny nano-particles. She injected Janine. The gravity of what Sam said stifled my willingness to protest what she was doing to Janine.

"I was gathering information on Voss and Scarlatti," I said.

"Good, because right now we have a big fat goose-egg." Sam handed Janine and me new contacts cases. "Put these on. Like your tracking chips and auditory implants, your contacts were designed not to be damaged by an electric pulse. We designed them at very low voltage, with shields for just such an occasion, to protect our warriors from brain damage."

"I don't understand," I said. "I thought tonight's mission was over."

Sam put her injector into its case and dropped it into a black bag next to her. Then she pointed to the red dots on the map. "All but ten of the boys were caught in this area: some by us, most by your cops. Five escaped south." She pointed to red dots moving away from the Institute, in the same direction I'd imagined spotting Mom.

I clenched my fists under the table. Janine placed her hand on top of mine. If ever I doubted Mom was part of the Underground Railroad, those illusions vanished as three green dots surrounded the red ones. I needed to create a diversion so she could get away, but how? Sam wasn't directing this capture.

"Another five boys escaped the Institute and vanished off the tracking system."

"Dead?" I offered.

"The tracking devices don't require a live subject."

Glad to know I'm a live subject. "Shielded?"

"Outside help," Sam said. "They didn't get far."

I forced breath into my lungs and tried not to show my anguish. *Mom?*

"You've caught them all," Janine said with nervous enthusiasm. She clutched my fist.

"These five masked their tracking devices, escaped from the Institute, and hid in a garbage truck, if you can believe that. The truck shouldn't have been there. Lieutenant Scarlatti is all giddy because Scandia and Montrose found them."

I felt as if punched in the stomach. I placed my hand on Janine's arm to keep her quiet, and took a deep breath. "We need to catch Voss and Scarlatti delivering the boys."

"That brings us to the rest of tonight's mission," Sam said, "and why I deputized you. On the surface, Voss and Scarlatti are heroes for capturing escaped boys. We both know they orchestrated this to capture a particular boy, Seth McDermott, brother to the boy you fought in the arena. They're transporting him to the facility you looked at earlier, along with other boys they've captured."

"For genetic experiments," I said.

"You've done your homework."

Janine studied me with a mixture of suspicion and curiosity.

"They've created new gene-altering therapies," I said. "They tested these procedures on differentiated stem cells, and on lab animals. The last testing stage uses the boys as human guinea pigs—" I caught myself. *Don't be hasty. Sam has an interest here.*

Sam sat back, her face stony blank as I've been told mine got when I held secrets. She said, "We'll hold some of the boys below

225

the arena, until we can find more secure permanent quarters."

I wanted to suggest driving them to the border, but this chat was already taking too long if I was to find a way to help Morgan and Mom.

"It'll give me time to interrogate them," Sam said, "until Devotte gets an injunction to return them to her custody. The cops will hold the rest, except for the five boys Scarlatti captured. That's where your new mission comes in. I want you to go back to the facility across the river and wait until I can arrange enough resources."

I squirmed in my seat, while trying to keep anxiety out of my face. "What do you want me to do?"

"We don't have time to discuss details, many of which are not final. Your mission is simple. Scout the area. Don't get caught. I want you to verify Scarlatti and friends are there with the boys. Let me know who else is there. Can you do that?"

"I stand ready to deliver." *And to get out of here.*

"Before you go … you said you had hard evidence."

I hesitated. "Can I speak to you alone?" I tracked a figure 8 on Janine's wrist and nodded for her to leave. Her face twisted into a tortured pout.

"If you think that's necessary." Sam reached for the door. "Still protecting your baby sister?"

Janine hesitated, glared at me, and climbed out of the vehicle.

After she closed the door, I fished out the chip with "SAM" written on it.

"What was that all about?" Sam asked.

I didn't want to give Sam the chip, my only leverage. I didn't want to help the mechs, and yet, I couldn't risk it falling into Voss' hands. I made sure it was the correct chip, and placed it on the table. "This should have enough evidence to convict Captain Voss and Lieutenant Scarlatti."

Sam's eyes narrowed with the question: *Where and how did you get this while I was watching?* All she said was, "You have been busy."

"Good police work." I smiled. *You have no idea, or do you?* "You should find logs of activities. Voss and Scarlatti arranged the escapes, stole government funds, and more. This goes higher, much higher."

"Don't go there." Sam left the chip on the table. "I suspect that's a blind alley."

"With something this big, Governor Battani and Adrianne Picard have to be involved."

"You'd better have rock-solid proof before you go down that road, something more substantial than your gut feel."

"They were both at Battani's mansion," I said. "Picard was involved with the death of that boy."

"Or she covered for someone."

"In exchange for digging this up, I need a favor."

Sam leaned forward. "We're not negotiating, soldier. You're on a mission."

"I'm not withholding evidence, Sam. I ask—"

"For masking your implant? For going off the grid the moment the boy you once helped tried to free his brother? Your implant works fine. Shall I prove that to you?"

I shook my head and forced steady breaths. "You didn't give me much to work with, Commander. I did well in spite of that." I pointed to the chip. "You said to dig deep."

"What favor do you want?"

"I don't know. I was hoping to earn some goodwill."

Sam laughed. "You're much too young to talk like that." She picked up the chip and examined it. "Let me see what you've got." She pulled out a portable chip-reader.

THIRTY-FOUR

Sam said nothing about Mom, as she deputized Janine and me. I took those together as a good omen.

I didn't like the idea of Janine joining me on this mission. She had already seen too much. I couldn't be sure she'd go along with another escape under Sam's eyes. For that reason, I wished Morgan were in my head so he could help me figure out what to do. All this for a boy I didn't know and would never see again. What did that say about me?

Janine and I rode on separate cycles Sam provided, with advanced-technology helmets to conceal our identities and provide night/infrared vision. Under glaring floodlights, police trucks took boys away from the corner of the Institute. Armored mech-vehicles picked up other boys to take to the arena. Most of the boys looked to be around Seth's age. None looked threatening. If only the public could see what I saw. What then? *People believe what reinforces their deeply held beliefs. Seeing does not alter that.*

The moment Janine and I crossed the river to the south side, we left the city lights behind. The night sky grew darker as we rounded hills that blotted out any evidence of Knoxville behind us. It had been only two nights ago that I first stumbled upon this facility tucked between hills on a winding country road.

"The governor and Picard have to know about this place," I said into my helmet.

"You need to concentrate tonight," Sam said. "Don't try to connect dots that aren't there."

"If I'm right—"

"Enough chatter. I tracked the garbage truck across the bridge onto the road you're on. Then the signal died."

"Satellite blackout?" I said. "That proves—"

"Keep your eyes sharp. They'll have surveillance. When you get close to the property, hide the cycles and proceed on foot."

We reached the crest of ridge, with the glow of lights ahead. We hid the cycles on the left side of the road and climbed a hill on the right, guided by the helmet's night-vision. Anyone who found the cycles might check the other side first.

Janine followed close behind me in silence. She gave off a glow of excitement and fear as a halo in my helmet's infrared. I stopped now and then to listen, praying Mom wasn't nearby, trying to help these boys. This was a dangerous game, and yet not a game. I needed to help Morgan in a way I had never felt before toward anyone except Janine.

Curious about whether reporter cam-swarms were tracking me, I checked my wrist-com. The newsfeeds looped the time before the pulse and then the roundup after, with praise for the police effort in catching all the boys. My heart sank. There had to be public cams showing what happened, but the government could screen all communication through the towers and confiscate disharmonious messages.

When we reached the crest of the hill, close to where I'd been before, Janine stopped me and drew a figure 8. Then she traced out on my back: "We're not helping them again. If they escape, I have to arrest them to protect R family."

"Are you in position yet?" Sam asked. Her voice resonated in my brain.

"There's concertina wire," I said. "We have to be careful."

I reached the spot above the wire and recalled cutting my finger the other night, but that was at the warehouse. "Won't they have infrared sensors?" I looked for signs of flashing red lights.

"Stay outside the outer barrier and you'll be fine," Sam said. "What do you see?"

"It's hard to see much of anything in the dark," I stepped up the night-vision contrast.

"Concentrate on the buildings."

Faint moonlight reflected off solar panels atop two well-lit six-story buildings connected by a three-story building. Low-intensity floodlights shone against darkened windows and outward toward a ten-foot wall topped with shiny wire. Nearer to us, in shadows, was a ten-foot chain-link fence, topped with wire. Coils of concertina wire also circled the side of the hill. Below, a second wire barrier glistened in moonlight.

"They don't want anyone sneaking in." I played with a blend of regular, night, and infrared sensors. "Why doesn't this show up on GPS maps?"

"You know the answer," Sam said.

"Then the governor has to be involved."

"Drop it, and focus on scoping out the facility for me."

"The government has to be involved in altering satellite mapping and screening reports on the captures."

"I said drop it."

I scanned to the right. Alongside the compound, two windmills lazily rotated. "Why put windmills where the hills block the wind and solar panels where there's no morning or afternoon sun?"

"Good question," Sam said. "Look in infrared. Tell me what you see. Wind and solar can't supply enough energy for this facility."

"They're for show, in case someone stumbles onto this place."

Sam didn't answer.

In sharp infrared, the back of the compound lit up like the sun. I had to blink and dial down the intensity. "Is that nuclear?"

"That's my guess," Sam said.

"See, it has to be government—"

"Enough chatter."

Using infrared, I scanned the buildings floor by floor, looking for Morgan and Seth. I had no plan. Not that mine ever worked. There were few images on the upper three floors of the towers, and no hint of gender. There were no images on the second or third floors of the towers or the connecting middle section. No images appeared in front of the buildings, in the cars or utility trucks. Then I saw the garbage truck, in shadows along the left side of the building. I zoomed in and turned up infrared magnification.

Five images remained inside the garbage truck. A large image stood behind the truck, Hank. Four other images stood nearby. A fifth approached. "Are you getting this, Sam?"

"Zoom and play with the focus so we can see their faces."

"We can do that?" I fiddled with controls until individual faces filled my screen. I had to hold my head steady. At this magnification, the vibrating images gave me nausea. "That's Hank talking to Scarlatti," I said.

I turned to look at the faces inside the truck. Seth sat impassive in the corner, surrounded by three little boys, as if none of this fazed him. Morgan crouched, ready to pounce.

Don't do it.

I wanted to use this high-resolution infrared to scan the hills for Mom. I couldn't betray her. I returned my attention to outside the truck as Scandia and Montrose pulled Morgan out. "They're moving the boys inside," I said. "It looks like the emergency-room entrance to our hospital."

"It's a hospital of sorts," Sam said. "Think of the supplies they've brought in."

I scanned the first floor in infrared. The left side, the hospital side, had dozens of images prone on beds. Few walked around. "Why take the boys to a hospital?"

"That's what I'd like to know."

The right side of the complex had a few heat signatures standing by what might have been workstations. I wished infrared could show the rest of the inside. The thought of losing more privacy sent chills up my spine.

"I don't see enough people for all those supplies, Sam."

"Try belowground."

I scanned the basement. The helmet's sensors weren't strong enough to penetrate that much earth and concrete—or whatever else shielded this facility's activities. "I need a closer look."

"Wait."

"For what? For them to—" I couldn't finish my sentence. This was what Morgan had feared.

"I'm trying to assemble the right players," Sam said. "Stay put. Give me eyes on what's happening."

So she could transfer Morgan back to the arena. *No way.*

While scanning the emergency-room area, I took Janine's hand and gave her the figure 8. I wrote on her back, "I need you to hold something for me. Don't let anyone know, including Sam."

I handed Janine the second chip. "If anything happens to me …" I couldn't finish the words. I bit back tears over my birth mother and keeping this from Janine.

"Don't do anything," Janine wrote.

"Stay here and watch my back," I said to her. "I'm going to get a better look." I started downhill. With night-vision, I could just make out the coils of concertina wire.

"Soldier, I told you to stay put. I don't have jurisdiction here."

"Cops do." I kept moving. I had to give Morgan and his brother a chance.

There was silence on the other end.

I stopped, listened, and didn't hear Janine. I moved farther down. The brush was thick. In the dark, I climbed over a log and came face-to-face with the wire. I backed up, moved around, and reached the bottom of the hill. In night-vision, the road stretched back toward Knoxville. Faint red lights flashed to my right. Infrared images popped up from both sides of the road.

"Get out of there," Sam said.

"Too late," I replied. Flashlight beams shone all around. There was no way to climb up. If I did, they would grab Janine. "You wanted to see inside the facility. Now you'll get your chance."

"Show yourself," a terse voice said. "Before we shoot."

I removed my helmet and hid it among the bushes.

"Submit," Sam said. "Say nothing. I'll do what I can to get you out."

"I'm sorry, Sam. Keep Janine safe."

"Stay alive."

THIRTY-FIVE

Perhaps I'd let myself get spoiled. When Captain Voss arrested me for fighting Dara—long story—they didn't get me to lockup before Sam bailed me out with an offer to join the Mech Corps.

Four gray-uniformed guards approached from different sides and surrounded me. Each shined a light in my eyes, blinding me. I tensed, imagining myself in the arena fighting three boys at once. I had mech-gear back then.

"Don't fight," Sam said, anticipating my thoughts.

I can take them.

"Snipers have trained their weapons on you," Sam said in a firm yet not angry tone. "This is no time for heroics."

One of the gray guards grabbed my right arm. "Come with us."

Another guard grabbed my left arm and pulled me forward. When I resisted, they carried me. In the glow of flash beams, I looked for the telltale glint of cam-swarms, but didn't see any. I also didn't hear their mosquito-like buzz: no mobile cams. The guards marched me toward the hospital end of the facility. There would be no public display of my disobedience.

I considered using my mech training to break free, grab my cycle, and escape toward home, but the second cycle would lead them to Janine. If she stayed low, they might think I was alone. Then she could give Sam the eyes and ears she needed.

I didn't fight them because I wanted to see inside this facility. Maybe I could help Morgan, lend him my cycle, and ride home with Janine.

Without my night or infrared vision, the asphalt road was dark, lit now and then by two flashlights scanning the sides, and distant floodlights around the facility. My four companions wore night-vision infrared goggles.

We reached the emergency-room entrance. A sign above the door read "BGTI—Biogenetech Informatics."

"I see it," Sam said. "Stay calm. Don't talk. When they scan you, close your eyes so your lenses won't transmit."

Fighting my impulse to flee and make things worse, I glanced at the garbage truck. No one was outside. They must have taken the boys in already. I held that shot for Sam, then scanned the well-lit area nearby. There was a loading dock toward the back of the building. Little nodes protruded from the roof and the overhang that protected the entrance. Cams, no doubt.

A gray-uniformed guard with tight-cropped black hair frisked me from neck to ankle, poking and prodding for hiding places. I closed my eyes. She found my stun gun and pistol. After she relieved me of weapons, the guard restraining me shoved me toward the entrance. "Keep moving," a terse voice said.

I glanced back but offered no resistance. The dark-haired woman with olive complexion bore the insignia "BGTI" on her gray uniform jacket, along with what looked like captain's bars.

"That's Antonia Rossi," Sam said. "Don't irritate her. She's an intense fighter with a short fuse. She tried out for the Mech Corps; didn't make it to the first tournament due to disciplinary issues. If you think Dara has a temper, this one is worse. Be careful."

I smiled and moved through the emergency-room lobby. It looked like any Knoxville hospital, except it had no patients. I looked around for Sam's benefit, and for possible escape routes. I was inside two barriers of concertina wire, a chain-link fence, and a stone wall. I had no idea what other security they had, and I was on my own.

Lights brightened as we crossed the empty lobby, past the vacant emergency-room counter. Long beige corridors stretched to the right and left. Rossi pushed me forward, into a small room that looked like our station's interrogation cell, with cams and a full-wall mirror.

"Wait here," Rossi said, as if I had any choice. She slammed the door.

The full weight of my situation settled in when the door's lock clicked. Cams and the observer behind the mirror, could watch me. *Morgan, where are you? How do I find you? How do I help?*

I heard voices other than Sam's. I leaned against the door. The voices grew sharper, as if a speaker were next to my ear.

"Why bring her here?" Voss' high-pitched, squeaky voice.

"We need to find out what she knows," Rossi said, "and who she's working with."

"You said you wanted to catch her red-handed," Director Devotte said. "Let's finish this so we can deal with the boys."

"Move away from the door," Sam said in a whisper.

I rolled away and stared at the mirror, wondering who else was here. My knees shook, ready to collapse. *Hold it together. You're a mech-warrior.* Not quite.

The door opened. In marched Voss, Scarlatti, Rossi, and Director Devotte. I suspected Scandia and Montrose were with the boys, or behind the mirror. The only ones missing were Governor Battani and her friend, the mega-entrepreneur Adrianne Picard.

I backed up to the wall, took a deep breath, and tried to hold my face stony-blank. "You caught all the boys."

"I said be quiet," Sam yelled into my head.

I winced and scanned the faces for Sam's benefit. Voss' round face sagged with worry. Director Devotte drummed her fingers on the table, no doubt eager to return to her Institute after another embarrassing night of escapes. Rossi stood across the room, waiting.

Scarlatti looked annoyed to have to deal with her useless partner again. I expected her to say something like, "Aren't you dead yet?" Instead, she said, "You're under arrest for aiding the escape of boys from the Institute and interfering with police matters."

"I wasn't aware this was a police hospital," I said.

Sam's voice blasted into my skull. "Are you incapable of shutting up?"

"You think this is a joke?" Scarlatti said.

Director Devotte held out the palm of her hand. "Enough! A blast like that required outside help. So did the coordination." She turned to me. "Who did you tell about the stakeout?"

I clenched my fists in my pockets. "I didn't tell anyone." I didn't have to, with Morgan and Sam in my head.

"You're hopeless," Sam said. "I can't help you if you won't help yourself."

"One of the boys you helped told us everything," Scarlatti said. "How you arranged for the garbage truck and guided them across the alley. Fortunately, he signaled for help after you took him from his home."

The Institute wasn't Hank's home. I kept that to myself. "What happened to innocent until proven guilty and boys can't testify in court?"

"Annabelle!" Sam yelled. I cringed, afraid the others could hear.

"I knew you couldn't resist helping boys," Scarlatti said.

I shifted my feet and pressed myself against the wall. "You admit you hired Hank to stage the escape."

"In order to catch you. This was a sting, and it worked." Scarlatti grinned as she took out a set of cuffs and a maroon prisoner collar. "You're under arrest. Anything you say can and will be used against you."

"See?" Sam said. "Even she's telling you to shut up."

I turned toward Devotte. "I'm curious. You could have locked down the facility when you learned about the escape. You didn't. You wanted these boys to escape. You're in on this, like a few days ago when you unloaded the two boys. You sent them here, even though they don't need medical attention. You could transfer boys at any time. Why the charade? Why kidnap them?"

"We're not kidnapping anyone," Voss said from behind Scarlatti. "This entire operation was sanctioned to flush out the Underground Railroad. We have evidence that links your mother to the Mech Corps commander *and* the Underground Railroad. Your entire family is going down."

I was mortified. *Say it, Sam. Tell me I'm going to prison with the rest of my family.*

"Why aren't you laughing?" Scarlatti said. She couldn't help smiling. "This is quite funny. You thought you were so clever. Your entire family did. What do you say now, smarty-pants?"

I wanted to ask what evidence they had, but I didn't need more secrets revealed to Sam. *Damn you.* Sam used me to get at Voss. Mom and I were collateral damage. I prayed Janine hadn't heard this.

"Who are you working for?" Director Devotte asked.

"No one," I said.

I heard a big sigh in my head. "Since you're already in the deep end, you might as well get me some evidence I can use."

"I'm not buying that," Devotte said. "Did your mother put you up to this?"

Which one? "No. I'll confess to what I've done if you tell me who you work for. Is the governor behind this? How about Adrianne Picard?" I made sure to scan the faces for Sam, in case she could read something I couldn't. This time, Sam remained quiet.

"Don't spread rumors," Voss said. Her jowls quivered as her face reddened.

Scarlatti looked tongue-tied.

Director Devotte held out her palm. "She's baiting us, can't you see?"

The only one who remained calm and silent was Antonia Rossi, the black-haired woman in the gray uniform who had escorted me into the building.

"What do you think?" I nodded toward Rossi. "Is the governor or Picard involved in these kidnappings? Does Picard own this facility?"

Rossi stepped out of the shadows and approached me. Her olive complexion glistened in the LED lighting. "I run this facility," she said in a brusque tone. "Now that you have that, give us your confession."

"You have your answer," Sam said. "Be careful. This one is cunning, physically intimidating, and has an agenda."

"Very well." I hung my head, and watched her face. "I went to catch boys. I caught Hank."

"He said you knew Morgan."

"I met him in the arena. My duty was to arrest him, and bring him and the others in."

"That's not what you did," Rossi said.

"Hank, the one you hired, jumped me." I looked at Rossi and froze my facial expressions. "While I was down, he told me everything. He bragged about how you promised him and his dad safe passage to the Outland if he helped you kidnap boys for this facility." I was surprised Rossi didn't interrupt me.

"Why didn't you bring him in?" she asked.

I said, "You hired the assassins to kill Senator Scott, didn't you?"

Rossi's eyes were intense, her body relaxed, as Sam was during a fight. I expected her to punch me like Dara used to do. "You're getting off subject."

"What did my mom ever do to you?"

"Control yourself," Sam said. "You're dealing with a tough character."

"You can't prove anything," Scarlatti said.

"Hank told me where to find evidence," I said, "which I've tucked safely away. Attempting to assassinate a government official won't go well for you."

"Hank didn't have that information," Scarlatti said. "He was merely a messenger."

"Would you stop prattling?" Rossi said to Scarlatti.

"Is she wired?" Voss asked.

"She's clean," Scarlatti said. "I checked her for wires and transmitters. Besides, the pulse fried her electronics."

Not all, I wanted to say, but it wasn't polite to correct adults. "Why kill the senator?"

"She claimed she had a legislative responsibility to investigate," Rossi said. "She got too nosy."

"Dig deeper," Sam said.

"What was she close to finding?" I asked.

Rossi's eyes narrowed. "You owe me a confession."

I braced myself. Fear sifted into anger I needed to control. "First, tell me why you attempted to assassinate Senator Scott. Did this have to do with money you skimmed off our police station's budget?"

"You have no idea how much good we do in this facility," Rossi said.

"Enlighten me."

Rossi turned to Scarlatti. "Are you certain she's not wired?"

"I checked her twice. Not a murmur."

"I guess it won't hurt," Rossi said, "since you won't get a chance to tell anyone." She brushed Scarlatti aside and faced me with unnerving calm. "This facility is a biogenetics lab. We push medical cures as far as we can by using stem-cell proxies, and on animals."

"Which the state forbids," I said.

Rossi nodded. "They demand cures with minimal human risk and side effects. We're talking about full cures for cancer, heart disease, brain tumors, and many more diseases. With our budget crisis, think what these cures could do to lower the cost of National

Healthcare. We could balance the budget within three years with what we'll soon have available."

"That'll make you a hero," I said. "What did the governor promise you?"

"The governor?" Rossi chuckled. "She has no idea. Plausible deniability. After we have results, you're right. The governor will give us anything we ask for."

"Adrianne Picard owns this facility, doesn't she?" I was getting close. I felt it. Euphoria spilled into despair. The information might help Sam, but I wasn't getting out of here alive.

"Yes," Rossi said, "but she has no idea what goes on here, just the results."

"She wouldn't approve of our methods," Devotte said. "That's why we have to move boys and supplies this way."

"Why so much toilet paper and adult diapers?" I asked.

Rossi laughed. "The meds have unfortunate side effects."

"*Eww.*"

"You can't have it both ways," Devotte said. "Our leaders want a healthy, all-female society, but the implications are messy. It's one thing to say you want a female-only neighborhood. That requires expelling the males, which upsets mothers, sisters, and daughters. Our job is to handle the mess so our leaders can sleep at night."

"The governor and Picard have to know," I said.

"They don't," Rossi said, "and you won't be able to tell them. Otherwise, they'd close us down to set a good societal example. Then it would cost a fortune to open elsewhere. They have to be politically correct, but that won't get them their cures."

"What are you doing with the boys?" I asked.

Rossi smiled like a proud mama. "Those from the Institute allow us to try broad spectrum cures for autism. While that condition affects many more boys than girls, it still afflicts thousands of young women across the country. Once proven, we can offer them this cure."

"What does it do?"

"It alters gene expression and brain chemistry. The short version: it rewires the brain to fix the mechanisms that causes autism."

I turned to Devotte. "How would it benefit the Institute for the boys to lose their mental capacities?"

"Sometimes it has the opposite effect," she said. "The procedure can take a mild autistic and turn him into an idiot savant, able to handle some of our toughest technical challenges. One of them can replace ten of our regular wards."

"You're programming these boys to be cogs in your machine? What about failed experiments?"

Rossi sighed, yet retained her relaxed-alert pose. "Unfortunate outcomes have to be disposed of. Since we use viral vectors to insert specific genetic changes, we can't allow normal disposal and decomposition."

"Why?" I asked.

"We can't allow the boys' contaminated DNA to get out into the environment."

Despite expecting this, I was shocked. "So boys come in. Meds and biological waste go out." I couldn't believe I said this so calmly, but I wanted Sam to hear.

"Pretty much," Rossi said.

"Boys are human beings."

"Not when a society decides they don't need them anymore."

"This is no better than using slaves or women in the past," I said.

"Think of all the advances medicine made on their backs."

A True Believer. "You're also developing biological weapons to use against the Outland." I was fishing. I could almost hear Sam hold her breath.

Rossi turned to Scarlatti. "You told me this one was stupid. She seems remarkably well informed." She returned her attention to me, with a scowl. Her eyes bored into me. "Twenty years ago, we hit upon a virus that altered a woman's uterus to reject seed with the Y chromosome."

"I thought women chose female babies," I said.

"That didn't move fast enough for our New Harmony leaders, so we introduced the virus into the food and water supplies. We also modified a strain to make all males infertile. If we release this into the Outland, we're a generation away from their extinction *and* the end of this war. This is for the greater good. By the way, one of the drug's side effects is male lethargy, which could end this war much quicker."

"While Picard makes trillions off EggFusion Fertilization and other medical miracles," I said.

"Why shouldn't she be rewarded for benefitting society?"

"Giving you fat illegal bonuses along the way."

"That's how the real world works, sweetie." Rossi's voice sounded almost friendly. "I've been more than patient with you. Now it's time for you to fess up, as you promised. Who helped you?"

"Hank was a nervous boy. Something startled him. I took control. He begged me not to turn him in. He told me this was his only chance to reach the Outland."

Rossi moved closer. "My patience is wearing thin. Who put you up to this?" She no longer acted interested in my guilt or innocence.

"He was convinced you'd kill him for failing you. He feared you'd bring him here. He told me where to find evidence that you laundered government money, along with videos of your Outland raids, and recordings of informants. He called it his insurance policy."

"He didn't have access to any of that," Scarlatti said.

"Shut up," Rossi said.

"You always were more trouble than you were worth," Voss said. "Today, we finish this. I'll relish the look on your mother's face when we haul her in."

THIRTY-SIX

Antonia Rossi grinned and grabbed my arm. "The state has better uses for you than the Mech Corps, or being a useless police officer. We need human hosts to try our latest meds."

"Stay calm," Sam said into my implant. "The next few moments will determine whether you survive, and with what scars."

Thanks for the pep talk, Sam. And for breaking my concentration.

"Maybe you won't willingly give up your accomplices," Rossi said, "but while suffering through med trials, you might change your mind, if you still have one."

I thought of my friend, sent to the Nashville Rehabilitation Center. The image that came to mind was from the movie *Girl, Interrupted*. Though I knew what was coming, I was shocked at the end.

Rossi tightened her grip on my left arm and motioned for Scarlatti to open the door.

"Here goes," Sam said. "When I give the signal, imagine you're fighting Dara in a back alley. She'll kill Janine if you can't stop her. She wants to make an example of you and your sister. She'll fight you to her last breath. This is your life-and-death fight."

I got that. Now let me think.

Scarlatti unlocked the door and held it for Voss and Devotte. Scandia and Montrose straightened up across the hall.

"You can do this," Sam said. "Despite Rossi's intensity and drive, you're better trained, better than you think. You're more motivated. Think of Janine."

Stop bringing her into this. I was already feeling edgy.

Scarlatti joined Montrose and Scandia near the lobby. Rossi held the door and pushed me ahead of her. I didn't see anyone else. "Be patient," Sam said. "Wait for my word. I have agents moving into position outside the building."

On the wall, across the corridor, hung a picture of Adrianne Picard with the governor. How cozy. In the reflective glass, I saw Rossi hold the door to the interrogation cell as she pushed me out. In that instant, she turned to close the door.

Adrenaline surged, an energy boost like after mech fights, when Sam patched me up with her experimental meds so I could continue training. I was through waiting. This was my moment.

I thrust my body into rotation, rammed my elbow into Rossi's throat, and shoved her back into the room. I yanked the door shut, locking it.

Scarlatti went for her weapon first. Voss moved to my left. Scandia and Montrose moved back and reached for their weapons. Devotte faded back toward the interior of the facility. They all seemed to be moving in slow motion.

"You're all under arrest," I said. Bracing myself against the doorframe, I launched a lightning kick to Scarlatti's throat. It gave me intense satisfaction until I realized I'd just hit an officer. "Anything you've already said—"

Scarlatti clutched her throat and collapsed to the floor. Scandia and Montrose had their guns out. Voss grabbed me from behind in a huge bear hug, squeezing the air from my lungs. I popped up my legs and knocked her off balance. Swinging my legs down and in, I kicked her below the knees and dropped to the floor. As she fell on top, her weight suffocated me. I followed through on my roll and thrust her toward Montrose. The sergeant fired two shots before Voss landed on top of her. Blood pooled beneath the captain.

I rolled out of my throw and kicked Scandia in the gut. She fired twice but tumbled backward, missing me. As she fell, Scandia hit her head against the wall.

She regained her balance and swung her gun around. I kicked her gun wrist and slammed her against the wall, winding her. She collapsed onto the floor. "—will be used against you." I grabbed her cuffs, rolled her over, and fastened her wrists behind her. I took another set from her belt.

Devotte turned and ran down the corridor. I sprinted after her.

"Get out of there," Sam said. "I have mechs and cops on their way in. Your work is done. We've taken out the guards. Captain Chou is in charge of the cops. You can trust her."

I reached Devotte. She turned, pistol in hand. I spun into a kick. She fired twice. I kicked her wrist hard and felt the crunch of cartilage. Howling, she swung her left fist. I moved, caught her arm, and cuffed her wrist. She pulled free and swung the cuffed arm toward me. I swept her legs from under her and sent her crashing to the tile floor. She tried to get up. I pulled her wounded wrist to her back and cuffed her from behind.

She cried out, "God, please, I didn't mean anything."

I dragged her by her cuffed wrists toward the lobby, toward the others, while shooting and turmoil intensified outside the hospital entrance. When I reached Scarlatti, she still gasped for air. She grabbed her gun. I kicked it away and stomped on her wrist. Then I rolled her over and cuffed her with her own cuffs.

The door behind me swung open. I turned in time to see Rossi, red-faced, holding a gun. I spun into an arc so fast I felt lightheaded. The gun flew from her hand. Her face looked stunned, ashen. She recovered and launched herself at me. "*Ya-foo-chun.*"

She hammered me in the stomach and sent me reeling backward, farther into the facility.

"Okay, it's too late to leave," Sam said into my implant. "This is it; that fight for your life you prepped for."

My stomach wanted to heave. Another jet of adrenaline had me on my feet, kicking and swinging back. I was a puppet with Sam pulling the strings.

Unlike Dara, Rossi was quick. She jabbed, punched, and kicked. Though smaller than Dara, she made up for that with skill, ferocity, and what Dara lacked: creativity. I punched; she blocked. I kicked; she jumped away. She charged again, a relentless barrage of chops, hits, and kicks. Each time I fell back, the exit faded behind her.

"Stop playing nice," Sam said. "Kick up your game. Don't let her push you into her familiar territory."

Thanks for the warning, Sam.

Rossi advanced. I looked for patterns. She varied her approach. I pulled a punch and kicked her legs, caught her. She didn't go down. She grabbed me before I could reposition and threw me to the tile floor. She punched my ribs and went for a chokehold.

"Dig deeper," Sam said. "You can handle her. Move now."

I punched her throat; she moved and deflected my arm before going for my throat. Another gush of adrenaline, and I rammed both fists up below her rib cage. She gasped for air and drew back. I shoved her aside and went to cuff her. She recovered and rammed her right fist toward my throat. I shifted aside and threw my weight into her elbow.

"*Gaw-fu-sh-cra. Ahhh*," she cried out.

I pulled back her right wrist. "You're under arrest." The forearm twisted independent of her upper arm.

She cried out and slammed her foot into me. I fell back. Screaming, she rotated on her limp arm and jumped up. She kicked me in the side with both legs and dropped me to the tile floor. Off balance, she crashed to the floor. I rolled away as she scrambled on knees and one hand toward me. With a strong left grip, she grabbed my arm and twisted to break it. I yanked free and tried to get on her injured side so I could cuff her. Despite her injury, she rotated quickly and grabbed at me with each approach.

"It's over," I said. "Cops and mechs are on their way. You can hear them outside."

"They'll never get past the blast doors," she said. She grabbed my left ankle with her good arm and pulled me toward her. The look in her eyes was pure, murderous hate, worse than Dara.

"Finish this," Sam said. "We're taking down the doors. Montrose is trying to crawl out from under Captain Voss."

I'd forgotten about Sergeant Montrose.

Rossi yanked my ankle again. I lost my balance and kicked out with my right leg. I caught her left elbow. She howled and released her grip. I crashed to the tile, spun back to my feet, and climbed onto her back.

She bucked me with her feet while I pulled her left wrist up behind her and cuffed it to her right.

"Kill me," Rossi said. "Do it."

"Don't," Sam said.

I dragged her by her left shoulder toward the others. "You need to face justice for what you've done."

A blast like an earthquake rattled the emergency-room entrance, and my teeth. Plaster fell from the ceiling. The picture of Governor Battani and Picard fell to the floor. The glass shattered. I hoped that was a good omen.

I leaned Rossi against the wall next to Devotte, and reached for

Rossi's gun. A second blast shattered glass in the lobby. I ducked.

"Long live Harmony, long live the Union," Montrose yelled.

I turned. She'd crawled out from under Voss' bloody weight, and clung to the tile floor, the dead captain's body a bloated barrier.

"Put the gun down," I said. "It's over." I couldn't get close enough to disarm her. She still had five shots. I froze. She had a clear shot, and I had no cover. My legs felt rubbery, my arms drained from multiple adrenaline rushes.

Another blast tore a gaping hole in the front of the building as the glass doors collapsed into the lobby.

"What are you waiting for?" Rossi said. "Do it."

I crouched down and prepared to fire.

Montrose turned her gun on Rossi, Devotte, Scarlatti, and Scandia. With one shot left, she aimed my way. I shot her in the shoulder. She aimed at her head. "For New Harmony." She fired as the first mech-warrior entered the building: Dara, by the size of the mech-gear.

Dara aimed her machine gun and rifles up and down the corridor. "Is this all of them?"

"What took you so long?" I asked.

She removed her helmet. "You promised me an arrest."

"The crime scene is yours. I tried to arrest them. Montrose killed them all."

"I see. Even Captain Voss?"

I nodded and set the safety on Rossi's gun. "It's your takedown."

Dara removed her right glove and reached for my hand. "You did great. I'm sorry I've given you such a hard time. You'd make a first-rate warrior."

"Don't you dare say anything," Sam reminded me.

I smiled and shook Dara's hand. *You're not rid of me yet.*

Janine stepped out from behind Dara and punched my shoulder. "Don't you ever do that again." Noticing Dara, Janine stepped back and smiled at me. "I'm proud of you." She winked. I got the feeling Janine liked secrets, as long as she was in on them with me.

I led her toward the lobby. My thoughts turned to Morgan and Seth. It was time to help them. "You need to wait here," I whispered to Janine.

THIRTY-SEVEN

I headed toward the interior of the facility, toward where I hoped to find Morgan and Seth. I didn't get three paces before Sam's voice blared in my head. "Stand down, soldier. You might have turned the crime scene over to Dara, but you need to debrief Captain Chou. Now!"

Janine pulled on my arm. She must have received the same message, plus one to make sure I didn't wander off. I wiped a red smudge from her cheek and checked her for bleeding. She looked tussled, like after one of our basketball games, but fine.

She pushed my hand away. "I'm okay, Belle. Sam wanted me to stay away. I couldn't after they captured you. We need to get you treated." Like a mirror, her face told me I must look a mess.

"This facility's director, Rossi, was working with Director Devotte and Voss," I said.

Janine pulled me aside, cocked her head, and drew a figure 8 on my arm, as if to say Sam had already briefed her. Or she didn't want me to talk about it with others crowding around. I needed to get away from Janine and Sam so I could help Morgan.

Two more mechs entered the lobby, followed by Brooks and several other cops.

Captain Chou marched up to me and shook my hand. "You've made quite a mess." She waved her hand over the dead bodies while cops from her station carried in stretchers. "Congratulations on a tough assignment. I'd be honored to work with you. And your cheeky sister. She saved two of my officers on the way in."

247

Janine shrugged and grinned. I took her hands, looked her over more closely, and studied her eyes.

"I'm okay, really."

I let go, and gave Captain Chou a quick recap of what had happened. While I did, I studied the corridor and lobby, trying to figure out how to free Morgan. *Where are you?*

Cops in pairs carried the bodies out, except for Voss, who required a gurney.

"They were determined to die rather than be arrested," I said. "That tells me they were protecting someone."

"That's enough speculation," Sam said. "I need you outside in my office. Now!"

Janine tugged on my arm. I didn't like how she'd become my chaperone.

Captain Chou stopped me. Her face softened. "I'm sorry about the attacks on your mom. I had no idea my cop-interns were involved. It's a lesson that we have to remain vigilant against those who would undermine our social values. Disagreement is one thing, bloodshed is another." Chou joined her cops, escorting the bodies outside.

Dara and two sister mechs blocked me from the facility's interior. There was no way past them. I followed Janine out. Floodlights illuminated the shattered hospital entry. The glass had splintered into spider webs, yet remained intact on the lobby's tile floor.

I located Sam's armored vehicle with its darkened windows among a cluster of armored trucks. Several mechs guarded the periphery of the parking lot; more scouted the hills surrounding the facility with their mech-floodlights.

Janine clung tight to my arm, no longer the frightened girl I used to comfort at night. I patted her arm.

I opened the door to Sam's mobile command center and helped Janine inside. I entered to face Sam and Adrianne Picard. The slender blonde looked not much older than me. Her face showed few signs of the decades of running her biomedical empire. Her dark eyebrows furrowed. Her azure eyes pierced through me as Sam's did. There was not a wrinkle on her soft face, no crow's feet, and no creases around her lips. When she smiled, the facial muscles moved with the fluidity of a child's.

Janine sat across from Picard and watched me study the legend of the Second Civil War. During several moments of awkward silence, I considered asking her about her involvement.

She extended her soft hand and shook mine in a firm grasp. "Again I'm indebted to you for cleaning up a mess."

I eased into the seat beside Janine and tried not to wince from pain rippling up and down my body. "I …"

"There's something you want to ask me." Picard tilted her head.

"Was this your facility?"

Picard nodded. "I suspected Rossi was undermining my express orders. I shared my concerns with Sam."

"You called Sam from Governor Battani's residence."

"I did," Picard said. "What you found shouldn't be allowed. However, it wouldn't serve the people's interests to have a scandal. Heads would have rolled. But Rossi would have dragged the governor down with her."

"Montrose and Rossi chose death over—"

"You want to ask if others were involved," Picard said. "There will always be those who pervert the values of their society for their own benefit. Some say I've done that, by choosing youth over aging, while reaping financial rewards from EggFusion Fertilization. I provided the means for women to have children without men. I did not choose that path either for individuals, or for our society. Our citizens made those choices for well-documented reasons.

"I will not apologize for the experiments I've done on myself with rejuvenating stem-cell treatments. I choose youth. I refuse to use meds on other humans I wouldn't use on myself. Consider me a guinea pig: a lab specimen for treatments that'll benefit millions. Yes, I get the first treatment. I also take the risk if the treatments fail." Picard smiled, satisfied with her political speech.

I suspected she knew more about what had happened. Sam's glare told me not to pursue that. "Will you shut down this facility?" I asked.

"Until I can verify that my procedures will be followed and I find a new director."

"We'll have to find a new director for the Institute, as well," Sam said. "Lieutenant Brooks will stand in as acting captain for your police station."

"If you don't mind," Picard said, glancing at the van's door, "I need to shut down the facility and lock it up."

Sam stepped outside with Picard, and then returned. While I waited, Janine squeezed my hand. It was good to have her back, but she was keeping me from helping Morgan and Seth. After they moved the boys, I might not get another chance.

I studied the screens on the table. Dozens of green mech signals, including Janine and me. There were also red dots for five boys, not far from the interrogation room. We were all pieces on a chessboard.

Sam closed the door. "You made a good impression. That could help you down the road."

I took a deep breath while Janine clutched my arm.

Sam sat across from me. "I was worried about you. It got dicey after they locked you in the interrogation room. This time you didn't lose focus."

"Unlike the arena, this was life-or-death," I said.

"I'd like you to reflect on this," Sam said. "You couldn't have pulled this off seven weeks ago. I hope you recognize your growth. You're ready for the next step. I had to hold you and your sister to secrecy to be sure you could handle it."

"I swear, Commander, Janine didn't have to tell me you were working with her."

"No need to be defensive. I'm not angry. But under no circumstances can either of you tell a soul, not even your mother that you work for me, or what happened tonight."

I nodded. "All guts and no glory." I studied the table map for any indication Mom was here.

"You'll have your mech glory, if that's what you seek. This isn't a game, Annabelle. I believe you two could be first-rate mech-warriors. You need to learn to trust me."

"How can I, when you withhold information that could get me killed?"

"Belle?" Janine grabbed my wrist. "You can't talk to the commander like that."

Sam held up her hand. "It's okay. Annabelle has a point. Let me ask you. What would you have done better if I'd given you more information?"

"I would have known where to look," I said. "You planned for me to get captured, didn't you?"

Sam grinned. "You like to buck authority and act impatiently. You need to learn patience. Tonight, this worked for you. Don't believe it always will."

"Why didn't you tell me?"

"Then you'd have second-guessed how to play your capture. I take considerable effort to understand recruits, so I can best place them for their own good, and that of the corps."

I shook my head with another insight. "There's no way I could have defeated all six of them unless … that injection you gave me. What was it?"

"You're right," Sam said. "I couldn't send you into the lion's den without some advantage. The nano-bots and meds allowed you to spike your performance when you needed it. A weapon they couldn't frisk you for."

"It felt like superhuman strength."

"Not superhuman, though it won't be allowed in the Olympics. That injection gave you an edge in speed and strength when you needed it. It allowed you to outmaneuver Rossi, so you had time to take down the others and face Rossi alone."

"Sam, don't ever use me or Janine like that again. I'll do my duty. I'll try better to follow orders, but if you want my trust, don't use us."

"I'll take that as your agreement to continue your training," Sam said.

I hesitated. I saw no other choice. "I'm ready. Please give Janine another year."

"No way," Janine said. "We do this together."

I knew better than to argue with her when she dug in her heels. "What do we know about Montrose? When she shot everyone, she looked possessed by the devil."

"Not much," Sam said. "She was a clean junior officer, toed the line, and followed orders."

"A boot-licker," I said.

Sam chuckled. "What you certainly are not. She played a role."

"You mean like Janine and I did."

Sam nodded. "I wish you could have brought Montrose in alive."

"She wouldn't let me," I said. I kept watching the movement of warriors on the tabletop screen. "Rossi admitted to calling for my mom's assassination. Is there any way to find out who else was involved?"

"Rossi has a personal gun collection that includes a .60 caliber sniper rifle. Captain Chou will search this facility, and Rossi's home. I'm sure she'll be able to confirm Rossi provided the rifle and killed the sniper. She would not have delegated something so sensitive."

"I can't help thinking … the governor appointed Voss. She was about to promote her."

"Stop right there," Sam said. "Your mother and the governor have issues. Don't let that cloud your thinking. Otherwise, you'll lose focus. I can assure you, the governor was not involved in this matter."

"How can you be so sure?"

"I suspected her as well. You've wounded the bad guys. The governor is embarrassed by her connection to Voss. Be careful. If others are involved, they'll be very angry. That's another reason you shouldn't tell a soul of your involvement."

"Sam, can I speak with you alone?"

Janine gave me her worried look.

THIRTY-EIGHT

After Janine left and Sam closed the door, I tried to stand. I think better on my feet. My head bumped the van's roof. I settled into a seat across from Sam and steadied my nerves. She rattled me even when she acted nice. Especially then.

"Did you come to confess?" Sam asked.

"What do I have to confess?"

"You helped Morgan and his brother escape." Sam's eyes bored into mine, as if she could read what was in my heart and soul.

"If you know, why keep me?"

Sam stroked her chin and leaned back. "I knew you wouldn't kill him in the arena, even at risk to your own life. You found a way. I admire your resourcefulness. Dara is a terror, but she's not resourceful. I couldn't use her on a delicate mission. I knew Morgan would contact you. You couldn't stop yourself from helping him."

"Then why?" I asked.

"I can deal with what I know. It's what I don't know that blindsides me."

"I swear I'd never do anything to disgrace the corps, Commander." I closed my eyes. Saying this felt like a betrayal of my family.

"I know," Sam said. "That makes you a valuable addition to the Mech Corps. That data chip you provided was a treasure trove. Voss and Scarlatti were very busy girls. Over the past six weeks, they orchestrated nine escapes. Twenty-nine boys disappeared, all delivered to this facility. We have evidence Scarlatti arranged the two attempts on your mom, apparently at Rossi's insistence. I wish we could make them face judgment."

"Sam, you and Picard both said I've done a great service tonight."

Sam's eyes narrowed.

"You told me to dig deep for allies and information?"

"Yes."

"I couldn't have done this without Morgan and Seth. Seth dug into Voss' records to create the chip."

"He also hooked Morgan up so you two could communicate through our supposedly secure channel."

I took a deep, shaky breath. "Is there anything you don't know?"

"I detected a piggyback onto our signal. Quite clever. We tried to trace it to locate Morgan. The signal kept changing. When you made the bargain for information in exchange for helping him, I let it ride."

"You let me make a complete fool of myself."

"Annabelle, you're no fool. You believe what we do to the boys is wrong. I respect that. In fact, despite what you think, I don't disagree."

"Then why continue the arena fights?" I asked.

"Aside from their training benefit, the governor requires this. For political reasons, I'm not in a position to deny her."

"For services rendered to the state, could you let Morgan and Seth cross the border?" *There, I said it.* I clenched my fists to keep from shaking.

Sam leaned forward and studied me. "That's an unorthodox request."

"It's the right thing to do, Sam. That's what you teach us, isn't it? How can you punish them for helping us?"

Sam took a deep breath and sighed. "It's my job to enforce the laws of the land. I'm charged with doing what's in the greater good. Taking down Voss, Devotte, and Rossi was a greater good than capturing Morgan, which is why I let you continue."

"Sam, please. I gave them my word."

"I know you did. It's vital that no one escapes from the arena. Now that we've captured the last boy, we've met that goal. For services rendered, I'll grant you this. Don't think this excuses your gross insubordination."

"Which you counted on."

Sam laughed. "I'll see that Morgan and his brother are escorted to the border."

"Can I escort him, and have a moment to say goodbye?"

Sam's eyes narrowed. "Don't push your luck."

"I want to see it myself, to know it isn't some trick."

<∞>

Sam took the wheel of her armored vehicle while Janine and I sat in the back with Morgan and Seth. I wanted to be alone with Morgan. Sam insisted Janine escort me. I suspected Sam was watching us while she drove the hilly roads east in the dark.

"I'm so sorry for how you both were treated," I said.

Seth sat facing Janine. He alternated between what looked like counting on his fingers and gawking at my sister. Janine studied Morgan and me. A puzzled look etched her face as I was sure she tried to make sense of how this boy could touch me so deeply. I detected flashes of jealousy that someone else had caught my attention, plus curiosity. I'd become a new puzzle for her to solve. I loved that about her, always inquisitive.

"I can't thank you enough," Morgan said. "For everything."

In the dim compartment lights, his eyes twinkled. He couldn't say what he wanted to and neither could I. I wanted to reach across the narrow gap that separated us, touch his cuffed hands, and tell him, what? That I didn't want him to go. That I wanted to go with him.

Janine's eyes bored in on me, as if she saw what I felt, and it was more than caring for his safety. My right foot found the gap between his cuffed ankles and withdrew. The heat on my face was a hot breeze on a summer day.

There was so much I wanted to ask him. Where was the rest of his family? Where would he go? How would they get by in the wilderness when they were used to city life, Institute life?

The vehicle stopped. Sam opened the door. A second vehicle stopped nearby and shone its headlights into the opened door. It cast ghostly images across Morgan's face. He closed his eyes.

"Everyone out," Sam said.

I stepped out of the vehicle. Sam pulled Morgan and Seth out. I had visions of my birth father running across this very border. When he reached the other side, mech-warriors in gear surrounded and killed him. I trembled at the memory.

Sam removed the ankle and wrist cuffs from both boys. "Your passionate supporter has negotiated your release. We'll escort you across the border and provide two days' provisions. If I ever catch you on our side of the border, I'll hunt down you and Seth and do unspeakable things to both of you."

Morgan's eyes teared up. "You'll never see us again."

"Then we have an understanding." Sam handed them each a backpack and a flashlight, as if she'd planned this all along. "The border is over there. I suggest you head northeast, to avoid the local militia on the other side. I thank you for assisting Annabelle on a complex mission."

Morgan nodded. He took his brother's hand and turned toward me, his eyes moist. "Thanks for everything. I owe you my life."

I wanted to take him in my arms and hold him. The moment passed when he faced the border and jogged off.

THIRTY-NINE

Sam dropped Janine and me off at the station so we could pick up our cycles. "Be at the base in the morning to continue your training. Secrecy still applies. You two had best get your stories straight about tonight before you see your mom."

"Do we have to wear the contacts, or can we have some privacy without you yelling in our ears?" I asked.

"You may. You only need them while you're on assignment."

"What about the audio implant?"

Sam raised her finger to admonish me, and evidently changed her mind. "Very well. I'll provide you a shield if you promise only to use it when you're off duty."

I nodded.

She handed me a thumb-sized chip that looked a lot like the jammer Morgan had given me.

As soon as she drove off, I removed my contacts, put them in their case, and had Janine do the same.

<Before you jam the audio, I wanted to thank you again for everything. You're amazing. I know Sam's listening, but I couldn't leave without telling you I'll miss you. I'm signing off for good. I can't leave any trace.>

I wanted to yell at Morgan not to go. I wanted to hear his voice again before he disappeared. I longed to tell him how much he meant to me. But I figured he already knew.

"You okay?" Janine asked. "You've been acting peculiar ever since ... well, ever since the arena."

I smiled, took her hand, and pulled her toward the cycles, which sat alone in the parking lot. I lingered for a moment, in case Morgan said something. Then I jammed the signal. "I'm glad that's over so we can resume being sisters."

"No more secrets, then," Janine said, ever so serious. "He was just talking to you, wasn't he?"

I nodded. Being with Janine was like having the mech-link connection, like having Sam and Morgan in my skull. I felt Janine in my head again, rooting around to figure out what made me tick. It gave me comfort to feel that connection. Maybe having my sister as a mech-sister wasn't such a bad idea.

"Earth to Belle. Where are you?"

"I'm sorry. Yes, he was in my head just now, and from time to time. He signed off for good so they can't track him."

"It sounds weird to have a boy in your head," Janine said. "Didn't you feel violated?"

"At first. Then I got used to his voice. He wasn't such a bad sort, kind of nice, really."

"Are you sure that's all? I don't think I can ever forgive you for getting me involved in …" Janine cut herself short.

"Not everything you learned in school is true," I said.

"I know." She smiled and looked up at me. "I'm not the goody everyone takes me for. It's easier if people think I am. What was it like?"

"Dangerous. Scary. Comforting, amazing."

"You wanted to go with him, didn't you?"

"Part of me did, but I couldn't leave you. Besides, I have work to do here."

She hugged me and clung tight.

I whispered into her ear, "You have something of mine."

<∞>

On the way home, all I could think of was Mom. Sam had overheard the allegations that Mom was helping the boys. By the time I reached our home, my stomach was in knots, imagining cops arresting her. The place was quiet, too quiet, but it was well past midnight. Lights were out, except for a nightlight in the living room and the light from under Mom's door.

"I need to talk to Mom," I said to Janine.

In the pale light, Janine looked concerned, but went upstairs without a fuss. I knocked lightly on Mom's door and entered. She was wiping dark smudges from her face. She turned away, checked in a handheld mirror, and looked my way. "You're quite late."

I locked her door and pulled her into the closet, where I turned on a flashlight and triggered her electronic jamming device, just in case. "I know, Mom. I saw you at the Institute."

"Oh, dear."

"That means others might know." I almost said "Sam."

Mom held my shoulders. "Don't you worry about that."

"I'm proud of you, Mom, but I can't lose you. I shouldn't have asked you to help Morgan."

"I'm sorry, Belle." She closed her eyes. "They captured him and his brother. There wasn't anything I could do."

"I know. I have something I'm scared to look at alone. It might tell me something about Dorothy." I held up the second data-chip.

"Where did you get that?"

"You don't want to know."

She pulled an e-reader from the top shelf and plugged in the data-chip. I held my breath as the screen scrolled through its contents. I hoped to find an address, so I could write or visit. A get-out-of-jail judgment would have been ideal. I feared she might be dead.

Splashed across the screen were dates next to symbols the shape of old-style letters, hundreds of them. I frowned and opened one: *To my dearest Annabelle.* Others were addressed the same. Mom studied me and looked over my shoulder.

"I told you how much she loved you," she said. "She never forgot. I knew she couldn't, any more than I can forget George."

There was no address, no location. The words were mostly the same. *I can't bear not seeing you. I hope you're in good hands.*

The best, I wanted to assure her.

"Breathe, Belle. Let it out. It's okay."

I took a deep, unsteady breath, and tried to keep my poker face. It shattered all around me. My birth mother hadn't forgotten me. She cared. My mother loved me. All these years she'd suffered, not knowing what became of me. She sent all these letters into the vacuum of electronic space, never knowing if they would ever reach me. How proud she would be to know that in helping a boy, I learned the truth.

I will find you, Dorothy Montgomery.

ACKNOWLEDGMENTS

I want to thank my wife, Sue, for taking this ride with me. I am also grateful to my writing groups for their input over the years: The Troubadours, The Barrington Writers Workshop, and the Algonquin Area Writers Group. I especially wish to thank my editor, Arlene Robinson, for her patience and diligence in making up for my editorial shortcomings and helping to make this a better story.

OTHER STORIES BY LANCE ERLICK

THE REBEL WITHIN (Rebel Series book 1)
Action-oriented science fiction thriller.

Orphaned at age three when the elite military corps took her parents, Annabelle (16) is a tomboy who rebels against a conformist society. The state pushes her to become a cop intern to catch escaped boys. Then she's forced to choose between joining the elite military unit that took her parents or being torn from her beloved sister and adoptive mom.

The Rebel Within turns our male dominated world upside down. After the Second American Civil War, the Federal Union pursues a utopian society without men by rounding up the remaining males, and enforcing Harmony. Central to their plan is EggFusion Fertilization and Female Mechanized Warriors based near Knoxville.

In this world, Annabelle faces a cop intern boss who hates her, a military commander who demands too much, and an amazon bully who won't leave her alone. She meets a handsome boy who escapes prison. As she tries to survive rigorous military training and hunt for her imprisoned birth mother, Annabelle must choose between capturing the boy and helping him escape, while she wrestles with the consequences of her actions.

REBELS DIVIDED (Rebel Series book 3)
Rebels Divided was written as a standalone dystopian, science fiction thriller. It is also part of the Rebel series, three years later.

The first time he sees her, they meet as enemies and she doesn't kill him. That's worth something. Geo (19) is a rugged frontiersman who hungers to see more of the world than the impoverished Outland glen where he and his pa hide from local Rangers. To prove himself, Geo fights Union Mechanized Warriors and Outland Rangers to protect friends, neighbors, and refugees fleeing the Federal Union. Annabelle (19) is a tough yet fragile tomboy who lost her parents at age three to the Mech Warriors. Then she's forced to become a Mech.

After the Second American Civil War, the nation divides into two 'utopias.' The Federal Union enforces Harmony and an all-female society with the help of EggFusion Fertilization and Female Mechanized Warriors based near Knoxville. The Appalachian Outland promotes rugged individualism, but Thane Edwards holds a monopoly of power with his Rangers, loosely modeled on the legendary Texas Rangers. The Union's Tenn-tucky governor and the Outland warlord conclude a secret deal, pledging Annabelle to the warlord to provide him heirs, and putting a bounty on Geo and his pa.

When Annabelle refuses the arranged marriage, Thane Edwards kidnaps her and her beloved sister. She escapes, but can't find her sister without help. That's when she tracks down Geo, a sworn enemy she feels connected to. While trying to survive, and pursued by their own and opposing military forces, Geo and Annabelle wrestle with attraction and mutual distrust as enemies. Yet, only together can they confront Edwards to rescue her kidnapped sister and gain justice for the murder of Geo's pa. Time is running out.

MAIDEN VOYAGE (short story)

The Maiden's Ark is an all-female spacecraft that left Earth five years earlier. A distress signal says Earth is lost, stranding lunar and asteroid colonists. Then someone sabotages the ship's vital fertility lab. As chief of security, Nina must tread carefully between Returners with whom she sympathizes, the dictatorial captain who strips her of her duties, and an estranged lover who betrays her to the captain. Under constant surveillance, Nina digs into solving the conspiracy while she avoids being arrested or killed for digging too deep.

WATCHING YOU (short story)

At the intersection of global tracking, pervasive networks, mass storage, and the Patriot Act, we have the ability and some say the obligation to know everything about everyone. Can privacy survive? Can the individual endure?

Harold is a second-class citizen and a low-level worker in a government surveillance system charged with reviewing "criminal activity." He has private thoughts about a woman he's forbidden from approaching, and he will not be deterred.

ABOUT THE AUTHOR

Lance Erlick grew up in various parts of the United States and Europe. He took to stories as his anchor and was inspired by his father's engineering work on cutting-edge aerospace projects to look to the future. He writes science fiction, dystopian and young adult stories and likes to explore the future implications of social and technological trends. He is the author of *The Rebel Within*, *The Rebel Trap*, and *Rebels Divided*, three books in the Rebel series. In those stories, he flips traditional exploitation to explore the effects of a world that discriminates against males and the consequences of following conscience for those coming of age.

Find out more about the author and his work at LanceErlick.com. Go to that website to sign up to receive occasional email newsletters with links to free short stories, and updates on new releases and other writing developments.

www.ingramcontent.com/pod-product-compliance
Lightning Source LLC
Chambersburg PA
CBHW060406180626
46817CB00007B/2536